To Rachel,

None of this ever happened.*

Stunning Lofts

love,

Tom X.

* This may or may not be true.

PRINTED IN FRANCE
First Edition, September 2005
ISBN 2-916262-02-4

STUNNING LOFTS

TOM GIDLEY

M
METRONOME PRESS*

Time flies
time crawls
like an insect
up and down the walls

The light pours out of me

The conspiracy
of silence ought
to revolutionise
my thought

The light pours out of me

The cold light of day
pours out of me
leaving me black
and so healthy

The light pours out of me

It jerks out of me
like blood
in this still life
heart beats up love

The light pours out of me

The Light Pours Out of Me. Lyrics by Howard Devoto, 1978

There are many beautiful places in the world, and a few of them belong to me. A street in a village near Bari, every surface whitewashed to dazzling affect on a Mediterranean summer's day. The lighthouse at the tip of a tiny Welsh peninsula, approached in a small boat at dawn under cover of rolling black clouds. That inlet from the sea somewhere on the south west coast of Sweden that suddenly becomes a twisting stream set in dense woodland, lined by a scattering of modernist houses. These are some of mine. I think about them and the others quite often, to keep them with me and not allow them to fade away.

The ones that have really stayed with me, become my own Beautiful Places, have been moments of almost sublime bliss. Times when I have felt as if I might be the only person in the world, relaxed and completely connected to where I am. I've experienced a profound sensation of inner peace, tucked away and shielded from everyday concerns. They have all had a similar effect on me, stirred my emotions and imprinted themselves on my memory. They don't need to be beautiful to be Beautiful Places, of course. It's a subtle combination of location and a brief moment in time, an encounter when the world stopped spinning and allowed me off.

But how do *they* feel? Don't they miss me? Doesn't that platform floating in the stupidly perfect waters of Barbados remember my body, stretched out flat across its warm surface? Aren't the grooves I made in the thick ferns covering a hillside in Warwickshire by repeatedly tumbling down it still visible? Do all my Beautiful Places get along just fine without me being there – didn't I make an equally enduring impression on them?

I have trouble accepting that the places where I experienced such tranquillity still exist, long after I visited them. I've never tried to capture my Beautiful Places in photographs or on video – it would be futile and would only rupture the moment as it was happening. But how can I be certain they are still there? Whenever I think about these moments there is almost an element of regret that I've ever had them. I feel the childish greed of wanting to have them again, to stomp my feet and demand that I go back to each and every one of them, over and over. Travel through time and space to the exact second they occurred. I could of course set about revisiting each place, but really, what would be the point? The experience I had there couldn't be replicated and the original would suffer as a result.

I know that everyone has, to some degree, their own collection of such experiences. That you could ask almost anyone to name a place and time they were happiest, most content, and their eyes would probably mist over as they wistfully recalled it. But no one can share mine, just as I can't theirs. It wouldn't matter if they had even stood on the same spot at the same moment. They couldn't possibly duplicate my Beautiful Places.

I appreciate that this may not seem a particularly sensible or rational perspective. I never discuss the matter with anyone else because of the bemused response I would be certain to get. They would think me an idiot, or at best nod and smile and try to remember not to get talking to me again. That's perfectly understandable and I wouldn't gain anything from sharing my views with them, either. I simply have to accept the reality that all the places do exist, and always will, and that I will die and they will remain, regardless of my extinguished memory.

Or will they? What proof do I have that the moment my eyes close for the last time a shutter won't come down and close off the whole world as well? That everything I knew of it and experienced was for me only, and that each person has their own world that expires when they do?

I thought this room was decorated with luxurious wallpaper but now I can see the design is painted directly onto the walls. The quality is startling. I'm transfixed by the silvery grey surface, the delicate overlapping fronds of huge palms picked out in light chalky green. I touch the pattern gently with a finger and the paint turns to dust.

This was once a very grand spa resort, a magnificent villa set high on a hill against a backdrop of mountains. The rich and famous would come from all over Europe to take the waters, the long winding road constantly lined with Bentleys and Rolls Royces. Extravagant balls were held several nights a week. Artisans were brought from a town in Germany to hand-paint each of the couple of hundred rooms in a different colour scheme and repeat motif. During the war it was occupied by German officers and since then has gradually fallen into ruin. I read about it a few days ago and decided to make a special pilgrimage from Genoa. I climb the twisting road and find it easy to get in through the broken fence for a better look. I pass through the wrecked lobby and walk carefully up a marble staircase missing its handrail, examining the rooms on each floor. Everything removable has long since been taken, while the walls cling on to their eerie magical surfaces.

The building contains graffiti that marks the years of its decline. In the fifties and sixties it was used for late night candle-lit dances, the ballroom floor still being sound at that time. There are hearts carved in the plaster walls, initials etched inside them and dates from over thirty years ago. As I move up the hotel the signs of occupation become more recent. In the late seventies it was squatted for a while, and I feel a tingle of pleasure when I see a slightly charred door lying on its side, 'The Doors' logo drawn in marker pen across it.

I wonder at the things that each of these rooms has seen, the countless fingers that have touched the patterns that mine do now. I climb again and the ceiling suddenly disappears. The shattered remains of the roof lie all around me. I'm standing in a huge open-air suite of rooms, looking directly at the snow-capped peaks beyond. The sky is such a deep blue, if I reach up I'm sure to touch it. Jolly accordion music drifts up from the spa at the bottom of the road. The light breeze drops, the cicadas briefly give up their manic sawing, and everything becomes very quiet and still. I feel totally connected to this moment. I know that this will join my list of Beautiful Places.

I was standing next to the water dispenser. Brian was telling me about something. I wanted some cold water and he needed some hot for a teabag he'd put in a plastic cup. That isn't something I would do, pour boiling hot water into a disposable cup. The thin plastic shell instantly becomes very hot and wobbly, making it almost impossible to get back to your desk without spilling it and scalding yourself. But if he's happy with the situation, in full knowledge of its inherent dangers, then so be it. It's a free country.

We'd been standing there for a while, waiting for Sarah to finish filling her mug, and he started to talk about a car he was thinking of buying. I'm not really a car person, myself. In fact I'd say I'm rather anti-car. I live in a city with a public transport system that works well enough to satisfy my needs. I have never wanted to drive, ever. And from my experiences as a passenger in cars I think I would probably kill someone quite quickly during a fit of monumental road rage if I did. I just don't like cars.

So his words were not of the greatest importance to me. They were lost. Wasted. He might just as well have stood there flicking his lips with a finger and making baby sounds. But it was obviously a subject of considerable importance to him and he wanted to discuss his potential purchase with someone who might have some opinion or knowledge that would help him. He went on at length about boot capacity, safety features, fuel consumption and various other aspects of his tedious investigation. I wanted to ask him what colour it was. But I didn't. I nodded seriously, then I smiled inquisitively. I looked out of the window at the busy junction below and that's when I started thinking about some of my Beautiful Places, and then specifically about the abandoned hotel high in the Italian alps. I can fill a whole afternoon thinking this way. If I get bored with the overall concept I focus in on the individual examples and examine them in detail. I drift in a warm reverie, refining the memory of a place down to the texture of the sand beneath me, the colour of the wooden bench I'm sitting on, the way the light plays on the wet granite I'm leaning against. It can go on forever, believe me. I like thoughts that do that, that fracture and fragment into ever more abstract and yet increasingly specific ones. A very good way to kill time in a place like this.

When I looked back at Brian I was surprised to see an expression of mild irritation on his face. I gazed down at my cup thoughtfully and slowly tapped a finger against its ribbed wall. I hoped this would give the impression that I had only seemed to be paying no attention whatsoever to his car questions, and had actually been very deep in thought about the chosen vehicle. But when I looked up again he was a bit red in the face and was sort of breathing hard. What made him think I would know anything at all about the car? Why shouldn't I have just told him that as far as I was concerned he and all the other drivers could go and gas themselves? I shrugged and smiled politely.

'What do I know?' I said.

I'm watching the sun go down. I hear someone call my name, and when I turn she's walking towards me, her sandals swinging from her fingers. I'm not sure I recognise her but she smiles, links her brown arm through mine and we both look out to sea in silence, hypnotised by the gentle lapping motion and the soothing sound it makes. The sun slides into the water, pouring orange light across the surface. I have something to say to her, this person I may or may not know, something important, something that could change everything, alter the course of our lives. But as I turn to tell her the sun's burning edge drops below the lip of the horizon and there is a deafening roar as a giant vacuum sucks all the light and heat away and I'm spinning in freezing nothingness until

I lie still, hot on one side, cold and aching on the other and the streetcleaner pushes his bastard machine away from me.

If I move, it will begin. The story starts when I open my eyes, raise my head and take part in it.

Curl up tighter. Delete the day.

See only a huge hand, the jagged curve of a nail, all yellowed and cracked, a sore gap at the base where the quick should be. Dried blood.

Dried blood?

From the fight, the fight I'd forgotten about. A scene that began when we finished the cans and ran out of fags. 'Want some I'll fucking give you some.' Can it really have been today? It seems like weeks ago. I can't recall who I hit but I can see their miserable defeated face, all flat from years of people taking out their disappointment on it. I planted a punch on his nose and through a fog of drink was surprised that it felt so soft. His eyes were gently closed as it landed, he didn't even try to move or defend himself. Which was just as well. I'm no fighter at all. I will have to remember who it was though, I don't want any trouble when I see him again. But then he won't have any more idea about it than I have, probably won't even remember it ever happened.

My eyes are still locked on my hand. The deep terraced lines of my fingerprint, intersected by a half moon scar, from… where did that come from? It was a long time ago, I know. I was only small. It really hurt, I howled out loud; it was the first time I experienced the cold clarifying shock of real pain. You are Flesh You can be Torn and Hurt. We were playing hide and seek. I slipped into the shed, shut the door and held the bolt tightly. His older brother pulled the door hard; my finger got trapped in the lock, and the harder he pulled the more it tore into my finger. He was very sorry and spent ages putting a fancy bandage on it. Who, though? What was his name, and his younger brother's, my pal? It's not important and I've remembered how I got this scar so I can let this line of thought go.

How did I get here, end up at this awkward spot last night? Does it matter? Of course not. It doesn't matter at all. London's been up for hours, it must be early afternoon at least. My face is hot and stiff where the sun has crept around and burnt it. My eyes flick about, I watch without moving. I'm stuck, a regular fixture. Glued to the spot. The world of work carries on regardless. Let it. It doesn't want me, I don't want it. Frankly I'm surprised anyone does, but there you go, it takes all sorts, doesn't it. It's starting to rain now, big drops land on my face. I sit up and look around. I'm the only one left on this side of the square, the grass opposite is crammed with people, their stupid faces turned up to the light, craning their necks for every last ray before their hour of freedom is over. The sprinkler comes round again throwing another arc of cold water over me. I have to get up.

My legs are sore. Sore from all the lying down, standing up, the endless walking walking walking. I must try to walk normally. Try to walk like all the others, not like myself on a bad day, a day like today. Limp for one second and they're onto you, they've got your number. Limping Not Allowed. Limping Not Taken into Consideration. Limping Shuffling Stumbling Staggering Simply Not Fucking Tolerated At All. Marching Pushing Shoving Fucking Goose-Stepping Approved of and Appreciated. It's not right and something should be done about it. I shall write to The Times and lobby my MP. Questions will be asked in the house. I will create a right stink about it.

Oh God I need a crap. I need a crap and I'm hungry. Both holes demanding attention, what's a man to do? Which end first? It's not fair, they should have more consideration.

I bend over and have a quiet word.

Stop complaining and wait your turn, you arsehole.

Two upside down policemen wobble towards me between my legs. I jerk upright and nearly pass out with the rush of bad blood. I sit back down and try to look casual, disappear from their sight, but:

– What're you doing?

– Nothing, officers. Just hanging about, you know.

– Yes, so we see. Busy day, is it? Been up long?

Just smile, don't get lippy.

– Yes, officers, something like that.

– I thought we had a word with you just yesterday. I thought we had a chat about you not using the facilities of this square. I could have sworn we came to the conclusion it was in everyone's best interests if you pissed off for a while.

– Did we officer? I don't recall.

– Well we did.

– OK.

– No, not OK.

– No?

– No. Not OK at all, actually.

Oh fuck, the other one's on his walkie-talkie. They can't be serious, they can't seriously be arsed enough for all this.

– Not a good day today, you see. Big punch-up earlier and a tourist got thumped. Accidentally, no doubt. But it does mean that your lot are off the street, pronto. Don't get up, mate, or I'll do you for resisting, and neither of us want that. Stay where you are and we'll have you in the back of a nice van in a minute. Not the end of the world, is it? Station cells will be the only cool spot, day like today.

– Yes, officer. I suppose so. But you see, I've got to visit my mom. She's poorly, down at St Thomas's. Got to go today; she might not pull through, you see.

– Really. Sad, that. Personally, and you can take this anyway you like, I don't imagine the sight of you would do your 'mom' much good, really. I think the image of you leaning over her nice clean hospital sheets for a peck would finish your old 'mom' off. Now here's the van and I've had enough of talking to you, nice as it's been. John, grab his stuff. Up you get, mate.

– But.

– Look it's hot, you're nicked, follow that pile of shit you call your belongings in there or you are truly fucked. Thank you.

The temperature in this place is ridiculous. It's usually too warm and nearly always airless, but on a day like this it's unbearable. I feel the radiator next to me and it's hot, the heating is on full blast on a sunny spring day. I pick at it with a finger, apply some pressure with the tip. My fingernail sinks into the thick globular paint. It scores a line through the gloss that is slowly returning to its liquid state, softened by the hot metal beneath it and warm sunlight above. The nail runs smoothly along, following the ridges and contours of the cast iron carcass. I lift my finger and examine it. Ancient yellow paint, reborn and rejuvenated, is smeared like a lab sample along the pad.

My nail is filled with a rind of different colours that reminds me of a programme I saw recently, about scientists trying to understand when the polar ice fields last melted by taking an enormous plug from deep underground, and examining the results. It was to determine whether in the comparatively near future, the ice would melt again and the world's water level consequentially rise by up to six meters, wiping out about a third of all cities and ports. It was quite interesting. I especially liked the long plug earth sample itself, the uniformity of its shape and the variation of the material, all the colours and textures like those seaside souvenirs you used to see, glass phials full of sand in multicoloured bands. I can't remember how the programme ended but I can't help feeling that the scientific conclusion, ultimately, will be 'yes'. It occurs to me that most of London, in that case, will be underwater.

I like my flat and the idea disturbs me. It's a relatively tall block, and I'm up on the fifth floor, but even so. What a disaster for the property market, especially anywhere near the river. Where I live would be totally submerged, quite possibly. Most of the East End would vanish, just like that. Limehouse Basin couldn't be better named, really. The exodus from most of the City would be unimaginable. As if the hillier parts of North London, especially Hampstead, aren't expensive enough. We could all find ourselves fighting over shitty pebble-dashed terraces in Wales, or Scotland. Nightmare.

I scrape the rind onto the edge of my desk and then use the adhesive edge of a Post It Note to lift and deliver it to the bin. I'm impressed by the adhesive quality of the Post It Note. Perhaps that's because I'm using it for an unintended purpose, the removal of paint rind from the edge of a laminate surface. I usually find that a Post It Note stuck with good intentions in a easily noticeable place, a computer monitor or filing cabinet, say, will almost certainly flutter away soon after, only to be found some time later, with a footprint on it, once the note is no longer of any relevance. Other people seem very keen on Post It Notes, and use them at every opportunity. But for me, the potential joy of Post It Notation was destroyed the very first time I tried to be good and kind and left a note reminding Sarah that the meeting at 3.30pm was now at 4.45pm and in Edgware Road not King's Cross. That first time the glue failed me, failed Sarah and I in our communication and left poor Sarah stranded and defenceless in the midst of the Dickensian depravity that is one of London's central termini, it was all over.

I do keep a pad on my desk, but it's for show, really. It's like that here. A good idea, I was told early on, not be too individual in terms of desk presentation. Oh God, I ask you. As if the work were not tedious enough, as if the monotony of waiting for something, anything of challenge to come along were not great enough, we were expected to keep our desks as anonymous as possible. People very rarely come into my cubicle, as they refer to them here, and the drabness of it was making me feel miserable every morning. A simple desk framed on three sides by a beige hessian covered freestanding screen behind the computer, a small window to my right, and another ugly mottled green hessian divider behind my chair. My domain, in all its glory.

I put up with it for a while and then placed a small selection of shells from home around my keyboard. Nothing flash, no conchs, just a few things I'd picked up over time from different beaches. It seemed very innocent.

A couple of days later Margaret came in to give me a file. If you need a file not related to a current job, it's Margaret's responsibility to go into the archive room and retrieve it. She seems quite nice really, but always grins excitedly when you ask her for something, which slightly puts me off; can she genuinely derive pleasure from such a tedious activity, and if so, what does that say about the state of her mental health? She entered my cubicle, and placed the file on my desk.

'Ooh!' she said. 'Shells!'

'Yes.' I said. 'I thought I'd really try and cheer the place up.' I presumed she would detect this gentle dig at our miserable surroundings and appreciate it.

'It looks lovely! What a great idea, I've always said we should be able to bring things in from home.'

The effect was staggering. I was dispirited at what I had started. Within days, people I had presumed to possess some intelligence and a modicum of taste were all busily revealing their true natures. Oh the twisted idiotic mentality, the profane simplicity of my fellow workers, the total lack of any individuality that was proudly put on display. Teddies, gonks, monitors adorned with bits of glittery paper. A framed picture of a television actor I vaguely recognised, a Leeds United rosette, a miniature West Ham uniform on a tiny hanger.

The situation was clearly out of control. I had opened the floodgates. Years of repressed self-expression had been released, creating visual chaos. Only then did I really understand the firm I work for. The company had been formed from a government body, dealing with the mundanest aspects of town planning. Despite its heady climb to the lowest rung of architectural design, the office still retained the depressing working conditions of a bureaucratic outpost.

Brian organised a meeting at which it was decided that the personalising of workstations was perhaps permissible, but that obscuring monitor screens was unacceptable and items that presented a health and safety risk would have to go. And that football colours were possibly not such a good thing either. That made me laugh. What did he imagine he was preventing, by invoking a rule only usually enforced in pubs and clubs? Did he think the flagrant display of team allegiance could possibly spark an inter-departmental skirmish, a running battle between workstations of planners, surveyors and secretaries? The whole issue definitely marked my card with Brian. I was a troublemaker, a firebrand. But that's all right, I think. He knows I do my job more than adequately, that I'm always looking to improve things, try and make the world a bit better.

I leaf through the document on my desk and make some notes in the gutter. This is funny, as the notes concern guttering. How apt, how amusing. It is possibly the most miserable problem I've yet faced here, or at least the most uninteresting. A large civic building needs its entire guttering and drainpipe system replacing. I'm to provide a recommendation based on the projected costings and schedules provided by a number of contractors. These will all specify the same type of plastic pipe, in either black or dark grey. This will last up to thirty years. The existing guttering and drainpipe system is cast iron, and was made specifically for the building in 1825. It features various symbols associated with the civic pride of the borough and has the date in bold relief on each hopper, held aloft on a shield by a lion and a unicorn in each instance.

I have read the assessment and it's knackered, there's no doubt. And there isn't a company left anywhere that could make it again. But the recommendation I would like to make would be to rebuild the factory, train a skilled workforce, and remake the entire thing, perhaps to a more contemporary design, possibly commissioned from one of the many graduates that constantly write letters begging for their talent and enthusiasm to be put to use on even the most mundane brief.

But I won't do that, because it's a bit beyond the budget, would take a very long time to complete, and would suggest I'm about as wrongheaded as a person could possibly be in the modern world. I'll write to three of the contractors we use day in day out, see which is the cheapest and give them the job. Life's so much easier, that way.

An octopus can get through a hole, no matter how small, as long as it is larger than its beak. I saw one do it in a TV programme once. The screen went very dark and then this great monster swam into view. Its fat body undulated towards a group of rocks with a gap between them no bigger than a coin. It wriggled and throbbed, pulsating its softness against the hole as it oozed through it. The hard pointy beak followed, then the last tentacles whipped out of sight. It was horrible. I was standing on Tottenham Court Road looking in a shop window. I couldn't hear the narrator and wasn't prepared for such a clear and vile illustration of my condition. I staggered away and retched against a wall.

When I'm at my worst, this is how it feels. As if my brain is pushing against a tiny hole with rough edges, beating itself raw, unable to imitate the octopus and force its way through to somewhere else, somewhere calmer and clearer. Bad thoughts are going around my head, poisonous notions. My sick perspective. A perverse pixelation that bitmaps everything, renders life crudely. I can't help it, and it isn't always like this. I can go for weeks without even thinking about it, simply existing, taking life as it comes, no questions asked. But the dark octopus returns, and all I can do is numb myself with drink, confuse the beast as best I can. I've been OK lately but it's no surprise I'm thinking about all this today, given the night I've had. I couldn't sleep for the terrible sounds coming from the next cell. Someone whimpering and screaming until the early hours of this morning. It sounded worse once it had stopped. I can hear it now.

Where are we going? I thought they would drop us in town but we've crossed the river. What are the bastards up to? They think they're so funny. 'Want a lift, any of you?' 'Where are you taking us?' 'Never mind. Bit of a day out, a mystery tour, that's all. Get in the van. Now.'

Mystery, bollocks. We're in south London now. Not really London at all to me, an unthinkable destination. The river is a watery warning sign: You Are Now Leaving Civilisation.
– Here we are, ladies. Everyone out. Now we won't be seeing any of you round our way for a while, all right? And if you'll take my advice you won't hang about here long either. Local police aren't as friendly as us lot, and the kids seem to enjoy kicking your sort to death. Anyway, have a good one. Be lucky.
Yes, yes, all right. Fuck off.

I don't want to stay with this lot, they're pathetic. The worst sort to get stuck with, wretches without a clue how to exist. They're huddled together, jittery from lack of sleep and desperate for drugs. 'Where are we anyway?' 'Fuck knows.' 'I think it's Peckham.' 'Peckham? Don't think there's a hostel in Peckham.' 'D'you think he meant it? About the kids? Seem to remember reading about something to do with that, in Peckham.' 'Bollocks, a one-off, I bet. Could happen anywhere. Soho, Knightsbridge, anywhere.'

Their conversation isn't helping me. I must try to think. Maybe I should start walking south and just keep going. Get out of this shitty city altogether and keep going all the way to the coast.

No, that's not as good as it sounds. Little scavenging to be done on the way there and you could die out in the open, even at this time of year. I'd have to get a lift but there's no chance, not in these clothes. My jeans are tattered, all grimy and split at the crotch. My feet in my knackered sandals look like I'm wearing thick black socks, but I'm not. How have I let them get this bad? It doesn't take long to fall to pieces. No, there'll be no lift.

These fools are looking at me now, like I'm responsible for their troubles. I stare at the busy street, so different to town. It's more aggressive and noisy, though people don't have the crazed consumer glint in their eyes. Everyone looks tired and poor. The Three Mustykeers are still debating their stupid situation. 'Come on, let's get this sorted. Think of Jimmy.' 'Jimmy? What about Jimmy? Jimmy's dead.' 'Yes he's dead but he slept in Brixton for years, and walked up to Soho every day. Barefoot, usually. Said he liked feeling London under his feet.' 'As I remember, Jimmy died from fucking septicaemia or something as bad. Pigeon shit rubbed right into the split skin on his feet. So I'll pass on that one, alright?'

I've had enough of all this. I start walking away and they don't notice.

Let's have a look at what I've got. A total of thirty-five pence. A penny a year, brilliant. What an achievement, give the man a medal. I mustn't get maudlin though, I still have some pride, don't I. More than that lot anyway, their lives all buggered by bad luck and craven stupidity. I'm not to be confused with them, I chose my own way of life. I don't drink as much as them, don't do lighter fuel or glue or even poppers when someone gets lucky and feels like really celebrating. Poppers, I ask you. Stupid what it does, stupid to waste cash on it, but I understand the urge. Sometimes even that can make you feel like you're winning, like you're joining in again, back in the swing of things, with everyone else. I prefer other ways. Like when I get lucky begging and find a pub that doesn't cotton on and chuck me out before I've managed to buy a pint and drink it. Amazing, when that happens. It's been a while.

Some idiot handed me a fiver, so I turned my T-shirt inside out and went to The Angel. I marched straight through a busy lunchtime crowd and up to the bar. A few people turned to look and sniffed the air as I passed but I didn't care. I looked around casually, even nodded at a couple of tossers, I'm someone with friends, about to meet mates for a lunchtime swift one. And then I got served, just like that. Victory. I went out into the garden and had to fight the urge to tip my head back, open my throat and pour the lot down. It tasted fantastic. I finished it too quickly though, and really wanted another, but when I went back inside, the manager was standing there with his arms folded across his fat stomach. I gave him a friendly smile. 'Cheers, mate,' I said. 'Alright, son. Fair play. Now off you go,' he said. 'Alright, see you later,' I said. 'I'll call the police next time I see you,' he said. I handed him my empty glass and left feeling good. I walked back to the square with the taste lingering in my mouth, the flavour of lager without the metallic taint of a can.

What does that sign say? Camberwell one mile Elephant and Castle one and a half. Left or right. I'll walk up to the Elephant and then on to Borough or Lambeth, stay out of town for a bit but get clear of this area. From there I could go to the South Bank. I've slept there before, several times. It's quite a good place to be, at this time of year. All that concrete soaks up the heat during the day and keeps you warm well into the night. I might even find a few drinks, outside the NFT. It gets very busy in the evening, people are always rushing off without finishing their drinks and the staff are too pushed to keep checking. I can sit on one of those long benches for a while, pour a few unfinished beers into one plastic glass, admire the sick sunset over town with everybody else. Everyone relaxed and friendly. Not towards me, obviously. Nobody's going to sit down with me for a nice chat about whatever's on, what they've just seen, something good, no doubt. Godard or Herzog or Kurosawa or whatever. How do I know? How do I know about Godard and Herzog and Kurofuckingsorearse? I just do. I saw all those films, years ago. I think.

I slow down.

It's terrible when this happens, so frustrating. I hate it when the holes appear, the unseen gaps in my memory that rise up and throw me completely, pitch me sideways like potholes in the road. I should remember simple things like that, but it's the simplest things that are often the hardest to remember. It was ages ago. I used to go regularly, to see… film films films films, that's what I'm thinking about for fuck's sake.

I come to a standstill, then pace about, my foot probing the pavement for the edge of the abyss. I'm frightened.

I can't make the connection, I've forgotten it all, I don't even know what I'm doing here. Why am I in the street, where have I just been, where am I going? I scream and the traffic screams back and I'm close to tears now, this is no good, no good at all. Why is this happening? Why is my face wet? What's going on? All this, over some stupid films? I wipe my face and take a few deep breaths. I spent the night in the station, I've come from Peckham this afternoon, I'm going to the South Bank, I will find a drink and relax.

The hole closes and I step over it.

I looked up from the stub of my folded and graffitied free-ads paper and stared at the building. It took me a moment to translate the gapped lettering on the wall as the name I had circled in the paper. Pl mag Hou e was a thirties mansion block shocked into premature decline by the pushy young sixties estates that had surrounded it and then quickly stopped swinging. Its plumage had long since lost its shine as well as a couple of its letters. I was on time so I walked through the empty car park and into the central courtyard. Tiered open walkways spiralled up above and it took me a few minutes to find the right stairwell entrance. Long corridors of doors sprouted off the landings and I stopped on each and looked over the ledge.

I reached the top floor and paused. I wanted a second to catch my breath, but also to decide whether to knock. I'd seen a lot of flats by now and I usually knew even before entering whether it was a place I would consider living. Days could be spent going through the motions of keen examination and questioning when about three seconds in a building told me everything I needed to know. I looked along the hallway. Plants and shrubs were dotted outside some of the doors, and the concrete floors were clean. I walked along until I came to the number.

A heavy fug of paint fumes hit me as I walked in. The virginal white walls nicely offset the nicotine ceilings and highlighted the 'dead pensioner' furniture. It was just what I'd been looking for. The lounge was a good size and led onto a small balcony. I peered out of the greasy windows at the patch of open ground and the surrounding estate. It was suffering much more than this block, which by comparison had somehow found a certain dignity and peace in its old age.

There was no point going away to think about it so I took the place right then. The woman made a few noises about other people coming to see it but that didn't bother me. Desperation and experience had led me to carry rent and deposit around in cash, and I didn't want to cross half of the East End with it in my pocket again. The woman was thrilled with her thick envelope and couldn't hand over the keys quick enough. I knew it must be a sublet of a sublet of a sublet or something but then so were most of the flats I could afford.

That was two years ago. I moved in that night and spent the next few days cleaning the windows and tidying up the sloppy redecorating. I don't think I've done anything to the place since then. I don't really see the point when it's a rented flat, and the furniture looks all right with sheets over it. The police should think about renting a place here. The amount of petty crime, domestic violence and vandalism that takes place on the estate opposite is amazing. There's always something to watch from my lounge window. It upset me to begin with, but after a while I got used to it. It must be a terrible place to live, I think. Bright lights in shatterproof casing burn all day and all night along each corridor, giving it the ambience of a high security prison. Which it is, in a way. I don't think many of the flats can be privately owned and those that could move must have done so a long time ago. So many are empty, its face is a checkerboard of security grilles and shuttering ply. One day there'll be no one left there and I suppose it will get pulled down or sold off to be redeveloped. If they could just hang on a while longer I might be able to afford a mortgage and buy one of the dumps.

I wouldn't want to give the impression that my place is spartan, or I live a semi-monastic existence here. Not at all. But it's a bit small for entertaining, and it can take quite a while to get here on public transport. I've got a couple of pictures on the walls, ones I've carried around from flat to flat for years, even before I left college. One is a poster advertising an exhibition by the artist Yves Klein. It is a full-bleed black and white photograph of the artist jumping out of the upstairs window of a small house. His head is tipped back and his eyes are turned slightly upwards, expectantly, his arms spread like wings. The blurred motion of his action is set against the still background, the empty Parisian backstreet with a lone cyclist further along the road, riding away. The ordinary patched asphalt below him seems menacingly anticipatory. 'Leap into the Void, October 1960', it reads up one side in tiny letters.

The other is a poster I bought outside a Killing Joke gig when I was fourteen. It was the first concert I ever went to. It's a simple black and white image, framed with a thin red border. Two long columns of Nazi soldiers facing each other form an arch with their saluting arms. The Pope is walking towards the camera between them. Or at least I think it's the Pope. It could be some other high-ranking church official, but I prefer to think of it as being the Vicar of Christ, the Supreme Pontiff, himself. He is flanked by senior German officers and has one arm raised in salutation, dispensing a papal blessing. He is smiling, modestly. Please, enough, you're all too kind. The words 'Malicious Damage' are printed very small beneath his feet. I remember the night I bought it so clearly, coming out of the venue in a state of intense excitement, drenched with sweat and my ears ringing. I recall seeing the band merchandise on the pavement and pushing through the human traffic heading for night buses to take a closer look. I was used to seeing all kinds of images and statements used by bands, but something about this poster took me by surprise. It was very simple, and there was a lot going on at the same time. I persuaded the man selling them to let me have one for the change I had saved to catch a bus. I walked all the way home with it rolled up under my arm

The corners are a bit tattered on both from the sticking and unsticking of Blu Tak so I got frames for them when I moved here. The frames granted them a sort of permanence; sometimes I wonder what significance these images can have in my life after all this time, and why I don't replace them with something else. Especially the Killing Joke poster. But the Yves Klein is a beautiful, surprising image, and so in its own way is the Pope blessing Nazis – it was the first photograph I ever saw that really made me think about how radical a picture could be in a unexpected context. I still like the posters and it would be a nuisance to take the backing off the frames so I leave them as they are.

A few shelves of books. A stack of records I haven't played since my turntable broke. Piles of CDs, a box of tapes not opened since college. A decent television and video recorder and a rather nice leather armchair I bought not long ago. Two woven rugs purchased in a sale because they would have been way beyond my budget otherwise. My computer, which I use for my personal work. And my bed, which I saved for and would say is one of my few luxury items. I don't sleep well, and I need a good bed.

I work in an office that deals exclusively in making places look nicer, temporarily. I can't think of a better way of putting it. We take nasty, dirty old inner city streets and squares and buildings and make them a bit neater and tidier. It's an alright job in an alright company. But you have to appreciate I don't fit in well where I work, and the work itself, my job, isn't really 'me' either. I think it's the rather ephemeral, surface nature of these improvements that bothers me. We don't actually 'build' anything. There is no vision of genuine urban renewal, or whatever. No utopian buildings or groundbreaking housing schemes. We apply a veneer, not even a veneer, more like a thin plastic film, over decaying reality. It's more often than not a question of deciding what shade of purple to paint a decrepit tower block, rather than admitting the tower block is a terrible place to live, and determining how best to improve it.

So much of what we do is really about control, prevention. I know as well as anyone that in a big city like this things would be impossible without an element of control. I'm not going to start standing on the left of the escalator, or wandering into the road without looking. That would be annoying to others and dangerous, too. It's the subtlety of our schemes that gets to me. The way it's all dressed in nicety to camouflage its true purpose. Brian would no doubt despair if he heard me say this. He would go on about urban navigation, the relationship between pedestrian and pavement, or something. I don't know, maybe he's right. I suppose a lot of the work is about safety, or simply getting people to work on time. It just bores me so much I sometimes daydream about acts of vandalism so dreadful an army couldn't put it right. Another Great Fire of London to give me a level playing field, a chance to start from scratch. Not that I'm an extreme person, particularly. No more extreme than most people, when they're thinking to themselves.

I've found them. I've walked all over town today, even though my leg is throbbing, but I had to work out who did it, and find them. I've been attacked before. I'm familiar with people venting a bit of frustration on me at night, giving my body a kick on their way to the tube. You go out for a nice meal but your girlie gives you the elbow and you're ever so upset about it and you get shitfaced and then your true nature takes over. This was worse though. When I woke up I couldn't remember anything at all about it, I just sat there staring at the gash in my calf, my jeans all stiff and stuck with dried blood. I thought really hard and after a while a voice came back to me, and then another. 'Here he is, look, Taddy, here he is. Kick him, hit the fucker. Where's my tenner you cunt where's my money give me my money you thieving shite. Taddy Tad come on man gotta go come on.' Tadpole and Mikey, I'm certain of it. A pair of vicious bastards, the only difference between them being Tadpole's stupidity and his willingness to do anything Mikey tells him to. He set him on me while I slept in a doorway on Berwick Street.

I've been down to Embankment and up again but I can see them now. I step back off the street, move to one side to get a better view. The smell of chips from somewhere behind me is such a distraction but I keep looking. There they are, in Princes Circus. What a joke, just look at them, two bodies slumped on a bench. Suits stepping over and around them. Empty cans are scattered everywhere; they must have been thieving today. How funny, there's a fine public sculpture for you. Cast the fuckers in metal and bolt them down. Princes in the Circus, lifesize bronze. They've got Churchill and Roosevelt over on New Bond Street, why not Tadpole and Mikey here? They're a dirty blur of filth, slumbering garbage. Mikey in his red bobble hat, even in this weather. Taddy next to him, leaning on his shoulder and snoring peacefully. Like a couple of old dears in front of a gas fire. My leg twitches, urging me to do something about this.

I walk further along and cross over, round by the pub and back past the umbrella shop. The street brings me round behind them. I stand there, considering the possibilites. Should I grab a bin and smash their heads in? They'd never even know about it. That's no good, it's the middle of the day, people are all around us. A gang of motorbike couriers are eating sandwiches just a few feet away, and the roads that surround this island are packed with cars. And I don't think I'd have the strength or will.

I step in front of them and take Mikey's hat off. He twitches and turns over, but doesn't wake up. I lean over and put it on Tadpole, wait a second and then pull it down firmly. A subtle intervention, but one with all sorts of ramifications and possible consequences. I'm hungry and the scent of fried food is still in my nostrils. I'll eat a bag of chips and come back in a while.

These chips are good. I like the people who run that shop. They must all be members of one family, I think. There's a strange picture on the wall, a framed black and white photo of a teenager in basketball gear shaking hands with someone the size of a dwarf. Britain's Tallest Man it says underneath. Poor bastard. He looks a bit like the people in the shop; perhaps he's a cousin or something. I eat the chips as I wander around Neal Street. I don't like it here anymore. It lost its individuality years ago, became an extension of Covent Garden. It's hard to believe that it was ever a run down warehouse district, not always a mecca for tourists blind to the naffness of it all. And I really hate all these hippy shops. Expensive rubbish. An ecofriendly money machine. The cheese shop just about sums it up for me. It fills the street with its ripe stink, completely overwhelming on a hot day like this. It amazes me that not only does no one complain, the fowl stench lures them in.

I've remembered something very funny, connected to that shop. It must have been a couple of years ago. Who was it? Oh yes, yes, it was Suntan. Oh God, that was good. A gang of us were walking around, waiting for the hostel up there on Endell Street to open, trying to avoid police, who hate us in groups even more than on our own. We walked down here, down Shorts Gardens, from Seven Dials. Then the evil smell wafted up to greet us. We were all pissed and I started pretending to gag. We went past the doorway and saw a big queue trailing out onto the street. It was all too much for Suntan, too good an opportunity. He marched over and dropped his trousers, and launched into a mock market-trader rant: 'Here you go, anyone want some best knobcheese? Come and get yer Lovely Knobcheese, exotic and genuine, fresh from the source!' On and on, oh God, thought I would die laughing. The fools didn't know which way to turn. The queue dissolved; a bit too much association, obviously, between his antics and that smell. We all fell about in the street, pointing and laughing. Superb. We clapped while Suntan pulled his jeans back up and took a bow. What a day. A rare thing, and hard work, raising a genuine laugh, a real funny moment, that doesn't involve somebody else's real misfortune.

I finish my chips. Poor Suntan. It took months for them to identify him. There aren't many Asians on the street, perhaps that's why he was always fooling around, trying to make people laugh, even the total psychos it's best to avoid. That was his undoing, I'm sure of it. They found him in a closed skip miles away, I don't remember where. Burnt. The police reckoned he must have been alive when he was set on fire. But Suntan was only small. The image of him burning, his thin arms clawing at the metal sides, made me think of those photos in the paper during the Gulf War. Iraqis sticking out of tanks, cooked to a blister and unrecognisable as men. Their gaping black mouths open forever in agony.

I wonder what his real name was.

I've been gone ages, I better go back. I walk up Endell Street and cross over by the theatre. No one's there. Shit, they've gone, I've missed it! I bet they didn't even notice, I bet the stupid fuckers just woke up and moved on. Tad's so thick he might end up wearing the thing for months before remembering it's Mikey and not him who's known for his trademark hat. No, wait, something did happen. There's a pool of blood, a slick of fresh red right here, where they were sitting. Mikey might have killed him. He could have woken up and gone completely mental, it wouldn't be the first time. Mikey's always been one to watch, especially after a session, when he wakes up. Horrible moody fucker. But Tadpole would have hit back, for sure. The pair of them are as bad as each other. No respect at all, not for anything, even themselves. Camaraderie of the street, bollocks. I wish I'd seen it. Never mind, there'll be talk. Someone will know what happened.

My feet were killing me. It was my own fault. I'd been suffering ever since I got a new pair of shoes. I'd set out with the intention of getting the same ones I always get. Men's shoes are very difficult to buy, because they are nearly all horrible, I think. Once you've found a style that you like, that really suits you, well that's it, isn't it? You just have to pray they keep on making them. But as I was walking along I glanced at a shop I would never consider looking in normally. There in the window were a pair of shoes that looked a lot like the ones I had on. I went in and took a closer look. They were virtually identical. In fact I'd say they were copies. The leather was a bit thin and not quite the right shade of brown but I bought them anyway. Why spend the extra? I thought. I felt a bit guilty as I left the shop and stuffed the carrier bag and shoes into my rucksack. Now I was really paying for it. My heels were rubbed raw. I'd worn the shoes to work for a couple of days to try and break them in and by the Friday I'd had to take a cab because I couldn't manage the steps at the tube. It was ridiculous. I had spent what I would in two weeks travelling to work in two mornings. So I had decided to ignore the pain and wear them anyway.

I sat at my desk and undid the laces. I caught the back of one heel with the toe of the other foot and prised the shoe off. I could almost feel my foot getting bigger, returning gratefully to its normal size. I levered off the other one while I played with my mouse and looking around to make sure no one was watching. I thought about reaching under my desk and placing the shoes in my bin without even looking at them. I didn't have any other footwear with me, and it would look strange if I got up from my desk and padded about in my socks. How would I get home? And I wasn't thrilled at the idea of the cleaning lady finding a pair of new shoes in my bin. It wouldn't really help my standing with her. I knew she had formed a strong opinion of me on her very first morning. I'd gone in early to finish off a document on the standardisation of street furniture in central Oslo, and I thought I had the place to myself. I was almost through with my corrections. The streets of inner Oslo need never be disharmonious again; no two lampposts would jar aesthetically, the height and diameter of any given bollard would match perfectly that of any other.

'People of Oslo, Rejoice!' I said. I turned around and there she was.

'Don't mind me,' I said. 'Just finished.'

She just stood there, frowning.

'Oslo. Unified urban image,' I offered.

She shuffled away towards the loos, looking at me sideways and sniffing.

I squirmed slightly and turned back to my screen to close the file. I noticed that the very first word was 'Srteet'. I swore under my breath and started going over it yet again.

I was not happy about the shoes. In fact it was playing on my mind. I knew they were a cheaper option, but they weren't even made properly. I'd noticed a tiny crack appearing on the side of each shoe, where my swollen feet were rubbing most. I tried to put it out of mind, but the cracks got worse and worse. I persevered with them until I got home one rainy night with wet feet. I took them off, and saw a hole in the sole of each shoe. That was it, the final straw. I would complain to the manufacturers

30th May 1994
Mr C G Clarke
Kent Shoes
PO Box 89
Cardiff

Dear Mr Clarke

I am writing to you to complain about the quality of a pair of Kent shoes that I bought several weeks ago.

Within a month the sides of each shoe had started to split, and by the fifth week a large hole had developed on each outer side. The soles have also worn out extremely quickly, and there are now holes on the bottom of each shoe.

I have worn this pair no more than two days a week, and always keep them clean and well polished.

Perhaps they are simply a slightly defective pair but I would be grateful to hear your comments on this matter.

Yours sincerely

10th June, 1994
Mrs S. Armer
Kent Shoes
PO Box 89
Cardiff

Dear Mrs. Armer
   Thank you for your recent letter.
Enclosed are the shoes I wrote to you about. I think you will agree that for such light wear and otherwise good condition of the uppers, the splits and cracks on either side are unusual. I look forward to hearing from you once you have completed your inspection.
Yours sincerely

9th July 1994
Mr C Clarke, Service and Returns Manager
Kent Shoes
PO Box 89
Cardiff
Complaint Ref. 034K Style 1442 1

Dear Mr Clarke

Thank you for your most amusing letter dated 6th July concerning my GLENDALE shoes, which I returned to you for inspection. Having given the matter some thought, I have realised, alas all too late, my mistake.

As you so subtly point out, I do indeed have mildly perspiring feet, and this can, as you say, cause problems. But having examined my eight other pairs of shoes, I quickly discovered the problem – cheap footwear. Having always purchased shoes from Church's (I believe the GLENDALE is a cheap copy of a Church's shoe, is it not?) I have enjoyed owning footwear which has only grown more comfortable with continued wear.

My mistake had been to ignore what experience had already taught me, that good shoes tend to be rather expensive, and that the kind of footwear manufactured by a company like Kent Shoes best be avoided, despite the initial financial saving. Your leather uppers are made from a low-grade material that is both stiff and thin. Despite your pathetic denials and insinuations, I maintain that the shoes in question have been subjected to only very light use (I run an office, not a building site) therefore I can only assume this is further evidence of their poor quality and general flimsiness.

Thank you for confirming my suspicions about your product. Kindly inform whomever at your Oxford Street branch it may concern (preferably that incredibly rude and bombastic Irish salesman) to stick my shoes where they belong – in the bin.

I do not expect any further correspondence on this matter.

I look in a shop window and don't recognise the reflection. A man on a crutch in pea green clothes. Not clothes exactly; an outfit, uniform, maybe. The words UCH OUTPATIENTS across my chest and back. It's another hot day, and these hospital clothes are lovely, all soft and light, laundered a thousand times. I look different and feel different. I haven't felt this clean for a while. I hobble along on the crutch gripping a plastic bag of nasty old things through the handle. It swings in the way every few steps, bumping my knees. I would stop and change hands, but I really want to get off the main road. People are staring at me and my leg is hurting badly. I have to stop and adjust the bandage, I can feel it slipping. There is a strong smell of sweet antiseptic. My leg is already wet underneath, fresh pus must be gathering. That's alright, that's part of the process, they said, and it will heal over.

I woke up yesterday and couldn't move my leg properly. I sat up and gave it a good rub and nearly passed out with the pain. Bastard Taddy. I had some memory of it feeling sore last night, I got annoyed and poured something on it. Brandy. Yes, that was it. I was under the bridge, and there was a woman I hadn't seen before, her eyes wild and empty in the darkness, a definite hospital case. She had a bottle she'd nicked, God knows where from. She held it tightly to her chest, rocked it like a baby. Her wrists were as thin and fragile as the neck of the bottle, a plastic identity tag dangling from one of them. I was already drunk and wanted more. I asked and asked until she handed it over, because she liked me, she said, in a strange strangled voice. I took a big gulp and then pulled up my trouser leg and doused the flaming wound. The pain made me yelp. 'Why'd you do that?' she screamed, pulling the baby back. 'I saw it in a film, a cowboy with an arrow in his arm did it,' I said. 'That's whisky you fuckin dickhead.' 'Oh. Sorry.' The brandy made my leg sticky and boiling hot, it hurt worse than ever. 'Serves you fuckin right,' she said. I think I passed out after that.

I don't really know how I got all the way up Tottenham Court Road to Emergency this morning. I didn't have to wait long, thank God, in fact I've never seen it so quiet. There was one person in front of me, a small thin man with a stomach that stuck out like a balloon. He clung onto it, groaning, surrounded by empty orange juice bottles. He was a real sight. He kept belching and frowning. When the nurse came out and saw all the bottles she started shouting at him. 'Mr Jones if you drink another drop of orange juice I will call security and have you removed. You say you have a sore stomach and that you need help. You are in pain because of all the orange juice you drank yesterday and today and we will refuse you treatment if you go and get another bottle. Understood?' He looked like a dog told off for shitting on the carpet. He looked so sick he might fall off the chair. The nurse stomped back through the doors and he slowly got to his feet and limped out towards the cold drinks machines, counting his change.

– What you got?
– What?
– What you got? What's in the bag?

It's a girl I see around often but whose name I don't know, a thin pale ghoul with the intense energy typical of many junkies. She's with a young man but he's of no consequence, she's the provider in this relationship. I stop and hold the bag behind me, but she's already got her nose inside it.

– Nothing.

– They give you something, didn't they? What they give you, pain killers?

– No, nothing. Some ointment but nothing like that, no drugs.

She looks at my leg, sees the bulk of bandages through the thin cotton trousers.

– Alright. Where you going?

She hops from one foot to the other and clutches her elbows, looking around nervously like a meerkat.

– Just down, down there.

I point with the crutch towards Charing Cross Road.

She's not listening, I'm not of any value now. She tugs at her feeble accomplice's arm while I'm still speaking and they jog into the road. A bus blares its horn and she waves her arm vaguely in its direction until they reach the other side. They run up to someone, I can't see who, a figure that takes a step back trying to fend off their attention.

Another bus blots them out and when it pulls away again they've gone.

Can just make out some letters on the underside, disappearing around the curve. A fragment, nothing more. H A B then it gets lost in a blur of some kind of fibrous material before ending in A T. There's some form of vegetation, slightly furry with sharp edges, drooping over the edge just in front, very green and lush. Especially against the smooth, slightly shiny white surface around it.

If I squint with my left eye shut, the half-empty coffee mug and the plate with remains of some salad on it are towering above me, even though they're sitting on the living room floor. But then, I am lying on the carpet, and they are on the rug, which has quite a thick pile. That's madness, a total injustice. How come they get the nice soft rug to rest on? They are receptacles, inanimate objects, they don't care where they're put, they have no feelings or views on the matter, and they aren't entitled to any. I too am presently inanimate and even, perhaps, a receptacle of sorts but I do have feelings. Hurt ones. My cheekbone and shoulder are painful from being pressed against the thin acrylic carpet.

Right that's it, I'm taking charge of this situation, I'm going to redress the balance in favour of me. Sorry, items of crockery, you'll just have to make do a few inches that way. I push them without moving, using the hand which isn't trapped under my stomach. They slide along and then tip off the edge of the rug. I sit up and see the pool of cold coffee slowly sinking into the ochre carpet.

Shit.

This is getting a bit silly. I'm bored. I'm at a loose end. I'm holding two loose ends and there's nothing in the middle. I'm very very bored.

This is why I try not to spend too much time here at home. As much as I like it and find it quite comfortable, I tend to get a bit stir crazy after a few hours. I haven't really learnt the ropes of living alone, even though I've been doing it for years now. It just hasn't quite clicked yet. I'm sure it will. I think it will become a doddle, my preferred state of being, probably shortly after I meet a really nice girl and just before we decide to be wed and buy a little house together and have kiddies. At that moment, it will all make perfect sense. I will be a master of solitary existence, a true devotee of life lived alone. *Then* I'll be depressed. *That's* when it will kick in, I know it. Just my luck. I'd better get something to soak that coffee up or it will leave a stain.

I'm exaggerating, of course. I really don't mind being single, and I've become quite used to not sharing bathrooms and kitchens with a hoard of vulgar college mates. It's just that on a night like this, a clear, warm early summer's eve, when everyone's out there, eating and drinking, trying to decide which of the innumerable social pleasures they will engage in, I get a bit annoyed that I don't know more people. This is the price one pays, I suppose, for revelling in domestic bliss through the long winter months, tucked up in front of the television with a few beers and a takeaway, completely oblivious to the chilly world outside. The doorbell would be ignored, the phone off the hook, mobile switched to voicemail, during a snug winter's night in.

Thinking about this reminds me of the time when I broke my leg. I was young, it's a long time ago, it wasn't a particularly traumatic experience. I fell out of a tree, hit the ground, one of the others came up and said 'You alright?' and I said 'think so', then sat up, tried to stand and said, 'bust my leg though' and fainted and that's about all I can recall of the incident itself. I was a menace on crutches. Once I'd been caught lending them to a mate to pin someone's head to the ground and then seen trying to drag my leg back up the tree, I was made to stay in each night until the bone had knitted.

I lay there in my room each evening listening to the others outside, shouting and laughing until after it was dark and parents could be heard issuing threats in vain. I had been dreading it, fearing the intense boredom and loneliness, the envy I would feel not being able to join in. But actually I liked it. Detached from all the activity, reduced to a spectator of the hyperactive mayhem in the field below, I saw and heard things differently. Or rather, I chose *not* to see things.

For the first couple of days I would hobble to the window and lean on the sill to watch whatever was happening. Then one night I lay down, closed my eyes, and found myself analysing through sound the relationships of the kids I knew. I detected all sort of nuances that would never have occurred to me had I been there in the thick of it, too busy running about to listen to what was actually being said. If I stayed on my bed and looked only at the light on the walls and the shadows whose movements told me roughly what time it was, I created much more interesting and intimate pictures in my mind of what was going on outside.

For example. The night that Danny beat up his brother Michael for riding his bike through the gully and busting the front wheel. That incident seen from my window would have consisted of a patch of jostling corn containing two wrestling dots, accompanied by a bit of muffled shouting, under a sky all blotched and purple. Nice sky, rubbish fight. But enjoyed from my pillow with my eyes gently closed, it was much more entertaining. The squeak of Danny's front wheel, each time the buckled rim squeezes through the brake blocks, as Michael pushes the bike slowly through the field towards the back of the house next door, hoping not to be noticed. The clump clump clump of Danny's feet rising and falling in the tall grass from further away, catching up fast with Michael. The squeak becomes more urgent as Michael hears the clumping and tries to get to the edge of the grass and reach the back door. The squeak and the clump get closer together, there is a rattle of metal as the bike topples and Michael makes a break for it, hoping Danny will prefer to rescue his knackered bike rather than deal immediately with the culprit. The bigger feet continue past the steady clip clip clip of a free-spinning back wheel and Michael lets out a yelp of denial that's muted by Danny's fist. Then there is a confused battle of grunting, swearing and slapping, then the violent silence of a score settled, followed by heavy breathing. Two pairs of lungs are struggling for air, one recovering from the exertion of the chase and administration of punishment, the other fighting with physical pain and hurt emotions. Another rattle of metal as the bike is lifted, and the slow squeak resumes, getting closer until stopping just below. A slammed door and then silence, apart from some distant crowing and a hushed snivelling that continues for a while from the field.

I'm going for a pint, I can't stay here on the carpet until bedtime.

– What does he want?
– Says he don't want anything, wants to sleep that's all.
– Tell him to get lost.

– What now?
– Says he's been in hospital, needs to sleep indoors.
– Tell him to fuck off, there's no room, we got here first.
– Why don't we let him?
– Because.
– Why?
– Because there's no room and I don't want that smelly old fucker with us all night.
– OK, OK, just asking. Loads of room.
– We found it first, we've got to protect it. We can make this our base and we don't want to share it, do we? Do we?
– No, no, you're right.
– Course I am.
– Do you really think we can?

– Can what?

– Make this our base, like you said?

– Why not? Bet no one's been here for ages. No power or anything. We can try and fix that door tomorrow, we'll nick a lock.

– That's a good idea! We could nick a lock and some tools and we could do it up a bit.

– Yeah, well. No need to go mad. We won't be here long. Just need somewhere to dump our stuff during the day and sleep at night, don't we.

– Right. Good plan. Did you go up west today?

– Yeah. Told you so.

– Oh yeah. Did you see that guy, the one I spoke to yesterday?

– Who?

– You know the one. Can't remember his name. We saw him yesterday, in Leicester Square.

– What the one with the mad scars on his arms?

– Yeah him. Was he about?

– No. Why d'you ask?

– Dunno. Just wondered. He talks funny.

– You talk funny.

– You know what I mean. He uses funny words. Goes on about people, watches everything all day.

– Yeah, he's a real laugh. Keeps me in stitches.

– You know what I'm saying. He's always talking, telling you about things. He's strange.

– He's mad, if that's what you mean. Don't waste your time listening to him for fuck's sake or I'll stop hanging about with you before it rubs off. He's a nutter, or he was a nutter.

– I don't think he is. He seems really calm to me.

– He's calm because he's off his tits.

– No he isn't. He doesn't do anything apart from booze. He told me.

– Oh did he. Listen, get it straight, we don't have any dealings with his sort. Understand?

– Yes.
– Understand?
– Ow! Fuckin get off, I heard you! I won't talk to him.
– Good.

– Oh fuckin hell what is that now?
– He says it's cold on the stairs. Says he only came out the hossie yesterday, he had an operation on his head.
– Tell him he'll need another if he touches that door again.
– Come on, he can sleep in the hall bit.
– Do what you like, I'm sleeping.

It sometimes occurs that the place I choose to eat my lunch is the same venue as the one chosen that particular day by Sarah. And what's more, it's usually the case when this happens that there won't be a free seat at any other table or bench and so I am obliged to have my lunch with her.

This isn't entirely true.

I follow her at a distance, see which café or square she goes to and then check to see if there are any spare places to sit. If it's busy, and there aren't, and I'm in the mood, I go and join her. It can be good fun, as Sarah detests me.

I don't know why. Alright, I do, I know exactly why. Sarah is in her late twenties but acts and dresses much older. She has held the same job for several years and is good at it. The position mainly involves keeping the computer system up and running and deflecting criticism from Brian. She hates her job violently and would not reveal this under torture, I'm certain. As steadily as her career has ground to a standstill she has adopted the ways and manners of someone a generation away.

This process included, shortly before I arrived at the company, a very formal engagement to the forty-three year old manager of a central London branch of the Halifax Building Society.

So the Sarah I met on my first day was a rather aloof individual. My very first image of her was of a small, rather bird-like creature, tense in a tweedy suit and dominated by a large ring that dangled from one of her thin fingers and flashed madly. I went to shake her hand and the gem-encrusted symbol of her imminent betrothal was held so high I wondered if I was meant to kiss it. Her voice was smartly clipped and she almost shook with adrenalin as she spoke. She was high on the expectation of going on to better things and moving to some semi-rural enclave at any moment. It was just as well that she didn't literally hold her breath, as the engagement became lengthy by even the poshest standards and the subject of much discussion. Alas, disaster struck, and this financial magnate, this titan of the economy dumped her only recently for, it pains me to say, a slightly younger woman at his own branch. A fact none of us are supposed to be aware of. I know because Tony saw Sarah storm out of the office one day and when he looked in her cubicle he saw an open email on her screen from her beloved, bravely declaring his intention to terminate their engagement and announcing his new found love. Tony then sent me an email about it.

She hates me because I am a 'feckless, daydreaming idler', apparently. To me this translates thus: I am her own age. I am a daily reminder of the youthful ways that she so insistently cast behind her, imagining it would boost her flagging career, perhaps unaware of the gulf she was stepping into. She adopted the persona of an older woman from a different background and found herself still trying to shake free of a job and social station that clung to her, like a snake trying to shed its skin too soon. She entered a veritable no-woman's land. And then she has to come to work and see me every day, utterly unfettered by etiquette or ambition, and it drives her nuts, poor thing. She's a bullying snob of the worst variety and it occasionally gives me pleasure to bait her.

Today is one such day. Sarah has been on at me all morning, her tight face bobbing over the top of my workstation each time she drops another file onto my desk, a habit that she knows I don't like. It wouldn't be very difficult for her to prise herself away from whatever menial task she is engaged in and take the three steps around the corner of my cubicle. I wouldn't expect her to smile or anything.

I allow her a few minutes to settle in while I hover outside. She seems determined to get a whole table to herself and once she's secured one towards the back of the café spreads her bag and jacket across the seats. She seems more nervy than usual today; she fiddles with her hair, frowning into the tiny mirror of her compact. Then she takes a book out of her bag and holds it up in front of her face in a way that suggests she isn't actually reading it. I enter the café and slide along the seat opposite her and cough lightly. The book is lowered and Sarah twitches. Her eyes are a remarkable shade of hazel that deepens towards the iris, flecked with tiny shards of grey flint. They would be beautiful if they didn't confess so readily her brittle and poisonous nature.

'Oh. It's *you*,' she says.

'It is. In person. How the devil are you Sarah?'

'Oh drop it.' She holds the book as though someone has just placed it in her hands.

'Ok. Sorry. So, how's the book?' I gently hold the top edge of the pages.

Sarah tugs it back and quickly puts it in her bag. 'It's very good, thank you.'

'Have you got to that bit yet?'

'Which *bit*?' Her eyes glint as she leans back and a stray beam of daylight catches her pale cheek.

'You know. The bit that everyone raves about. The big twist.'

Sarah sighs and rebuttons her jacket as though I have been leering at her chest. She is particularly tense this lunchtime and I cast my mind back to try and think if I have done anything specific lately to piss her off. No, I don't think so. She picks up the menu and holds it between us but I can see the tip of her peeling nose sticking out one side. What is wrong with her?

The door opens and a man comes in on his own. I turn to look at him because the menu has twitched like an antenna. He scans the room and just as he's about to leave he sees Sarah's fluttering hand that has appeared in the air in front of me. He grins and approaches our booth, his eyes bouncing between Sarah and myself. He's probably in his mid-thirties, slightly balding with a round tanned face and he's wearing a suit that suggests he works in a better part of town. He moves towards my side, so I slide to the edge of the seat and he's forced to sit alongside her. Sarah has to shuffle further in to make room, tugging her jacket and bag clear as he sits down awkwardly. She gives me a filthy look and I smile warmly at them both.

The most summary of introductions are made by Sarah, the kind that are designed to inform one person that there is absolutely no attraction whatsoever between themselves and the unwelcome, uninvited other. Robert relaxes a bit once my credentials as work colleague have been established and we shake hands over the table. His elbow brushes against Sarah's hair and I'm pleased at the amount of annoyance this causes her.

'Robert, it's so nice out, maybe we should get a sandwich and sit in the park?'

This is not a question, it is a demand. Not a necessary one, as he is visibly relieved. Robert looks at me.

'That sounds nice. You don't mind, do you?' He smiles and I see a row of very good teeth.

'Not at all. That sounds like a good idea.' I stand up.

Sarah and Robert stare at me and then at each other. Robert swallows hard and Sarah bristles with anger. I wait for him to oppose me joining them.

'Yes. Let's go, then.'

Ah. So he's married.

This is instantly clear to me. Two people in the early throws of a romantic involvement would not willingly tolerate the presence of an irritating spectator like me. There would be no need for overt politeness; they would not go to such lengths to maintain cover. I will bet anything that not only is he married, but that he has never done anything like this before and he is absolutely shit scared of being exposed. If not, why would Sarah meet him in a dump like this instead of somewhere nearer his own office? Their edgy body language also suggests to me they haven't slept together yet.

Sarah is now so furious I think she might shatter into fragments if she bangs against the table. We go to the counter and order sandwiches. I stand in front of them knowing an argument is raging mutely behind me. We walk around the corner towards a square that is surrounded by long benches.

'I think we're in luck, not too many people on the grass.' I steer them both towards an empty spot before Sarah can protest. I drop my things and flop down languidly. Come on in, the water's fine.

Robert and Sarah look at each other and then lower themselves gently towards the grass. They behave as though sitting on the ground is an entirely new concept to them. Robert hitches his trousers up and Sarah has some difficulty adopting a suitably ladylike pose. Her legs are folded under her, both knees leaning one way. We start eating and I make a few light-hearted comments about the people in our office. Sarah tears tiny clumps from her sandwich and seems to get them into her mouth without opening it. But it is Robert who is fulfilling all my expectations, supplying the results I hoped for from the experiment I'm conducting here today.

His eyes have not left Sarah's legs from the moment we sat down. She is wearing a particularly tight skirt, one she would not have chosen had she known there was to be any grass-sitting involved during today's tryst. Sarah's physique is unusual. A small nicely formed head sits on a compact upper body, her arms and waist slender to the point of thin. From there down the change is swift and dramatic. Her arse and thighs are broad and comely, but it is the rest of her legs that are the real surprise. They are huge. Her knees would be more appropriate on a woman at least twice her size. Her calves are solid shapeless tubes that sit on bulging ankles. When she wears open fronted shoes a plate of embossed flesh stands proud of the surface. She looks as though someone has bound her waist tightly and then pumped air in through her toes. A cruel observation perhaps. But I know that nearly everyone at work, male or female, has made the same one.

Robert's eyes are cautiously fixed on the twin white masses of her knees that protrude from the hem of her skirt. I keep chatting away amiably while he glances down at the pink flesh straining against the side strap of her shoe. It's just as I suspected. This would-be Lothario is mentally backtracking before the game's even begun. What a coward. He's really not up to scratch. What kind of man is he to be put off by a pair of stout legs? What about her inner beauty? I am doing Sarah a favour. She would thank me if she knew.

They hardly seem aware I'm there now. She is looking moodily at the floor, still darting flecks of food into her tiny mouth and chewing over this precious moment lost forever and he is adjusting his clothes, taking peeks at his watch and fiddling with his mobile phone. I finish my lunch in silence and then stand up.

'Well, I'll leave you two lovebirds alone.'

They are both shaken back to life by my affirmation of their interest in each other. I tell Robert I look forward to meeting him again, and cheerfully inform Sarah I will see her back in the office shortly. Neither of them says anything. I swing my jacket over my shoulder and stroll out of the park. Just before I leave the gates I look back. Sarah's head is leaning on

Robert's shoulder, she's taken one of his hands and holds it in her lap. He is gazing up at the buildings.

– You watch this for us?

– What?

There's a kid standing over me. He's no more than a teenager. It's always the same at this time of year. The warm weather brings them here in their hundreds. It's easy to understand why. Tempers flair at home, the city seems appealing, it's exciting and parentless, escape from their tormentors. No need to have a proper place to stay, plenty of people to steal from. He can't have been here long. He still looks as though he's travelling somewhere, rather than having reached a very final destination. Give it time.

– Got to go and meet someone, can't take this. You look after it? I'll be back in a bit.

Why me? Do I look like a father figure, a good samaritan, a guardian angel?

– I'm not hanging around here long myself.

– Please, mate, I've got to get some gear. I'll split it with you. Just half an hour, please.

His eyes are all shiny with the need to get going and score. It's early morning and I like to start walking at this time, before the rush begins. He wasn't here when I lay down last night, and I don't think he's slept at all. He grins and grinds his crooked teeth, a horrible gritty sound.

– OK, OK, but half an hour, all right? And a word of advice: in future just stash it in some bushes or something, don't go offering your stuff to someone you don't know.

– Oh fuck, yeah. Thanks, mate. Back in a bit.

I nod and he sprints across the road, disappearing from view and my life in seconds. The bag is quite new, the zip still works and the handles are in good shape. I get up and have a look through it. A Walkman with layers and layers of Sellotape around it, a couple of grubby porno mags, jeans and a sweater. I swap our pathetic possessions over and throw the strap of my tattered rucksack over the railings. He'll find it.

I can't imagine why I thought the hospital smock and trousers would be a good idea. I must have looked ridiculous in them. They drew too much attention and didn't protect me from the chill at night. I couldn't do anything about them with my leg so bad and had to wait until I could get about without the crutch. Clothes aren't hard to find, though, and I had no trouble replacing them. People throw out decent things all the time. I took a detour out of town over to Notting Hill and went through a few bins. It took a long time to get there, with my leg still so sore, but I found what I'm now wearing within minutes of searching. There were a couple of old suitcases outside one of the big houses, and I knew instinctively they'd be full of clothes. Most of them were no good or too big but the second case was full of stuff I could use. So today I am sporting stonewashed jeans, a blue T-shirt, a grey sleeveless jumper and a tweed jacket. And, I can't quite believe it myself, a pair of old but sound brogues, which are almost the right size.

Dressed in this way, I feel much calmer again. Manners don't make the man, clothes do. I haven't been too bad lately anyway;

the whirring inside has been low and steady, and I've been drinking less. It can all change at any time, but for now, I'm in charge. I understand things properly. A night lasts a night and not several days. With a better sense of time comes a sense of proportion. The odds are stacked against me, the scales of injustice tipped over completely. It's not a problem, and there's no point fighting it. I'm OK, I'm still young, keep in shape, I learnt all the tricks early on. Got to keep your feet good, got to get a shave every now and then. Every day I see those who haven't realised this. The ones who make people gasp, stare in disbelief and revulsion. Characters who've unwittingly cast themselves. 'Ben Gunns'. It's so easy to get like that. Stop seeing your reflection in shop windows, stop knowing you exist. Start ignoring your smell, your hair, skin. And then one day you look up, and for some reason see yourself properly for the first time in a while, in a chrome door or a plate glass window, and you don't know what you're looking at. A bizarre stooped figure with his feet bound in rotting cloth and white eyes that pop out of a jet black mass of hair and beard. I know because it happened to me, once. Never again.

I check my pockets. Keys, map, pen. My notes. My evidence of the decline. I flick through my scraps of paper and find the one I was looking for.

> Base £5 Cash Note Removed of Crown for Every Breath's Experience That Royal Was RANT ACEUW ACEM Cannibal Power by English Asian or World Anthrophysic.

I've carried this one with me for a long time. I saw it written on a wall, in the underpass beneath Centrepoint, and scribbled it down immediately. People write all sorts of things on walls all the time, and I dutifully record a lot of it. But this statement made me sing inside and I had no idea why. There are times when I feel as if I'm on the verge of understanding what it means. It's nonsense, no doubt, but beautiful as well. A poem I can appreciate. I often wonder who wrote it and where they might be now. It could be a crumpled body in a doorway, a nothing I've passed blankly a hundred times on the street. It could be a man sitting down to dinner with his wife and kids somewhere in the suburbs, someone who once threw a coin in my direction as he passed without looking. There's no way of knowing. I fold it up carefully and put it back in my pocket. I've decided to give my new image a test. I'll hide my stuff in one of my regular places and walk along Oxford Street, all the way to the park, to that gallery. I'll go via Speaker's Corner. I haven't been there for a long time.

I noticed as soon as I moved here how many pubs there are. Every estate corner seems to have one; each must have a loyal group of regulars, all from just a few rows of council flats. There would very rarely be anyone else in these tiny run-down places. I tried a number of them in the first few weeks. Each was different and they were all the same. The same vague atmosphere of menace when I walked in, the sense that I'd stumbled in as a fight was about to erupt or some furtive deal was being struck. How odd that in the middle of such dense urban living the experience of walking into a bar was like that of walking into a village pub in the middle of nowhere; a place unused to the attention of strangers and bristling with repressed hostility.

But there was one that wasn't as threatening as the others were, where after a couple of visits I could at least nod in the general direction of the bar and get the most cursory of nods back. It was called The Flask. I called it The Broken Bottle. The seats were sticky and the surface of every table was pitted with cigarette burns but there were a few regulars about my age, and one or two who weren't even 'local', like me. Not that we spoke, of course. On a quiet night there could be a solitary person at each table, and despite the fact we had all seen each other there countless times, we would still all sit in silence, reading our papers or staring into space, like we were waiting for a doctor to appear behind the bar and shout 'next'. If it was the weekend it would get livelier and I had ended up once or twice chatting to people. But there was always a point at which the liveliness would turn to raucousness and I knew it was close to getting violent so I'd leave. I'd never stayed for one of the lock-ins I knew took place every Friday.

But then one night I met someone there, and the place changed permanently, for me.

It was a lovely evening and all the barstools had been taken outside by people, which made the pub seem bizarrely Mediterranean. I sat inside and read my paper for the third time and tried to drink slowly. It was boring. I got up to go and as I opened the door I saw her coming in through the saloon. I'd seen her there a few times before, but always with a man I presumed was her boyfriend. The last time I saw them together, things didn't look too good. They had that aura of solemnity around them that couples develop when they're on the verge of splitting up. No anger, or any other emotion visible at all. Just nothing left in common other than the fact they're together and the understanding that it's all in the past. It's always sad to see, because it's so familiar to most of us. When it's you in that situation the aura is tangible and impossible to escape. You know full well that it's hanging there, patiently waiting for one of you to get on and finish the relationship. But neither of you can, because the moment hasn't arrived yet. Then it does, and you're both upset and shocked and relieved that the aura has moved on to another doomed couple.

I carried on to the corner of the park and stopped. I was sure she was on her own. The pint I'd drunk had given me a tingling urge and a small amount of courage. I turned around and went back in. She was sitting where I had been a few minutes earlier. I looked at her while I bought another pint, ignoring the girl behind the bar frowning as she poured my drink. Her hair was freshly cut into a sharp bob and dyed jet black, framing her lightly powdered face and stencilled lips. It made her look like Louise Brooks in an ancient silent movie I saw one afternoon. Her nails were a deep red and as glossy as her hair. She was drinking a glass of white wine and reading a book. Her mouth was screwed to one side; she was engrossed in whatever she was reading. The aura had moved on, she had an air of fresh singleness, independence. I turned around as casually as possible, as if scanning the room for the first time.

'Do you mind of I sit here?' I said.

She looked around. 'No, no, not at all. It's very busy isn't it.'

I sat, gulped from my glass and nodded enthusiastically. 'Yes, it is. It's usually like this on a Thursday. It's Tuesday today, so that's. Unusual…' I glared at my drink and hoped she hadn't heard a word.

She nodded and turned back to read her book. I could feel the tips of my ears burning and wanted to finish my drink as quickly as possible.

Then she held the book to one side of her, a thumb marking the page, and looked at me. I smiled nervously and cupped a hand over one of my flaming ears.

'Why did the chicken go to a séance?' she said, staring right at me.

I stared back. 'I, I don't know. Why did the chicken go to a séance?'

She smiled. 'To reach the other side. Get me another drink, would you?'

I got up and almost ran to the bar and then rushed back to ask her what type of wine she was drinking. When I sat down again she was still smiling.

'Did you get it?' she said.

'It's, it's in front of you,' I said, pointing at her glass.

Her face dropped. 'The. Joke.'

'Oh. Of course. Yeah, yeah. Very funny. I liked it. A lot,' I said. My insides were churning.

The smile returned to her mouth and she nodded very slightly. 'You don't have any sisters, do you.'

I brushed imaginary crumbs from my trouser leg and took a deep breath.

'Two elephants fell out a window. Boom boom.'

My evening was over. It would be necessary to remain indoors for some time.

She raised her eyebrows, placed her book carefully in front of her and folded her arms. An arsenal of ten fanned iridescent nails flanked her pale limbs. She leaned back in her chair and laughed.

'I think you'd better get yourself another drink too, don't you?' she said.

She told more jokes, and I drank to deaden the panic I felt whenever the reality of the situation came back to me. I was in a pub, drinking, with a girl I'd just met. We hadn't even introduced ourselves. I could feel the lager numbing my senses and I didn't care. I was in heaven. Maybe not heaven, but a place that was very nice and I hadn't been to for a while.

We walked along a footpath flooded with rich orange light from streetlamps that fizzed in the warm night air. We came to a fork in the middle of the path. We stopped, and looked at each other.

'I don't live around here,' she said, smiling glossily at me.

'I live in one of those flats,' I said, pointing with my jacket at one of the anonymous council blocks.

She stared into the darkness and looked back at me with glazed eyes.

'Ooh. *Pouwsh*,' she said, in a plummy voice. We both laughed.

I hadn't thought for one second about the state of my place. It was only as I turned the key and opened the door that the detritus of single life hit me. I rushed in ahead of her, gathering up socks, shirts and empty Tesco bags as I went.

'Hey, you. Stop that.'

I stopped in the middle of the room, my arms full.

'You look like the world's worst burglar, standing there. Put that crap down, make me a drink and put some music on. Please.'

I hurried into the kitchen and got two beers out of the fridge, and rinsed out two glasses. I could hear her moving around. She wandered through the living room and bathroom, and then into the bedroom. The change in location had made me nervous again. I chatted to her as she carried out her inspection.

'So, I think I've seen you in that pub a few times, haven't I?'

There was a brief silence. I stood still with a glass and tea towel in my hands. I wondered if she had heard me.

Then ominously through the wall: 'Oh dear.'

'What, what is it?' I shouted.

She walked back to the kitchen and put her head slowly around the door.

'Curtains,' she said.

I stared at her. 'Curtains?'

'Curtains. The bedroom.'

The bedroom didn't have any curtains when I moved in. After a while I realised that the two blocks of flats opposite must have a spectacular view of me moping around each evening. But there is an enormous gap, an absolute chasm between a realisation like this and the business of doing anything about it.

'I. I don't have any,' I said.

'That's right, you don't. So it's curtains, I'm afraid.' She leaned against the doorframe.

My face dropped.

'Look, I think you're nice, despite your lousy social skills and your mucky flat. But there is a rule, a golden rule that you should have learnt by now. They say that boys don't make passes at girls who wear glasses, which is crap, because most boys will make passes at any girl, given the right moment. But there is another rule that does apply here. Nice girls won't sleep with boys who don't have bedroom curtains.' She gave my arm a squeeze. 'I made that up of course but I am a bit drunk and the thought of waking up at the crack of dawn to blinding sunlight isn't very appealing.'

We drank our beers, making the kind of limited conversation you do once the idea of calling a cab has been broached. I dialled a local firm and the bell rang almost straight away. How do they know? Whenever I'm in a mad panic they take forever. She said she would probably see me in the pub, and I said that would be nice. I was sobering up fast. My mind was busily trying to work out what real reason there could be for her to want to leave. What had I said that could have caused such a change in her? The doorbell rang again and she walked ahead of me into the hall.

'What's your name?' I said.

She looked back, smiling, shook her head and closed the door.

– Take responsibility for your own destiny. It's time – time every one of us took charge of our own future. The state can't help you. Your job, your career, is meaningless. There can be no real future for anyone living in ignorance.

Quite good, so far.

– I want all of you here to listen to what I'm saying and to understand. Today is the first day. The start of your life. This doesn't make sense to you. How can it be true? You are busy, you lead a full life, you have no need of deeper understanding. You can't see that actually you live in a bubble, your life is nothing but a charade. I know, because I have experienced it myself. I speak to you as a person who has passed through the darkness.

Fair enough. I'll go along with that.

– The darkness that mankind so readily lives in, but can be exited if one chooses. That decision is yours, my friends. And you are, all of you, my friends. My brothers and sisters.

Cheers, thanks a lot, mate. Fraternal greetings to you also.

Where's this going now, I wonder?
– Some of you don't believe me. Some of you are staring at me and you're thinking, how can he say that? How can he be my friend, he doesn't know me. But I do. I know all of you. The brotherhood of man is a reality you cannot escape. Whoever you are, wherever you're from, whatever you do, God knows you.
Oh for fuck's sake. How predictable. Very disappointing.
– God is with you constantly. He knows what you are thinking and what you are doing. But he cannot help you unless you help yourself. Accept him; accept the challenge of his love. Come to him and let him be your salvation.
I'm off.

The birds are twittering in the trees. They're all talking about me. They laugh and giggle, chat away to each other. Look at this one, they say. What a wreck. Not a hope in the world. Oh just look at his hair, his face, his funny walk. I don't mind, they have every right to their opinions. If they see fit to mock me, judge me a lost cause, that's alright. They are sparrows and pigeons, their own options are limited. I sympathise with their predicament, it's not so dissimilar to my own. We enjoy the same diabolical liberty. They move freely, do as they please, unfettered by responsibilities and demands, but they can only be what they are. They can't go to college and do a course, opt for a new start, give their dreams a chance, take a shot at changing their lives. So I can empathise and allow them a little relief at my expense. They are dirty little beasts though. They shit almost constantly, spread diseases, fill the skies with their stupid tiny bodies. I look up sometimes and it's more frantic overhead than on the ground. Black dots in front of my eyes, flitting about dementedly. I wish they'd stop, I could use some rest. I want to get to the gallery and away from my feathered antagonists.

The park looks nice. The flowers are all out – what are they? I've no idea. The grass here is very well kept. So nice during the day when everyone's at work. A few tourists, not too many. It's hot now, I'll put my jacket under my arm and put it on again when I get to the gallery, I don't want them to see my arms. It will be good to get out of the heat for a while. If I don't have any hassle I'll stay for as long as possible. Maybe wait until the afternoon's over and then go up to Euston. I could catch a train, head off somewhere else. I might leave London for good, move somewhere up north, to a seaside town. I'll get a job and meet local people, make friends with them. I will be known by all, a friendly type always willing to lend a hand. People are always knocking at the door of my cottage on the harbour, inviting me for a drink. I enjoy all the company and the deep respect in which I'm held. I've completely settled in and it was only a matter of time before the attractive, shy divorcee who runs the local shop fell deeply in love with me. We have two children and spend our days gathering driftwood and pebbles on the beach, our black Labrador frolicking in the surf.

I'll go to Euston and beg some money. Get some food and then start again with my keys. I've got to keep doing that, do it every night if I can. It helps keep me thinking. I like the weight of them in my jacket, they make me feel real somehow. I felt so aimless and lost before I found them. An odd find, not something that had ever happened before, as if they were sent to me by the gods, a brassy talisman to help me on my journey. They were sitting in the middle of the pavement, right in front of Saint Martin's, a great big bunch of keys, all different shapes and sizes. I knew straight away what I had to do, understood my mission completely. I stole a mini A-Z and that was it, I had everything I would need. Keys have a function, they fit locks and open doors. I own a set of keys, I have a function.

The gallery is quiet today, only a handful of people wandering around. Perhaps the show got bad reviews, or something. It makes me feel calm and steady being in here though, close to the cool stone floor. Maybe the exhibition really is a bit crap. It's not my sort of thing. I bet most of the people perusing the art don't have any more idea what it's all about than I do. Less, probably. There's a woman smiling and nodding at one of the pictures round the corner, like she gets it, finds it life-affirming and amusing. But it's not meant to be a funny picture, I'm sure. To me it's all a comment about death not life, but I suppose it's very hard to tell often, isn't it. Anyway, the space is nice and the attendants seem reluctant to bother me. And it's a lovely view onto the park.

It is really really quiet in here.
You could hear a pin drop.
It would clatter to the floor like a crowbar. The sound would be deafening, a cacophony of clanging metal on stone. Like a great big bastard metal crowbar dropped from a great height. Dropped from the roof of St Paul's to the floor far below, glinting and twisting as it falls, smashing to the ground, worshippers leaping out of its way, a great echoing explosion bouncing off the walls the tip cracking the stone floor the aisle the cathedral London the planet in two
Stop thinking like that.
It would though wouldn't it. It would shatter this reverential hush, this mind-twisting silence like
That.
Don't click your fingers don't click your fingers sit still sit still
Just look at the things, the art. Stare at it, come on, stare.
It's really too
FUCKING QUIET
in here.
Jesus, shut it, stop it now, don't want to get chucked out, not again. Like it here, want to spend the afternoon undisturbed. Take a deep breath, keep the mouth shut.
– Was that you?
– Hmm?
– Was that you, who just shouted?
– Me? No. Not me. Just looking at the art.

– I saw you.
– Saw me what?
– Saw you shout.
– Did you? Well what the FUCK are you asking me for then? You work in a GALLERY don't you? Don't they train you to LOOK and THINK? Isn't that part of the job description? An occupational necessity? A requirement of your post? Get your FUCKING HANDS OFF ME alright, alright, I'm going, look, I'm walking out. No bother at all. Thanks for everything, really. Great show. My compliments to the artist.

Tony, Sarah and I are sitting in his cubicle. Tony's workstation is larger than any of the others and can accommodate three employees, all sitting in chairs, as he is Team Leader. The other four peripheral members of the team stand around the entrance and sides of his cubicle looking in, as befits their status. They try to appear as casual and relaxed as possible although I know from my own experience that they are neither. Their legs ache already and they feel as though they are intruding on a conversation to which they are not invited. But then the three of us feel slightly odd too, having a group hovering over us as though we are detainees, or involved in a laboratory experiment. But we are sitting down comfortably, so we win, sorry.

David and John lean into the privy counsel and distribute printouts. There aren't enough to go round so I share with Sarah and Margaret shares with Judy. I was going to share with Tony but he says that he is Team Leader and will therefore need his own copy. Margaret giggles and is reminded by Tony that we have one hour, just sixty minutes, in which to resolve this problem. I am tempted to mention that the problem is something that was resolved well over a week ago, to everyone's satisfaction, but Tony had at that time provided us with calculations that had no relevance at all to the job. I know this because Sarah told me. But I don't say anything. Tony is looking tired and miserable.

'So as I said in my email, the factory called this morning, and apparently there is no way the finished structure will attach to the base and awning. I don't care who's fault this is or how it's happened but we have to sort it out now. So if each person can take a section, go through the calculations and specifications, and then Sarah if you would collate the results and see if they tally with the details faxed through from the factory, please.'

From the look on everyone's faces it is clear I am not the only one in possession of the facts. Sarah has evidently told the lot of them. I must have been mad to think she would tell me anything without it being part of some stupid plot. I wonder if she has told Brian. At which point, he passes by.

'Is that the Hammersmith job?'

Tony sinks. 'Yes, Brian, we're just sorting it out now.'

'You know if they don't start the steelwork today there's no way it will be up in time?'

'Yes, yes, I was just explaining to everyone the urgency of the situation.'

'Good. And have you discovered where the errors crept in?'

I am watching Brian, fascinated. This is the first time I have ever seen him applying the ruthless interrogative tactics of a top dog, a captain of industry. Of course Sarah told him. She is making an all out effort not to positively *beam* at Brian. Tony stares hard at the sheet of figures.

'My feeling is that we should just crack on and sort it out without any finger-pointing for now, Brian.'

'Well this is potentially the biggest contract we have at present. The chances of us getting the second phase of the project if we screw up on this are non-existent.'

Everyone is observing this with a mix of admiration and horror. Our office is unused to scenes of masculine competition. Brian is flexing enormous biceps that strain the fabric of his shirt and we are recoiling in anticipation of the mauling he is about to inflict on Tony.

'Actually, Brian, I have to admit it was my fault.'

They all turn to me. Sarah nearly falls off her chair. Tony's mouth is hanging open.

'You? What do you mean?'

'I was just about to apologise to Tony, before you came over. I completely forgot to call the factory last week and tell them I'd made a couple of mistakes in the measurements. Sorry, Tony.'

Tony smiles nervously. I'm sure he is wondering why I would take the flak for this, what fiendish scheme could I be planning? But there is no scheme. My ambitions here are very limited. Sarah wants Tony's job and I don't think she should get it through devious means. And while Tony is a very poor Team Leader he is infinitely preferable to Sarah, as I'm sure all the others would agree.

Sarah's cheeks have gone pink. There is something she would very much like to say. Something along the lines of, I know full well you had nothing to do with this problem and that you are covering up for Tony, why, I have no idea, but you are, and it is Tony who should be reprimanded for it and told his position as Team Leader is becoming untenable and it is I who should be given his job, me, the only decent intelligent person here.

But of course she doesn't say anything.

Brian looks at Sarah and back at me. His arms have returned to flab and he is confused. Perhaps Sarah got this wrong. Perhaps he has just been saved from making a real fool of himself by berating Tony without evidence, only for me to own up.

'Thank you for being honest, but you nearly cost us a lot of money, if they hadn't spotted the mistake before starting. But like I said, thanks for coming clean. Now please, get the figures right and get back to them ASAP.'

Tony sits up. 'Don't worry Brian, I'll get this sorted.'

I allow him to give me a harsh glare and look sheepishly at the floor to hide my grin.

It says here that an elderly Hungarian man living in Belgium is serving a term of life imprisonment for murdering two of his former wives and several of his children. The grisly murders occurred over many years, during each marriage. He was assisted in the killings and the disposal of the bodies by his middle-aged daughter, who claimed she had been abused since childhood and forced into abetting him. They used hammers and pistols to commit the murders and then chopped up the bodies. Bones and organs were bagged and dumped at butchers' shops. She also received a long sentence.

Now the interesting bit.

The man hired actors to impersonate the murder victims, telling them they were being filmed secretly for a movie about his life. So when suspicions were first aroused and investigators made enquiries, they were told the people were all alive and well back in Hungary.

Now the great part.

The chosen method of disposing of the remains was in a bathtub filled with a drain cleaning fluid so powerful that it dissolved them. The product has since been withdrawn from the market because of its excessive strength. The brand was called Cleanest.

What a shame. What a missed marketing opportunity this case that gripped Belgium for so long could have been. How fantastic the adverts for that miracle cleaning product…

'CLEANEST – Cleans Up after ALL the Family.' 'Life's a mess? Clean up with CLEANEST.' 'Problem people aren't a problem for CLEANEST.' 'Tough on troublemakers – CLEANEST.' 'Does exactly what it says on the label – and much, much more!' 'Trouble-and-strife? Not on your life!'

Rain rain go away and don't come back. If the rain in Spain falls mainly on the plain then the rain in London falls mainly on the fallen. I hate it when it rains. I can deal with the cold the heat anything but the rain. It takes so long to get comfortable again. I only really miss having a roof over my head when it's chucking it down. I don't know where it came from today. I'm usually very good at spotting any change in the weather but this has taken me by surprise. It was so nice this morning, even at lunchtime, a proper summer's sky, all blue with wisps of white cloud. Now look at it. Rain bouncing off the ground, drumming maniacally on the roofs of cars. People dashing in all directions, diving for cover as if caught in a bombing raid. I'd like to add a few drops of Cleanest to this downpour. I'd love to watch as the street dissolved, taking all the people with it. Hang on, that's the TV campaign sorted; De Niro does the voiceover, the image a typical busy London street scene. 'One day the rain's gonna come and wash all the scum off the street… Helped by CLEANEST, the detergent that doesn't take No for an answer'… Oh yes, that's brilliant. The special effects people would love working on that one. Close-ups of eyeballs and teeth going down drains, melted bodies swirling in the gutter. Superb. Such a pity they've gone and banned it.

My trousers are soaked. Jeans are a nightmare when they're wet. I'll have to wait for it to pass over and hope it heats up again. Just lie in the park and let the late afternoon sun dry me off. But then these jeans will be as stiff as cardboard; rainwater is so dirty in London. As if all the sweat and grime gets sucked up to the sky, condensed in clouds and then dumped back down again. I think it's dying off already, though.

'You know what your problem is, don't you?'

Being here with you. 'No. What?'

Tony leaned away from the bar, clutching the rail with both hands to steady himself. He looked like a cow in the final stages of CJD. His tie lapped at the dregs on the bar and his hair bristled up on one side where he had been clutching it. I swung my head round and looked in the mirror behind the bar. It's always tricky judging how drunk you look to others. I tried to catch my own eye but my reflection was either shy or disappointed with me.

Tony was looking very hard at one of my lapels. He leaned forwards, talking into an imaginary microphone.

'You live in a world of your own, that's your trouble. You just drift in and drift out again. The job doesn't mean a thing to you, does it?'

I smiled, gently easing him away from my shoulder.

'Your round,' I said. 'Your shout, mate.'

Ignoring his criticism rattled him.

'Fuck the round. I'm trying to tell you something, set you straight.' He brushed my shoulder with his fist slowly and for a moment I imagined feeding it to a rabid dog.

'Oh come on, Tone. We've been through this. We're just different animals.' Species. 'I can't get worked up about the job, anymore than you can, really.'

He grimaced and shook his head like something was stuck to it.

'No. No way. Not me. I am committed. I am a player.'

You should be committed. You couldn't even play with yourself. 'Of course you are, Tone.'

We do this quite regularly. We come to one of several bars around here and get wrecked. Getting wrecked was never verbally agreed on as the aim, just as it probably wasn't for any of the other people who are here. But it absolutely definitely without question is the goal. No matter what is happening in the world or even our own lives, the ritual is adhered to. We are committed to this, we are players here. We drink ourselves out of our minds, out of our suits. Out of our characters and into others. There are raised voices, there is passion. There are fisticuffs and brawls. Mostly forgotten and all put aside by the end of the week, when it all happens all over again.

I like it. I like coming here and watching people's inhibitions fall away. I like observing petty differences become vengeful grievances. Friendships are forged fast and as quickly forgotten. Relationships get strained, interfered with like drunken fingers in the back of a bra. It's great. This is my field of study, my arena of interest. I drink with Tony because he is the only person in the office who will come near these places. I don't really know much about him, that is, nothing beyond the circle of background information that informs our drinking conversation, a circle that warps and widens by the end of each session and seems to have sprung back to shape at the start of the next. I am aware that he has ambitions. He is Team Leader. He has started attending management training courses and these have so far resulted in nothing other than a tendency to get sarcastic and bristly after a few drinks. Which is fine, really. I don't have any great expectations regarding our friendship. I knew its limitations as soon as we met. Some people are like that; you quickly sense that you like them enough to be happy to meet for a few drinks but have no desire to know them much better. We all have our needs, and those needs change, over time. Right now Tony seems to need to avoid going home to his girlfriend Laura – who I've never met and no doubt never will – and to get drunk with someone who will put up with the undercurrent of bitterness to everything he says. And I need someone to stand next to while I enjoy the drama of the evening, though I'm fairly certain he is oblivious to this.

'I don't get you. I've said it before and I'm saying it again; I just don't get you.'

Tony is a bit taller than me, and wears nicer clothes. He is a couple of years older and better looking, too, but I've started noticing that the silly expression that settles on his face when he's drunk is occasionally slipping across his mug when sober. He should be careful about that. He has thick sandy coloured hair that's always pushed about, slightly dishevelled, in a way that suggests to me he went to public school.

'Don't take offence.'

'None taken.'

'I mean, it's up to you, isn't it. If you're happy always being in the same job, carry on. But I mean, you could *try*, you could *pretend* to give a fuck.'

I'd really had enough of this for one night. The group I'd been watching had moved on somewhere else and Tony had started his favourite theme earlier than usual. I wanted the pint he owed me, my last drink of the evening.

'Are you going to buy me that pint or not?'

He stuck his bottom lip out. 'Nah. Forget it. I'm full. Come on, let's go.'

We weaved out of the pub, crunching shards of thin glass underfoot. When we got to the street corner I stopped. Tony stumbled on for a couple of steps and then lurched back like we were attached by elastic.

'I think I'm going to walk it tonight, Tone.'

He looked at me incredulously with his tiny blank eyes.

'Walk? All the way? OK, you dreamy bastard.'

I forced a laugh and gave him a salute. He turned toward the tube entrance and I gave him the finger.

The air was heavy and warm, split open by overlapping sirens. It felt wonderful to be out at night. Everything looks different under streetlights in summer. Shimmering amber glazes cars like toffee apples. I swung my jacket over my shoulder and took long strides, my case swinging at my side, keeping time. I covered ground quickly and before I was really aware of it, I was within a few streets of my flat.

I passed a car that had been in the same spot for a month or so. I noticed it a couple of weeks earlier on my way to work and since then had been half-interestedly following its decline from innocuous parked vehicle to local eyesore, a heap of scrap metal stripped of all reusable parts. As I said, I'm not interested in cars, really, but there's always a certain fascination in seeing one get casually butchered, when all you see is the process and not the action, like a time-lapse film that starts with a plump robin and ends with a pile of unrecognisable bones.

The car had been heaved onto bricks and all the wheels removed. There was a yellow sticker on the side door window, which meant the council had finally noticed it, or someone had bothered to complain. I carried on and almost tripped over a house brick in the middle of the pavement. That could cause an accident. I picked it up and walked back to the car. I heaved it into the air in the direction of the windscreen, turned and walked away. It made a very satisfying sound; a smart 'boff' edged with a sudden snap, like footsteps over iced puddles. A sound as flattened as the windscreen. Very different to the clumsy clatter of a foot through a shop window, or the tinkling fallen teeth of a small windowpane hit by a stone. I carried on walking.

A light went on in a porch. A small dog started up its aggressive yapping accompanied by muffled cursing and the door opened. I stopped in its arc of light. A burly man in a vest stepped out. He looked each way and then back at me. I smiled and nodded. He took in my suit and case, then looked into the darkness around me, searching for the source of Fido's irritation.

'Fucking kids,' he grunted.

I nodded enthusiastically. 'Absolutely. Fuckers. Rotten little fuckers.'

He frowned at me. This was the kind of man I can only deal with when I'm drunk. He would scare the shit out of me in daylight. I'd sobered up after my walk and bit of shotputting; I didn't really want to get into any trouble, especially so close to home, on a street I use daily. It looked as though he was going to comment on my ungainly use of his own vernacular but then he shivered and looked down at his vest like he suddenly felt underdressed for the occasion. He rubbed his fat hams of arms and stepped back inside. The light went off and the yapping stopped.

I feel awful the next morning. My legs are stiff and my feet are pulsing; why on earth didn't I just get on the tube? I try to picture the end of the evening, leaving Tony and the walk back. It's too hazy, too much footage is missing. Christ, what a distance, in that state. I don't like walking around here at night on my own. I look at the time. I'll have to eat something on the way.

I don't have time to search for my sunglasses, so I stumble along the street squinting and grimacing. I pass a car with its windscreen folded in, a brick resting in the crease. I stop and stare at it, at the crumbs of glass scattered around. It looks stupid, dull and undramatic. And familiar. A man comes out of a house opposite so I shake my head, tut and hurry on.

I sit on the tube with my mouth shut tightly, convinced a cloud of foul vapour will escape and suffocate the whole carriage if I open it. I need to concentrate, read something, if I'm going to get through this journey. The man sitting next to me has his newspaper folded open, so I look sideways at it. I read through the items until I come to

SUICIDE PUZZLE

A man who committed suicide by jumping into the Seine in Paris yesterday was carrying a suitcase containing a beheaded female body.

I stare at the line and read it again. It's true. It has to be. It's come from Reuters and they wouldn't make it up. They didn't listen to a second-hand story in a late-night bar and send it round the world as the real thing. It's news. But it's... what? Mad? Not quite mad. It's sad. And ridiculous. What had happened in their lives to bring them together then leave him dredged from the river with a suitcase full of her? What sequence of disasters had led him to do whatever it was he'd done, what twist of fate had brought her into contact with such a man? I look up at the suit with the paper. He's reading another part of the page. I will him to look further down and read about the man and his luggage of headless woman. Go on, read it. He shifts in his seat and rattles the paper and I figure he's aware of the undue attention I'm paying him. I don't really want to make anyone feel uncomfortable on the way to work so I look ahead at the person opposite. It's a woman, a bit younger than I am. As soon as I look at her she looks away.

Naughty. You were watching me reading his paper, weren't you?

I give her a nice smile even though she's staring far too adamantly at the overhead tube map. I don't mind. At least I've stopped wondering what caused Madame to end up as the contents of some lonely nutter's baggage. Other people's lives. The mystery continues.

I get off at Holborn and join the queue for the exit. I stop off at a cheap café and pick up a bacon roll and a tea. I walk around the square eating the roll and try to ignore all the office types who stare as they walk past. What's so funny about a chap eating his brekkie on the way to work? Have they never seen a grown man with a bacon roll before? I finish it quickly and wipe my mouth with the serviette. As I go to throw it away I see it's covered in ketchup. I run my palm across my face and look at it. It's clean across the middle, with a thick red line top and bottom, where I missed with the tissue. I've been walking along doing a resounding impression of Coco the Clown. This really gets me in a foul mood and I give my whole face a vigorous rub with both hands. A motorbike courier slows to have a good look. I pick up my case and walk quickly to work.

Why do I seem to think better when just the other side of a hangover? It's so strange, completely illogical. Ideas come quicker when I'm still a bit rattled. I'd never've thought about that ad campaign if I wasn't all jittery from the last few days. Not a state I would choose to be in but it does seem to make things that bit sharper, more poignant or something. Doesn't matter anyway. Not as though I have a job, a family to keep in goodies by labouring in a crappy advertising agency or something. How I hate those people. They wear their occupation so clearly, like a big badge they're chuffed to bits with and want the world to read. Marching around with big voices booming into tiny mobile phones, prancing about dressed like clowns, oozing self-confidence and false charm. Cunts who spend their days devising idiotic schemes to shift shit no one needs and paid like kings for doing it. I go and have a look at them sometimes, to remind myself, but I can't stand it for long. Sitting in Golden Square is free entertainment until it starts getting to me. It's all I can do not to take them on, smash their silly heads together to try and knock some sense in, but really, what's the point? Their industry is as established as parliament, and even more insulated. Soho is a village, a hamlet full of village idiots. Half the woes of the western world start in London W1, I'm sure.

How much do I want a drink. I've probably got enough for a can. That's what I'll do. I'll get a can, and maybe stand outside The Coach and watch for a while. Wait for that bastard Norman to go in then grab an empty glass, fill it from the tin. So much less hassle when I can mingle, or at least go unobserved or commented on. It can be as enjoyable for me as it is for all the others standing there, chatting away. Sometimes I get so caught up in it I hardly remember that I'm not one of them, that come closing time when they all stroll off for a bite to eat or to catch the last tube home I'll be considering which alleyway or back street I'm going to sleep in. If I'm going to sleep, that is. Much better to do that in the safety of daylight rather than the menace of darkness. Can't ever be sure some psycho isn't going to let off steam by stabbing you or setting fire to your clothes or something. Like that poor bastard whatshisname; saw him one day wandering around as usual, saw him again a short while after staggering about with an arm like a balloon, looked like it would pop if you pricked it. Asked him what had happened and he muttered something about waking up on fire, the sleeve of his anorak ablaze, stuck to his skin, laughter as someone ran off. Jesus, it gives me the fear just thinking about it.

It's busy already. That's good. More to look at and less chance of being spotted by the kid collecting glasses. I can feel the cold can against my groin. I'm desperate to get it out before it warms up, must find a glass. Ah, here we go. A pint of your finest strong lager please, Norman. Pleasure, young sir. That'll be a fiver to anyone else, but to you, long-standing patron of this establishment, I'll charge not a penny above cost. Cheers, that's very decent of you. Look at that, lovely. Never know it wasn't his overpriced slops. Nice crowd tonight out here. Young, quite trendy. Some very fine looking females. Wish I could have a shower and a change of clothes, at least appear normal enough to look at them without waiting to see their disgust or disapproval when it registers. Very warm but I must keep this jacket on, don't need them seeing my war wounds as well. Not much of a conversation starter, or chat-up line. Happened once though.

I was standing here when a girl about my own age came stumbling out of the pub, very pissed. She almost knocked my precious drink out of my hand, and started apologising. Then she looked at my arm. 'Wow, oh my god, you poor thing. How did that happen?' she said. I told her I was involved in an accident that ended my professional skiing career. She looked a bit confused then smiled and nudged me. She chatted away for ages and it was irritating, frankly. She went on and on, asking me all about how I managed living on the street, how awful it must be, how important mental health care is and how little is done for homeless people. I tried to change the topic several times but she was too drunk to notice my discomfort or the people who had started looking at us. I hate it when that happens. Some people seem to think that a good long chat about my situation is just what I'm after. They feel a need to empathise, and imagine that they're helping but it makes me want to point out that they're just being rude and doing it for themselves, not me. I let her carry on because she slipped me half an e. But even that didn't seem adequate compensation so I got rid of her in the end by asking for her phone number.

– She's a dyke, you know that?
– No way.
– She is, I swear. Everyone knows about it.
– Really? But she's so good looking.
– Yeah, I know, no sense to it is there. Shame. She's got a great body hasn't she. Our loss their gain. Puts me right off though, knowing. Still, keeps it to herself, doesn't make a show of it so fair play. Not hurting anyone are they.

Four young men in bright Hawaiian shirts stand next to me. One of them is airing his profound views on the correct etiquette and acceptable limits for sapphic behaviour in modern society. The others nod sagely in agreement.

– Do you mind if I join you guys?

I say, smiling.

They look at each other. The philosopher shrugs and looks in his glass.

– Free country, do what you like.

– Really? When did that happen? Was it very recent?

He frowns and looks to his friends for help.

– What?

– When did the country become free? Only it was right out of my price range last time I checked and I'd hate to miss out if they're giving it away now.

The master of debate glares at me, gripping his glass tightly.

– I don't know what the fuck you're on about.

– Oh come on, no need to be like that. I'm not trying to wind you up, just thought I might have something to add to your conversation. I might prove to have something interesting to say, you could be impressed by my thoughts, my input.

The others are fidgeting about while my friendly interlocutor swirls the dregs of his pint around and then drains the glass.

– Whatever. We're off. Go and annoy somebody else.

One of his colleagues is emboldened by this bluntness and flicks a five pence piece into my pint.

– Yeah, there you go, five of your thoughts paid for in advance.

They all laugh at this surprising stab at wit and I stare at the coin fizzing at the bottom of my drink. I insert two fingers carefully into the lager and extract the five pence piece. They all watch aghast as I take the bottom of my benefactor's shirt and slowly rub the coin dry with it.

There is a burst of confusion as The Thinker explodes and his fist clips the side of my head. I fall backwards against the wall, jolting the people standing behind me and causing a ripple of shouting and pushing. The three stooges are leaning hard against Socrates, straining to stop him from making his point more forcefully.

– Come on, Jim, leave it, he's not worth it, just a tramp.

– YOU FUCKIN CUNT YOU TOUCH MY MATE WITH YOUR DIRTY HANDS AGAIN I'LL KILL YOU.

– Jim, calm down, man, come on, let's go.

There's hardly anything left in my glass and this annoys me far more than the frothing purple face spitting out insults.

– You seem to have spilt my drink. Could you get me another?

It goes quiet. Somebody whistles. Voice of Reason becomes quite still, blinks in surprise. The tension in his body drops and his pals sag. He pushes them off him, takes a few steps back and grabs a half empty pint glass off the roof of a parked car.

There is a loud 'Ooooh' and some squealing from the spectators as it detonates above me against the wall. I crouch in a shower of glass and beer. He stands in the middle of the road, legs wide apart, pointing.

– There's your drink you fuckin loser.

The wail of sirens edging along Wardour Street encourages his gang to regroup and they jog away towards Cambridge Circus, all slapping him on the back and whooping. I fumble around in my wet hair and pick out a few fragments of glass and rub the bottom of my T-shirt over my face. There are specks of red on it as I tuck it back in my jeans but nothing to worry about. When I look at the crowd of faces only one or two are still watching me. A barman leans out of the doorway frowning so I walk off to find a drink somewhere else.

It's another lovely day so I buy a sandwich and sit in a square behind Tottenham Court Road. Strong sunlight filters through the branches of the trees that dictate the central park area, its railings concealed by the dense summer greenery. This is a good place to sit and watch people. Without turning my head hardly at all I must have about fifty individuals within easy examination distance. At this time of day it's a mixed crowd. Small clusters of suits sit on the grass, making the most of the sunshine. Bicycle couriers sit with their backs against tree trunks, their mounts at their feet like faithful hounds. I can look at about twenty benches, no trouble. The winos that make up the hardcore attendees are joined by, well, people like me. Lunchers. Eating, reading, chatting, trying to ignore the occasional unsolicited remark by one the park's intoxicated residents. The heat keeps them in line, generally. They occupy whole benches; each sprawled out on his wrought iron chaise-longue. They lazily consult each other, engage in vague debate then flop back down. Empty tins mark the length of their day's work so far. Their rude ruddy tans indicate the years of their outdoors toil. We're a bunch of lily-white lightweights in comparison. Call sitting on a comfy chair in an office for a few hours each day work? These gentlemen make do with the hard unyielding wooden bars of a bench, all day every day.

One of them stirs. He sits up slowly, an empty beer can rolling off his chest and clattering to the floor. He stretches luxuriously and looks around the square, taking in the crowd that has formed since he dropped off. He stoops forwards and gives each of the cans at his feet a quick shake. An unintelligible curse suggests they're empty. He sits back up, rubs a hand like a purple boxing glove across his face while the other strokes his swollen stomach. The gossamer sheen of his filthy nylon rollneck reflects the light each time his glove passes across it. He surveys the flock for suitable quarry. Who will it be? The lone blonde, quietly going atichoo atichoo atichoo behind a romantic novel? Or the pair of illicit lovers, clawing at each other furtively? Either way, this will be good.

I'm distracted by a figure that passes the outskirts. I have a sense that he has been round at least twice in the last few minutes. As Rollneck staggers to his feet and lumbers towards the blonde I notice him again. He's looking for someone's office, surely. Nothing unusual about that; this particular square is surrounded by Georgian terraced houses long since converted into solicitors' offices. He's wearing a suit and carrying a briefcase, but there is something odd about him. He doesn't quite fit together. I squint through the hedges as he comes around again. He's hardly looking at the buildings at all, and what seemed a confident stride is more of an aimless stroll. I finish my sandwiches and walk to one of the gates. I time my exit to coincide with his next lap. A timid 'leave me alone go away' from behind isn't enough to divert me now. Here he comes.

I step out and cross his path. He barely registers my presence, his eyes on some imaginary horizon. He's about forty years old, with greasy hair heavily salted with dandruff. The sides of his nose are angry clusters of spots. The suit he's wearing is badly frayed at the cuffs and around the neck. There is a tear down one pocket and the other is missing entirely. His briefcase is a very dated oversized burgundy thing that hangs slightly open, panting as he walks. His feet bulge out of a pair of badly broken slip-on shoes. I walk on a little way and look back. The subterfuge returns; the distance restores everything to normality. People keep walking past without noticing him. It's an odd scene and it's disturbed again when he carefully places his briefcase against the side of a rubbish bin and reaches into it.

This scenario compels me. I find it difficult to stop watching him. I'm not sure I've ever really looked at someone like him before. His pathetic costume fascinates me. He's caught between two worlds, in a reality of his own making. He's found a level he can survive at, mentally. By imitating someone in the working world he must be able to get by, avoid slipping completely into the netherworld of homelessness, a place virtually impossible to return from, I imagine. But his grasp is so weak! He's living in a charade, too easily penetrated. His position is so tenuous it troubles me. He *is* in the other world; he only *thinks* that he is in some way part of everything he sees around him.

I'm suddenly aware that I've been standing here staring for a few minutes and a couple of people are looking at me, looking at him. I'm going to be late getting back. I'll have to leave him to it. I hope I don't see him again.

Spare any change please
Spare any change please
Spare any change please
Spare any change please
Spare any change please
Spare any change please
Spare any change please
Spare any change please
Spare any change please
Spare any change please
Spare any change please
Spare any change please
Spare any change please
Spare any change please
Spare any change please
Spare any change please
Spare any change please
Spare any change please
Spare any change please
Spare any change please
Spare any change please
Spare any change please
Spare any change please
Spare any change please
Spare any change please
Spare any change please
Spare any change please Spare
any change please Spare any
change please Spare any change
please Spare any change please
Spare any change please Spare
any change please Spare any
change please Spare any change
please

Oh come on somebody.
Spare a little change in your heart.
It's dark already.
My arse is going numb.
I can't sit here much longer, not tonight. I need to get going. Where will I start tonight?
Can't remember how much I got done yesterday. I'll have to look in the book.
Nearly everywhere from Montagu Square to Seymour St coloured in.
Shit that's a big area.
Did I really do all that?
Or is that what I wanted to get done?
No, it's right, I never colour in until I'm done.
So tired. Too hot as well.
I really need to get on though. So few pages here I've covered completely.
The streets look like veins where I've coloured them in.
All the arteries, all the tiny capillaries. But where's the heart? The Heart of the City. What a joke.
Ok, give this another five minutes, and then push off.
Come on you fucking miserable scumbags

99

Sarah has my pen.

I know it. I've suspected for a while that she steals things from my desk before I get in. It's only a biro and I have plenty of others in my drawer but it's the principle of the matter, one more example of her silly point scoring. I put a tiny dot of Tip Ex on the end of it a few days ago. I can see it winking at me now. Sarah's been flaunting it all morning, waving the pen around like an expensive cigarette holder. She's also smiling a lot, which she rarely does. I think she must be slightly unhinged. I'm fairly certain she has also been deleting files from my computer. When I left the office one evening last week there were loads of emails queued to be sent, and when I got in the following morning they had disappeared. No one had received anything from me.

But more worrying was the incident a couple of weeks ago. Judy filled her mug with water one day and spat the first mouthful over her keyboard, causing a small scene. Tony sniffed her mug and thought it smelled of bleach. Sarah said that the cleaner must have forgotten to rinse it. Margaret told me later that she had seen Sarah hanging around outside the office after work, as if waiting for the last person to leave. I'm not sure I want to know whether this is true; the thought that I might be working with someone pathologically vindictive is unsettling. But I have to do something about that pen – reaching in my drawer for another I find that the box with about ten remaining in it has gone.

Sarah comes by for the hundredth time today. She points towards me with my pen. The white dot is aimed right at me. She is prodding the air between us with it.

'Now, Brian is worried about some aspects of your last report, and he has asked me to see if you can improve it.'
Oh how she revels in this authority. I'm so scared. Really.

'Right. Do you know anything about the subject involved?'
I can't remember which report he might mean.

She frowns. 'Of course I do. That's beside the point. Your conclusions were sloppy, Brian says. I'm sorry but you really will have to go over it again. See if you can't round it off better.' She draws a circle right in front of my face with *my fucking pen*. I struggle to stop myself from reaching out and snapping her fingers.

'I'll do that right now. I've got a printout of it here somewhere. May I borrow your pen please Sarah?'

She stops conducting. Her eyes fall on the biro in her hand. She is missing it already. 'Erm, well, I don't have any spare ones myself, actually.'

'Really? That's weird. I'm sure there's a box of them under your desk.'

Her face hardens. The game's up. She's not going to play anymore. Without a word she drops the pen, actually *drops* it, as though it is worthless, a useless thing she shouldn't bother even holding. It bounces off the newspaper on my desk leaving a tiny full stop.

I put the pen in my pocket and open the file on my screen. It's a bit scrappy at the end, I have to admit. I go over the background notes again and find a few details I've missed in my conclusion. I'm glad I won't have to spend too long putting it right. I need as much time as possible to think this afternoon. There are a few ideas bubbling up to the surface I need to interrogate properly. I may have cracked another difficult section of my plans for London. It's a hobby, of course, and may never be seen by anyone, let alone implemented. But I have found that it exercises my mind, makes my job more bearable. The problem I set myself is a very real one. I started noticing a couple of years ago that getting home was taking progressively longer, the journey sometimes verging on being impossible. London is gagging on fumes; the streets are overwhelmed by the sheer volume of people. The struggle to use the tube at six in the evening can be frightening. Something must be done about it.

I've got files on my computer with all my notes and drawings. I put them on a disk and then erase them from my desktop, to continue with them at home, then whenever I update them I copy them again and bring them back in. I can't risk Sarah finding them. I feel a strong sense of satisfaction with this; the company is unwittingly funding many hours of my own work. It gives me great pleasure to know that the years spent here won't have been wasted. I make sure everyone is busy and then double click on a file. My reworking of the area from Buckingham Palace to Trafalgar Square swishes open. This is the section nearest completion. I often look at it before doing anything else, to give me a renewed sense of pride and purpose.

The palace itself is stripped back to its original size, the enclosed, hostile central square removed completely. A broad public path runs right through it from front to back. The silly gates facing the Mall and the pointless ornamental gardens on either side are gone too, the whole area pedestrianised. A border of small trees that allows people to walk freely through the grounds replaces the ugly mile of wall that surrounds the enormous gardens at the rear. A modern security wall stands around one small section of the house; there has to be *some* privacy, after all. The whole mall is paved over, market stalls (none allowed to sell souvenirs) lining it as far as Trafalgar square. Only buses run all the way around the square, and the National Gallery extends above the road to the very centre, enclosing the column. Each side of the gallery extension is a sheer wall of mirrored glass; a place for reflective contemplation, reflecting the world around it. Nelson protrudes from an aperture in the roof.

This is all quite reasonable, I think. Nothing about it is surreal, or wildly fantastical. How much better it looks already, just on my screen. I click on another file and a view of King's Cross appears. I frown at it. I'm having real trouble here, I can't seem to get started. There is a lot that needs doing to the area but I can't help wanting to leave a lot of what exists as it is. I'm not sure I *want* to improve certain aspects. The traffic has to be dealt with, of course, and the entrance to the station isn't an entrance at all, more of an emergency exit designed as an afterthought. But do I want to get rid of the crackheads, the junkies and the lunatics? It's irrational I know, but each time I work on this section I find myself thinking about how interesting it is around there, the number of times I've stood and watched some scene from another century taking place, those involved blind to the bustle of commuters around them. But then I remember the time I got involved in one such drama there, and how quickly I was glad to get out of it again.

It was very late at night, several years ago. I'd been to a club in town. The evening had not been a great one and it culminated with me swallowing a large chunk of hash as I was leaving. I decided to walk down to Trafalgar Square and get a night bus. I hadn't eaten anything all night and was fairly drunk. Within minutes I was stoned, more stoned than I had ever been before. I kept walking for a long time and when I next looked up I had no idea where I was. I stared at the street names, the buildings, and it was as if I had walked all the way into mainland Europe, for all the good it did me. By now the drug was fully in control. I was unable to feel irritated or scared by the situation and the freezing night air was of no consequence. I moved robotically towards the mirage of an all-night kebab shop and ate without thinking or tasting anything. With a full stomach and a head starting to function normally I carried on, and before long I was standing opposite King's Cross station. I was pleased to see a familiar landmark but very perplexed. I'd walked over two miles in completely the wrong direction. How was I going to get to Hammersmith? I'd have to get some more money out and find a minicab.

I heard a small insistent voice in my ear.

I turned and looked down. A small woman stood shivering next to me. Her hair was scraped back tightly into a stingy bun that made her spotty forehead bulge, and she wore a skimpy black top and jeans without knees in them. One leg was encased in dirty plaster and she jigged about on a crutch.

'You want anything, love?' she said, her teeth chattering.

The dope had worn off completely now, but it had left me very relaxed and contemplative. I didn't think I had ever seen a more brutal, graphic example of what working the streets can do to a woman. I looked at her more closely; her age was hard to guess. Something in the eyes and voice suggested about twenty but everything else argued more like forty. It wasn't that I was particularly sorry for her, or that I found her situation upsetting or pitiful. I don't think I felt very much at all, considering the night I was having. But it was as if I was seeing something very familiar for the first time, properly. I reached in my pocket and pulled out a five-pound note.

'There. You have that.'

She held it in front of her, open-mouthed. She looked up at me, still speechless with gratitude. This wasn't my intention. I'd simply given her all the money in my pocket.

'I don't focking believe it. That's, that's great thank you.'
She looked as though she might actually kiss me, and I wanted
to tell her it was nothing, a simple gesture of goodwill, when I
realised a figure in a raggedy tracksuit had been standing close
by and was now pacing around me, eyeing the note.

'Wus at for, wus at for, bizniz? Yew want biznz? Wot you
give er at for, eh?'

The woman scrunched the note in her fist. 'Fock off, Sal,
it's mine, he give it me, he don't want nothing,' she snarled.

I stepped backwards. Sal was in my face, pushing her to one
side. 'Got more? Givin it away?' I could feel the pitter patter
of his hands running up and down my clothes, expertly and
menacingly.

'I haven't got anything, I gave all of it to her.'

He turned without another word and jogged away as she
wobbled off as fast as possible around the corner. It would
be less hassle to get my money off her than mug me. I ran
across the street, jumped over a barrier and looked back. In
the darkness of a bus stop I could make out their silhouettes,
battling with each other against the Plexiglas. I could hear her
protesting aggressively and him shouting abuse. I hoped she'd
jab Sal hard in the groin with her crutch. I turned and ran, not
stopping until King's Cross was out of sight.

I will probably have to change the area quite drastically,
eventually.

Clear thoughts again today, percolating through cleanly, one after another. A clarity of vision connecting straight to my brain, not interrupted by bafflers that put a strange sick colour on everything I see. It's warm and I've eaten well, my stomach is full and I feel like walking it off. My appetite has been sated, but my eyes are still hungry. I'm enjoying looking at things again, free of my rage. I'm more aware of it all, how good everything can be. How London is a visual banquet for someone who enjoys watching as much as I do. So much going on, always something new to take in.

Plik

A woman in her fifties in a black business suit using three mobile phones. Three. One's gripped in the crook of her neck, another is held to her other ear and a young woman, who must be some sort of assistant, holds up a third to her face. The woman is reading details from the screen. She keeps shouting at the poor girl to hold it still, then barks more instructions into her neck. It's very funny, like a modern rendition of some old painting, an ugly queen gazing vainly into mirrors held up at different angles by an ill-treated lady-in-waiting. She cranes her neck forwards, squinting, and the phone drops from her shoulder and clatters onto the pavement, its battery skittering off into the road. There is a lot of swearing and shouting and I let out a laugh that chops cleanly through the air / the woman / the stupidity.

Plik

Pluk

The colours coming off that glass office building! The way the sunlight shines right through it from one side to the other, refracting huge prismatic patterns onto the others around it. A giant paperweight held up for inspection. Are the people inside aware of the free light show their workplace provides? Do they ever notice it? So beautiful, and unexpected. I've never seen the building at this time of day before; it's usually a fairly dull tint of green. I will try and remember it in future.

Plik

Pluk

Plik

I can see him at the top of the street, walking towards me. I've seen him a few times recently. He has the bearing of a man of some status. He's very tall, and walks with his shoulders pushed back, his hands often clasped behind him and head held up, as if taking a turn in the garden to inspect the roses or going to see his tailor for a fitting.

And what a head! This man makes people notice him without doing anything to gain their attention. Even at this distance I can see the flurry of activity that moves along with him. People gasp and stare or catch sight of him and move quickly out of his path, forcing their eyes away. His head is a mass of cavities and lumps. Tumorous growths sprout from his face and push through the thin hair on his crown, and where around one eye there should be structure there is concave softness. Purple lesions from unimaginable operations cover his neck. A head like a potato left in a kitchen drawer and forgotten.

As he gets nearer I alter my course to coincide with his. He's wearing a nice grey suit today, a white shirt with a stiff collar and a red tie. A swollen briefcase is tucked under one arm. He steps up to the kerb alongside a gaggle of tourists who stop talking and grin at the sky. I weave through the cars and approach him.
– Morning.
He peers at me through a thick welt that bulges over one eye.
– Ar, yeth, gerd morning.
The mangling his voicebox has suffered has robbed his speech of its posh clarity.
– Looks as though it will be nice again.
He raises his head, squinting and it makes a bumpy relief against the white sky.
– Oh. Yeth, yeth, it doeth, dursn' ib?
He smiles; or rather, the normal half of his mouth smiles and the fleshy warped half quivers and pulses uncertainly.
I smile back.
– Anyway, nice to meet you. Bye.
He nods slowly, almost bowing.
– You althow.
He crosses the road and I turn to watch him cutting a swath through the churning crowds. A giraffe unaware of the commotion of wildlife that surrounds it.

From the window I could see straight into an office across the road. A middle-aged man was sitting at a desk and waving his arms. A woman was standing near the door. She had a folder in her hands, held tightly to her chest like a shield. I couldn't tell whether she had just come in or was going out. She didn't appear to be saying anything. He was working himself up into a real state, banging his fists on the desk. The woman moved the file over her mouth. Then he slumped forwards and I had to sit up to see his shoulders heaving. The woman dropped the file and went rushing over to him and threw herself around his back. His hands flipped awkwardly over his shoulders and patted hers. He reached down his sides and smoothed the flanks of her skirt. They rocked gently like this for a while until she suddenly pulled back. She said something with sharp juts of her head. She wiped her face and walked away quickly, scooped the papers off the floor and left the room. The man stood up slowly with drooping shoulders and came over to the window. He leaned with one arm over his head and gazed at the traffic below.

I turned around and realised they were all looking at me. I was half standing up and half sitting in my chair. The meeting room has a much better view than the one behind my desk. The only time I can get an update on the torrid romance that has waxed and waned for months across the road is when we have a meeting.

I smiled and sat down. I really wanted to tell them about the scene opposite.

'Sorry, Brian. Could you repeat that last bit?' I said.

Everyone squirmed and Sarah fiddled with the imitation pearl necklace her fiancé had given her a week before giving her the bad news. She was grinning like an idiot at the client who kept his eyes fixed on the document in front of him.

'I wasn't speaking. Tony was.'

I turned to Tony. 'Right. Fire away, then, Tone.'

He didn't like being called Tone at work, especially since he was the veteran of so many management courses and interviews. He cleared his throat and adopted a quiet confident voice that said there is no need for me to pick you up on this because it is obvious to all that you are at fault and I am so magnanimous I will leave it there. And we are with a client.

'The costings, please.'

I flicked through the file in front of me. There were three different sections of the job being discussed and he could have been referring to any one of them. My mind was entirely preoccupied by the man in the opposite building who had still, after all this time, neither left his wife nor finished his office fling. I considered that pretty poor, really. His wife was either living in ignorance or was racked with anguish daily as he left for work, and his secretary was trapped in a hopeless romance with a man incapable of taking decisive action. Three people were being made unhappy by one. Four, if you included me. More, if there were kids involved.

'Sorry, Tony. I've only got the basic engineering brief here.

Give me one second and I'll go and print out the other two.'

Tony opened his mouth to say something but Brian touched his sleeve.

'That's fine, we'll move on to the schedule and come back to it when you're ready, thank you.'

I sat in my cubicle and put my feet on the desk. It was so peaceful with them all next door. The strange tranquillity of an empty place usually full of people. It reminded me of the day I left Junior School. The whole year were having a celebratory lunch in the playground and I went back in to use the toilet. I wandered into the school hall and felt a wonderful calm. It was like being in a church. I strolled around for ages, onto the stage, behind the headmaster's piano, taking in the atmosphere of a space I had only ever known packed with children and teachers. It was one of my earliest Beautiful Place experiences. How odd. I seemed to be on the verge of having a perfect moment, right there in my shabby cubicle. Could this possibly join my collection of Beautiful Places? I wouldn't have ever thought it possible, but I was wonderfully content, warm and calm.

'Are you coming back in?'

I swivelled round and saw Sarah. 'Yes, of course. The printer crashed.'

Sarah was in charge of the printer. She flicked her hair in irritation.

'I'm not sure about that. It was fine, before... Look just come back in. They can't stay much longer.'

She came to London to start afresh. A new job in a new city. After a few weeks she felt lonely. She wanted to meet people her own age. Nobody really socialised at her office and all her friends were hundreds of miles away. She placed an ad in a newspaper and soon after met a man whose reply she had liked. They got on well. They would go to the cinema or the theatre. They started to meet for drinks, once a week. It was after one of these nights out they ended up sleeping together.

Her world changed after that.

She looked forward to his call every day. Her job that had been everything, her reason for being here, lost all importance. As long as they could be together and as often as possible, that was all that really mattered. He said he felt the same, that something was developing he hadn't expected, that he felt a bit guilty for looking for a friend and it leading to this, these feelings. He lived a long way out of town near Burnt Oak, so they would meet at the small studio flat she rented just off Baker Street. She would make some food and he would bring a video and a bottle of wine. It was cosy and nice, but he would nearly always have to catch the last tube home or call a cab. He said he had started looking for somewhere closer, somewhere she could stay as often as she liked.

Then a week went by without hearing from him. His mobile was always switched off and he didn't reply to any of her messages. One night the phone rang and a female voice told her that her lover had a different name. And a wife, and a two year old daughter. And that she would never see him again. She listened and then hung up without saying anything. She ate some of the meal she had prepared for them both and went to bed.

The next day she put the few things he had left there into a plastic bin liner and put it out with the rubbish. She called in sick to work. When a week had passed she called again, and explained to her boss, who was very sympathetic, that she had decided to move back north. She stayed in the flat, living off the remainder of the money she had first brought with her. A few weeks later it had all gone and the phone, then the gas, then the electricity were disconnected. The managing agents of the flat called round and pushed a letter through the door telling her she had a week to pay her rent arrears or they would send bailiffs. She stayed in bed after that.

One day the doorbell rang and rang and rang and in a moment of bottomless horror she hanged herself by the cord of her dressing gown from a rail in the wardrobe.

And then when the bailiffs broke in a week later and found the body they called her best friend and she knew, knew straight away that that was the day she had rung that bell, it just had to be her fault. She came down from Scotland looking for her pal and rang her bell, decided not to shout through the letterbox just in case, and then got a call and then all the facts came together one by one with details added things she must have invented she didn't mean to but that's what the doctors said and it has finished her completely she killed her best friend lost her own life too and she has this this this terrible urge this basic need to tell me tell anyone anyone who will listen. She pulls at my sleeve, cries and leans on me, begs me to tell her what to do. Make her come back, please tell me it never happened.

These are the ones I avoid the most. A permanent look of bewildered panic; how did I get here? Life just got smaller and harder until it cracked without warning and they fell through the gap, onto the street below. A marriage that petered out, a job that ceased to exist, a long-term illness or the death of a loved one. Couldn't cope couldn't go on couldn't stop it happening. The reasons are ordinary and the maths simple. An equation that's not taught and learnt too late.

So many stories I don't listen to them anymore, because it's always the same, and it does my head in. I used to make time to listen, and try to sympathise, offer some consolation or advice, but I just can't anymore. Awful, awful stories, relentless, endless variation but always so alike and always the same ending. It's always those not long arrived who are keenest to tell you everything. Convinced that their situation is unique, that something must be done about it, someone must help them to work it out and correct the injustices done against them. They think it's important you know about it, that they keep the details clear, the memory of who they were and what happened fresh. After a while it fades for most, and a good thing too. You see them every day, the ones who clung too tightly and lost it, doomed to walk forever, going over and over and over the facts, the memories, editing and correcting, putting it all right in their heads. Driven insane by their distractions.

'Hello.'

It was a while since I had last seen her, and for a moment I didn't recognise the person standing over me. The black bob was now a crop, and the face was scrubbed and lightly tanned. The hands holding a pint and a glass of wine didn't end in painted talons.

'Hello,' I said. 'You look different.' I glanced at the pint glass.

'Yes, I suppose I do. The vamp act wasn't really working, I decided.'

To my amazement she sat down and carefully placed the pint in front of me as if I had ordered it. 'Cheers,' she said and made a fuss of clinking glasses.

'So you meant it then. That we would meet here, sometime. I thought you were fobbing me off.'

She studied my face as I spoke and I wondered if there was something stuck to my mouth.

'Try not to think and please, don't do what you were about to.'

'What was I about to do?'

'Introduce yourself properly. I don't think I want to know your name and I'm not going to tell you mine.' She leant in close to whisper. 'It's better if we're strangers.'

I held my hands around the base of my glass and turned it thoughtfully.

'Alright. You're on. And in that case I won't ask what you've been up to or where you've been.'

She approved of this. 'I think you're getting the hang of it.'

But inside I was bursting. I wanted to know her name, and where she had been, and why we had to play a game. She had left me with an empty feeling that I couldn't quite define. I had gone over and over the events of that night and I wondered if she could really have wanted to leave so quickly because of a lack of curtains in my bedroom. I had been back here more often than usual lately knowing each time that by trying to force another chance encounter I was jinxing the possibility of one happening. Now that I had accidentally re-entered the surreal otherworld she seemed to exist in I wanted to make it real. I knew that if I tried she might disappear forever.

'Oh dear. Maybe you're not too happy about it after all.' She sat up straight and looked around the pub.

'No, no, it's just I haven't seen you for a while, you know, since.' Why was I finding this so hard when another part of me was so happy?

'We didn't have an arrangement, did we? I did say we would run into each other sometime, and we have, haven't we. Besides, I've not been around for a while.' I glanced at her hopefully, 'and I'm NOT going to tell you where I've been, but this is the first weekend I've been over this side of town for a few weeks. So let's have a nice time and drink a toast to your new curtains.'

My mind stopped turning over. 'How do you know I've got new curtains?'

'Because I walked past your building and looked up and saw

them. I didn't think there would be more than one new pair of curtains put up recently on the top floor of that block.'

I laughed. 'That's true. So you've been spying on me?'

'That's very presumptuous of you. No. I just happened to be passing and I realised where I was and looked up, that's all.'

'To my curtains, then,' I said, holding up my glass.

'To your curtains.'

Then I told her the story of how I had bought them.

I had decided she was right; the light in my bedroom was intolerable after about 5am, once I was aware of it. I found my tape measure and a pencil, and wrote down all the dimensions that I thought I might need on a flattened out empty cigarette packet she had left behind. That was the simple part. From there on it had been a task of Herculean proportions.

I went into town and headed for the only place I imagined must do made to measure curtains. On the second floor of John Lewis I found something called the Express Curtain department. I narrowed down the choice to two fabrics – easy, as most were chintzy and shiny – and waited patiently in a queue to be seen by a man sitting at a small desk in the middle of the shop floor. When I got to the front he disappeared for about fifteen minutes. Eventually he returned and waved me over. I got out the cigarette packet and I pointed to the two fabrics, showed him my sketch, and explained what I was after. He nodded, smiled and went through the sample book in front of him. He got a small calculator out of a drawer, and did a few sums.

'Well, sir, given your measurements,' he looked at me over his glasses as he said this, which I ignored, 'given your measurements, I can tell you that the cost will be one hundred and eighty pounds for the one, and two hundred pounds for the other.'

The price was about double what I had imagined. But then I didn't have a lot of experience in home furnishings.

'Then I'd like this one, please.'

'Very well, sir. Now, I would suggest that you explain the drawing you have brought with you to me, one more time.'

I went through my measurements with him again and described how the rail would bend and the two curtains should meet.

'I am terribly sorry sir, but I have no idea what you are talking about,' he said, in an overtly courteous way. 'I was with you at the beginning, and I thought we were discussing the same thing, but now, I am sorry, you have entirely confused me.' He stopped and looked at me over his glasses again. I tapped the desk and looked at the 'Express Curtain' sign. I knew I had to stay calm.

'What point would you like me to return to? The beginning?' I said.

'Perhaps that would be wise.'

I went back to the beginning. I showed him my working calculations, everything. Eventually he held his hands out with palms raised, in a way that reminded me of Jesus as depicted in The Last Supper.

'Ah, now I have it!' he said. 'You wish to purchase *two* curtains.'

I studied him closely. 'Yes. A pair.'

He was in his element now, I could see. 'So sir, each of the measurements, they are for a separate curtain? You really did not make that very clear to me. Now I have it. You wish to purchase a pair of curtains, each to this size here.'

I don't think I said anything in response. I stared at my drawing, the two curtains I had carefully shaded in to make them appear more curtain-like, each with a measurement alongside. He got his calculator out again and did some more sums. It's double, I thought.

'The price is double, sir,' he said with satisfaction.

I held onto the edge of the desk with both hands. My knuckles were white. Being here, the middle of a crowded shop floor and trying to buy curtains was making me very unhappy. My lips started trembling and I heard a low whirring sound in my head.

'Right. It's double. OK, let's do it.'

He pressed on. 'Now, can sir tell me the exact distance from the curtain rail runner to the ceiling?'

Curtain rail? *Runner to ceiling*? I closed my eyes and tried to picture my bedroom windows. Come on, come on, you've stared out of the things often enough. Then it came to me.

'There isn't one. Curtain rail.'

His face dropped. 'So, you are here, ordering curtains, to be made *before* you have installed a rail?'

'Yes, I am here, today, to order curtains, and to buy a curtain rail.' I said, grimly.

He took off his glasses and rubbed his eyes. 'Sir. Sir, I would strongly advise that you install your rail, recheck your measurements and then return to see me.'

I lowered my head and looked up at him through my eyebrows. The desk edge was going to snap off in my hands.

'I am going to buy the rail and order the curtains, today. If we go through to the rail section,' I swivelled me head around, then back to him, 'we will choose the right rail, and then we will know, exactly, the dimensions we need.'

He put his glasses on and looked at me with a defeated expression. 'I would advise against it, but if that is what sir wishes, that is what we will do.' He stood up slowly and I followed him into the next room.

I kept the rest of the curtain-buying hell fairly brief, the whole rail-selecting saga, how the Express Service meant a mere three-week wait instead of ten, how when the delivery finally arrived it was a day early and so had to come again, a week later. But when I finished she was looking at her watch. Her eyebrows were buckled low and her face was tense.

'God, I'm sorry, that must have been really boring.'

She looked up distractedly. She seemed somewhere else

entirely. 'Oh no, not at all. But I have to go. I'm sorry.'

'No, look, *I'm* sorry, I didn't mean to go on like that, I'm nervous, that's all.'

She pulled her coat on smiling but couldn't hide the change that had come over her.

'The story was funny, and you told it very well, but I do have to go. It's just something I have to do that I really can't discuss or be late for.' She looked at her watch again. 'I've got to go,' she said for the third time.

And then she left.

Slipping again. Can feel it, feel its dark energy tugging at me, wanting a word. Wanting to whisper in my ear and then hug me so tight I can't breathe. Winding around me and slipping in. Keep thinking keep thinking don't let it. Can't stop it though. Wanted a drink badly and didn't give in. But it's happening anyway. So now I really really want a drink and if abstaining didn't work, if it has such easy access, what's the point? Maybe get drunk and lie still, let it have its fun, run riot with the head until it's done and goes again. Could hide out for a bit until it passes. If it passes. No! Stop it, take a deep breath. Now, keep walking.

How can I feel so cold? Got my jacket gripped tight to my chest but everyone else looks very hot. Can hardly see a thing, light much too bright today, got to keep a hand over my eyes. Can feel the street's heat through these shoes, but I'm shivering like mad. Thought these brogues were good, but they've broken down quickly. Must have been left for a long time unworn. Would have been expensive new. This helps. Helps to think about something like this. Keeps the mind ticking over, stops the thoughts taking hold completely. Just walk and focus on the shoes.

That's it, one in front of the other. Laces are knackered too. Keep tying the broken bits together, but they won't last. Doesn't matter, can always find laces. Funny what the mind holds as significant. Clear in the mind, the way I always notice empty shoes everywhere. Not just one on its own, in a bin or the gutter, but pairs, everywhere. All different sorts and sizes. Standing carefully side by side, as if their occupants just vaporised. Half expect to see a whiff of smoke coming out of them. Something worrying about seeing pairs of empty shoes in the street. Like a warning: get control, get a job, or you could be next. Makes me shiver.

Life's proved its point, I get it, thanks, it can stop now. Stop pushing me, prodding me about. I'd like to just stop altogether, sleep for all eternity. Could kill myself. Could have another go. No. No point. No release that way. Reincarnation guaranteed. Another lap to do; no thanks. How would I manage it anyway? Gas myself in the car? What car? Never had a car. Hate cars. Electrocution. With what, pray tell? What appliances do I own, what socket do I ever see? Pills. When was the last time anything as glamorous as a single sleeping tablet came my way? Smack. Needles? You must be joking. Wouldn't give them the satisfaction after all I've been through, all the jabs and tests and samples. Well that leaves drinking myself to death which will take time and is a terrible way to go. And hanging. Which I'd be bound to cock up so badly I'd strangle slowly, swinging about under a bridge while all the wankers walked over my head.

Stop this now, stop thinking about it, next line of thinking please.

Oh fuck this is hard. Where has it come from? Been doing so much better, not drinking, keeping clean, everything. Can't stand to think I might have to stop the night-time checks. Must keep that up, helps to keep going. Very important that. Warming up again. Can let go of the jacket.

Keep going, keep walking.

Too hot. Burning up now. Need to reduce the temperature reduce the risk.

A coin on the tongue to cool the mind. The Queen's head in my mouth, her mouth in my head. Sharp metallic bite on the taste buds, fake sincerity of the sovereign a bitter pill to
Stop stop don't think just walk

can feel my spine like a rod of hot metal in my back my cortex like a whip a snake thrashing bubbles in the front of the brain
betweentheeyes
the light is hurting my eyes the bright white light white floor too bright too white reflecting like laser beams off cars and shops burns a hole right through me
disappearing
in the glare   the rays shooting   through
me in and out of   me
light pouring out   n   o w
m   e   l   t
and   f u s e   w   i   t   h

'I'm thinking of having a nervous breakdown.'

'You mean, you think you're *having* a nervous breakdown?'

'Yes I mean I think I am having a nervous breakdown,' Tony said rapidly and then stopped, his bottom lip caught in his fingers.

I eyed him warily. I put my mug down and rubbed my eyes. I leaned back in my chair and hoped it would give the impression that I hadn't already reached the same conclusion.

Tony had recently returned from yet another management training exercise, which I'd told him not to go on. Each one left him more forlorn and miserable. It was like watching someone endlessly climbing a sheer wall of ice and constantly sliding back down, only to start again. He would improve gradually as the effects of each course wore off, and then be worse than ever after the next one. He was tired and irritable at work and I was sure Brian had spoken to him about it. I'd learnt more about him in the last few weeks than I wanted to. It had made me closer to him and completely changed the picture I'd had of his background. But the more I knew, the less I wanted to know.

Tony had clearly not had what would be called a beautiful childhood, and it was now a source of constant bitter reflection. It had gnawed its way through to the centre of his adult existence. Every nuance of the abuse he felt he had suffered at the hands of his cold and distant parents was apparently reflected in present day events, particularly his lack of professional success. I'd heard a lot about it and knew we had barely scratched the surface.

'I say that I *think* I am having a nervous breakdown because I'm not sure.' He turned towards me sharply, head up, eyes wide open. 'I'm not sure if any of it's real.'

I shifted about in my chair. I wanted very much to be listening attentively and considering suitable responses but all I could hear in my head was a song that was on the radio all the time and had been driving me crazy.

'You know I would like to help, Tony, but maybe you need to talk to someone qualified about this. I'm not sure I *can* help.'

Fazed by my directness Tony lowered his gaze to his tea mug and carefully ran a figure around its edge as if trying to raise a note.

'I'm sorry, about recently. I mean I know I've been a bit difficult. I haven't talked about this with anyone else. You're the one person I feel I *can* talk to.'

I must have shifted again. Realising he may lose his audience Tony moved up a gear.

'But as you've been such a good listener I thought I might be able to share this with you.'

I stayed silent. Whether I liked it or not he was going to give me my share. He looked wildly around the room as if searching for courage and support. I hadn't seen him like this before. I couldn't tell how much was genuine and how much for my benefit. I wanted to kick him under the table.

'I'm really really at the end of it, mate. I'm a total fucking failure. I'm supposed to be head of the team but I don't get on with any of the others, really. Especially Sarah. God, I hate her. She's evil. She's a. a…'

'Succubus?' I offered.

Tony looked confused. I realised that he had been drinking. 's.s.sukabus?'

'Succubus. Female demon. They're supposed to seduce men while they're sleeping, I think.'

Tony slumped over and laughed. I did too.

'I had a lucky escape, then.'

I wiped my eyes. 'What do you mean?'

Tony grabbed his hair and slouched on the kitchen table.

'Sarah. Ages ago. She'd just been dumped by that dickhead and she suggested we go out for a drink one Friday. I was bored so I said yes. We got drunk, or at least I did, and then she suggested we go back to the office. I fell asleep on the couch in reception. When I woke up she'd gone. She left a really horrible note on my desk. I didn't see it until I got in on the following Monday, but I don't think anyone else noticed it before me.'

We sat staring at each other and then collapsed in fits of childish giggling. But then the emotional release shifted his thoughts back again and lent greater force to his frustration.

'If I could just, just move up, you know, not be directly responsible for a group, deal with the bigger picture, I know I could do that. I've told you all this, I know. But in the last couple of weeks I've just. Reached the end. Brian says he won't let me go on another course. He says I should put more effort into the job I've got. Laura's moved out, said she couldn't take my misery any more. I'm going to do something. No argument, I'm going to top myself.'

He stopped abruptly and stared at me.

For the first time I saw that his eyes were rimmed violently red and his skin was no longer tanned but tinted yellow. He started heaving asthmatically, spasms of uncontrollable grief bubbling up to his mouth. I could too easily picture the ball of thwarted ambition, clenched in his chest. His hands gripped the tea mug so tightly his knuckles had gone white. Specks of tea appeared in the lap of his jeans.

We both sat in silence. Suddenly I felt anxious. The song had stopped looping in my head and I was gripped by the reality of where I was, of Tony's presence in my kitchen. It was as though the black vacuum of his mental distress really was going to suck me in. Guilt at my inadequacy had kept me listening over the weeks but now I felt cowardly for not being straight with him sooner.

Tony and I had always kept our conversations at work pretty much to a minimum. We would have a brief chat on a Friday afternoon to arrange what time and where we'd see each other later. I had perfected a technique of appearing occupied with my work when I was actually far far away in my thoughts. I didn't like this to be interrupted by the inane chitchat that often blew around the office like litter caught in the wind and of roughly equal significance. I was quickly labelled as a serious, slightly dull sort of young man too immersed in his job and that suited me fine.

And then one day Tony appeared at the gap of my cubicle. I didn't notice him at first. Then I heard an irritating tapping sound and saw him standing there, flicking his pen against two mugs clutched in one hand. He was smiling as though he might be in mild pain.

'Tea,' he said.

Tea, I thought. 'Oh, tea. Yeah, OK. Thanks.'

When he came back we sipped our tea in silence, and then after a few inquiries about what I was working on he made some remarks, things which in retrospect I see very clearly were the first vital testing moments. He was feeling annoyed about the course he'd just got back from. He was sure the leader had never done it before and that the tasks they had been set were not applicable to the cut and thrust of a modern office. I hardly said anything but by the end of that mug of tea he seemed a lot happier, as though I had provided the answers to some awful convoluted problems.

'I enjoyed that. Back to work, then,' he said.

'Yes. Back to work,' I said.

Each day after that Tony's face would appear over the lip of my cubicle and it would be time for our daily tea break and chat. Why didn't I say no then? How could I. It would have been churlish of me to protest that I was just too busy. He was supposed to be my mate, my drinking partner. He was the one person there who had a fair notion of my opinion of the place. He was also technically my superior and I didn't want to antagonise him.

I became less and less keen on our tea breaks. 'Tea break' was not the right term at all. It was the time of day when I had to apply myself the most. It was a job more involving than the one I was paid to do. Tea, welcome or otherwise, had become the sugary bond between us, and it was a very hard adhesive to separate. Tony felt it should be applied daily, and nothing put him off. Sometimes I would notice with relief that it was almost five when his feeble rap would play across the fibreboard divider. If I tried to ignore him the pantomime could become excruciatingly long-winded, the silent intervals painful. One day I was determined not to hear about his resentment so I slipped my headphones on when I saw him hovering by the kettle. In his desperation not to intrude, Tony crept up saying hello repeatedly. I hadn't switched the tape on and I was itching with embarrassment as I heard him hovering behind me. I turned and he jumped out of his skin as though he was in his own cubicle and had found me at his desk.

And our drinking was suffering. Nights out had become deeply introspective affairs, with too much soul searching and not enough looking around to please me. At least during our tea breaks he tried to be vaguely polite and keep the full darkness of his thoughts concealed. In the pub he was unbearable. Tony would spend most of the evening scowling at his glass. The first couple of drinks would slip by with a half-hearted display of gossip and banter. Then a few pointed observations would slide into sloppy sarcasm and from there we were in freefall. My hobby was becoming a distant memory. I had to closely observe his decline and try to cap the font of his misery before melancholy became malice. He would often end the evening by telling me to get lost.

One day at work he approached with steaming mugs of tea and I simply picked up my jacket and walked out without a word. I hadn't planned to, but I was past caring. My patience had gone. Or rather, my apathy was worn out: I had to defend myself. When I came back half an hour later he was at his desk and two full tea mugs sat next to the sink. A thick skin had developed on them.

That evening I had been lying on the sofa looking at the network of cracks and mottled stains on the ceiling. I had done this often. When I relaxed my eyes so my focus was somewhere just beyond the surface a face would appear. I'd seen it a number of times; it was someone I recognised. It had perplexed me for weeks. I lay there that night and suddenly the pieces fitted together and I saw Susan Sontag smiling down at me. The likeness was profound. I wondered if I would be able to capture it with my camera. The doorbell rang and she went away. Tony walked in without saying anything and I had felt unable to stop him. Now the full seriousness of his situation was here, in my kitchen.

The cynical spin I had used to keep his life one step removed from my own was unspinning fast. What had seemed like a necessary distancing act was now clearly nothing of the sort. He had bullied me into listening. If I was honest Tony had always slightly scared me. I had been a coward to put up with his mawkish self-flagellation. And now things had moved on and he was clearly in need of help. Help I hadn't been able to give him before and I couldn't offer him now.

I walked over to the window and focused on the street below. A man was swinging his arms around and a woman was punching his collarbone to impress her feelings upon him. Their body language was as crude as the expletives they were shouting at each other. I could hear Tony behind me. I could hear the thoughts colliding in his head, the blood tumbling clumsily around his body. My eyes refocused on the windowpane and I saw his blurred reflection, his face still staring at my back. I forced my gaze out of the window and back onto the dark street. The couple were still at it. She lunged at him and he toppled backwards over the low railing. Her drunken body followed his and the pair collapsed on the bare earth. He lay still with his limbs splayed while she writhed on top of him, her face buried in his as though devouring him.

I turned to say something but Tony wasn't there.

Another bright day today. People walking to work, walking to their own deaths. Strolling casually into the arms of eternal nothingness. I don't care. I'm walking in the other direction. I'll organise my own undoing, thanks. Call me old-fashioned, but I think a fucking good war's what we need. Get the city boys into a different uniform and the painted office bunnies down the munitions factory. Get the lads out there and get them dead dead quick. If everything's so bad, if nobody really gives a toss anymore, then a nice bloody long war should sort it all out. Make mincemeat of the pantshitters and hard, moral fuckers of the rest. The world's a different place now, and it wouldn't be the hun we'd be up against. No. Might be a bit tougher than we thought, too. Not much time for getting all worked up about the fucking Euro, not when you've got the Koran held upside down and a week to learn it in. Grandad, before the fluid filled his lungs and drowned him, used to talk about men back from the First World War who became schoolteachers, thrashing the daylights out of kids, their eyes full of fury and France. We could set the

131

clock right back if we'd just think of someone to pick on and do them. Do I sound unreasonable? Do I sound reactionary? Course I do. But I'm right.

It's a blustery day and much cooler than usual, a reminder to London not to assume too much when it comes to the weather. The light is sharp and unforgiving. I notice the make up on the faces of some of the women I pass in the street, the way every crease and line seems filled with dry powder when they cross the shafts of sunlight between buildings. I can't help thinking about dead skin when I see the whirlpools of rubbish blown up by the strong breeze. I imagine billions of flakes of skin being brushed off everyone and forming a solid mass in the air and this makes me feel a bit sick. I'm really hungry, that's what's causing the nausea. I normally get a sandwich or a pasta dish in one of the places near the office, but I can't be bothered to wait so I go to get a burger at Holborn. I'm five minutes into my lunch hour, so there's no need to rush, but I'm starving, so I march along.

Walking quickly is making me sweat so I loosen my tie, let my jacket hang unbuttoned. Everyone else seems to be wearing thick coats completely done up because of the cold wind so I hold my lapels together out of some strange idea of etiquette. I turn just before the tube and go into MacDonalds. I think about how much I hate the place for a moment and then order. I manage to eat and be out again before the atmosphere has a chance to really depress me. I can never understand people who linger in those places after they've finished eating, like they're taking in the ambience of a nice little restaurant. Maybe that *is* their idea of a nice little restaurant.

I cross at the main junction and head towards the bookshops on Charing Cross Road. I walk along thinking about what I might get when I catch sight of Lisa. It has to be her; I recognise the tan coat and swish of pale blond hair. We haven't spoken in over a year, for good reason. She said she would call the police if I called her again. The only reason I rang her was to try and arrange to get my CDs back. She went berserk as soon as she heard my voice. I let her keep them in the end.

She's only just ahead of me now, and I slow down to avoid overtaking her. She stops suddenly, and people walking behind almost run her over. She pulls her phone out of her bag and starts yelling into it. I stop and stand in a doorway. I can't believe it, she hasn't changed one bit. I'm fascinated to watch a scenario I was involved in so many times. People are giving her plenty of space as she stands there, gesticulating and stamping her foot. I can't help enjoying this. I feel vindicated. She turns suddenly and I can see her face is red and wet. Her mouth is jagged and trembling. She holds her hair as though it might blow away and I start to feel upset. I'd like to scream at her and ask her how it feels but at the same time I can't help feeling sorry; sorry for the whole time we were together. She puts her phone back in her bag, and starts to walk back the way she came, towards me.

I move out of the doorway but there is a swell of human traffic that blocks my way and almost lifts me off my feet. Then I hear her call my name, her voice instantly recognisable to me. I push my way along the crowded street, not daring to turn around, though I know it's obvious I heard her. I hear her again, her voice raised and slightly strangled, and I run down a side street. It's long and empty; I have to run fast to reach the next corner without her seeing me fleeing like an idiot. I pelt along, my jacket flapping around me, the burger I ate churning in my stomach and turn the corner without looking back. It might look odd if I stop now, so I carry on running. I can feel my heart beating wildly and I wonder at what point it might be alright to walk. I've reached Charing Cross Road by the time my legs decide for me and I start walking slowly, my hands on my hips like an Olympic athlete after a race.

I stop for a moment to get my breath back and try and calm myself. I lean forwards and let my mouth hang open. I look up at the window I'm next to. It's a shop selling cashmere sweaters and scarves that permanently displays discount signs, as though the place is on the verge of closure and everything inside must be an irresistible bargain. I've walked past often over the years, and the only thing to change has been the fluorescent signs when they've become too faded to convince even the tourists. I spot a travel rug, a red and green tartan blanket. Suddenly I'm reminded of a summer holiday when I was very young and we went to Wales. Only instead of driving there on motorways and A roads, Dad decided we'd take the scenic route, and after a few hours I was trying hard not to succumb to travel sickness induced by the constant bends and dips of Welsh border lanes. The memory is very faint, but I remember that eventually we had to pull over so mom could wash down the tartan travel rug I had emptied my guts over with water from a small tin camping kettle. In the confusion we drove off without the rug or the kettle. By the time this was noticed we were too near our destination to turn around. Mom and Dad had had the blanket since before they were married, I was told, over and over.

I'm still staring at the rug in the window and I feel hot tears streaming down my face. Christ, what is wrong with me? But it's no good and the more I fight it the more the memory takes a grip and before long I'm really in a state. I'm buckled in half leaning against the window with my eyes tightly shut, trying to control the weeping. I straighten up and move off Charing Cross Road and onto Long Acre. I dab at my eyes with a paper tissue but it stings and makes them raw. I feel myself calming slightly and I blow my nose. I'm not expected back for a while so I turn around and head towards a café that I know will be quiet.

What is the matter with me? I'm almost in tears again and I have to dab at my face with another tissue. I'm aware that people are noticing me and I press my thumbs tightly into my palms and quicken my stride. If I can just get to the café I'll be OK. I cut through the streets behind Soho Square and march straight through the doorway of Luigi's. I sit down at the back of the tiny room and breath deeply for a few moments.

I'm just about to go to the counter and order a tea when I notice the clock over the door. It's now 1:55. I'm due back in five minutes.

What am I doing?

It will take me at least ten minutes to get back to New Oxford Street. If I'd headed there straight after Car Blanket Memory intervened I would have only been a couple of minutes early. I don't have the time to scold myself properly and I leave quickly without looking at the surly woman behind the till. I run along Oxford Street constantly bumping into people and dodge cars across Tottenham Court Road. I can feel myself almost sucked towards the wind tunnel beneath Centrepoint. I look at my watch as I approach my building and see that it's 1:50.

What?

I look at my mobile and it says the same. The clock in Luigi's must have been almost fifteen minutes fast. This makes me really mad. I had plenty of time to drink a nice cup of tea and rest for a bit. Now I'm here, back at work, with ten minutes of my lunchbreak left. I can feel my collar tighten as the veins in my neck swell. There's a funny ringing sound in my ears and my eyes are hot again.

It's essential not to return to the office before the end of the allotted hour. No one does that; we all find the company a dull and stuffy place to work and since none of us seems capable of doing anything positive about it – like going to work somewhere else – there is an unofficial policy of taking a full hour for lunch every day. I look around, trying to remember if there's anywhere just here that I can go for a few minutes. My head's spinning and I'm still feeling over-emotional and annoyed with myself for being so sentimental. I'm about to walk back a bit to a sandwich bar I've been in before when I see Simon who works in the office next to me approaching. I try to turn around but he's seen me. He gives me a small nod and stops.

'You going in?' he says, giving the doorway behind us another nod.

I look at it too, like I've never set eyes on the miserable place before. 'Oh. Yeah, yeah. Hour's up. Might as well.'

I laugh like I've told a joke and he squints at me as sunlight cuts through the clouds. He nods again, slowly, and moves in a way that indicates I should do the same. It's useless, I'll have to go in. We climb the steps and I notice the small clock over the reception desk says 1:58. Forget all about tea and rest and car blankets.

Who are you? Me. And who am I? You. Right: so I am you and you are me. I'm glad we got that straight. Pleasure, anytime. Here's lookin at you kid, here's mud in your eye. Look at me, Ma, I'm on top o' the world. The world is like a great big onion. Onion? Forget it. Forgotten. You and me, then, happy as can be, all good friends. And jolly good company. Apparently. So they say. Do they? Don't know.

Who's that? Kenny.

– Kenny! Kenny, mate, me old china.

Ah, Kenny; got a plate in his head, has Kenny, not the right greeting.

– My nearest and dearest, how on earth are you on this fine morn? No? No? Well fuck you too then, fuck you your tin head and your mother and your sister. WANKER. DID YOU HEAR ME? W A N K E R.

Teach him.

Oops.

– Sorry sir, didn't mean to upset madam, how are you both?

Spare a little change, perchance? Hmm? An itty bitty liccle bit of change? No? Fine. FINE. be like that.

Do give her one for me, pal. A pox on your house. Ha ha! Ha. Hmm. Still never mind, all comes out in the wash, so to speak.

But I digress. Let us continue to sally forth within the confines of this capital city this broken hearted bastard of a borough this malevolent malcontent of a metropolis that sucks the joy from the unhappy lot who toil in it through the protracted birth of a new millennium.

– Excuse me miss, you've dropped your head. Head. Just there, behind you, look. HA! How can you drop your HEAD?

Perfect example, no sense of humour at all.

I'm going to. You're not. I am. I'm going to ask him. Don't. Too late.

– Excuse me, could I borrow your phone? I need to reach my financial adviser urgently. No, really. Between you and I, something big is going down. Must get a piece of the action, if you know what I mean. No? Look, I'll tell you. I'll share this with you. You can get rich too. Honest. Look at me, would I jest where money's concerned? That's fine, you keep walking, you lead and I'll follow. You'd prefer me not to. Fine, if that's all the thanks I get. Fine. Tell you what, how about you furnish me with some coins of the realm so I may repair to a stationary telephonic facility and thenceforth make a killing on the market? No? I could follow you all afternoon, if you'd rather. Gadzooks! Ten pence! You're a gentlemen, I'm overwhelmed, it's too much. Please take it back, I'm embarrassed. My best to your good lady wife You WANKER.

Aaargh

FUCK MY HEAD

Calm down.

WHY?

Calm it, stop shouting, you're making a scene. No trouble,

please. No need. Yes, well. That's all very well for you to say. In there. I have the body the limbs the mouth and
I WILL SHOUT IF I WANT TO
So there. This place is doing my
HEAD IN
I want
SLEEP
Sleep. Really really really need some sleep. But you, you bastard. You won't let me, will you, hey? You kick off then, don't you? On and on and on and on. What is your problem? Come on, tell me
Tell Me What You Want Me To Do
people, people walking denim shirt red skirt laughter on the face. Face smiling smiling laughter shout shout across OI YOU IDIOT GET OUT OF THE ROAD in the light blaring of horns in the sunshine shadows on the pavement cool love in the doorway a kiss flashing light off windows enough to make the world spin faster cling on cling onto to what is here
STOP
LET ME OFF
Too much too much information not enough processing to decide not to think to look to feel BANG
Must BANG
Stop BANG
The BANG
Feeling BANGBANGBANG

Can't see. Can't see a thing. All gone red.
Blink through blood.
Better. Banged it better.

Run, run run run. Shouting, someone chasing. Got to run away. Not my fault is it, nothing I can do about it. Got to stop it somehow.

Stop now, breathe. Lean in here for a moment. Wipe this red

gunk off my face with my T-shirt. Red doesn't go well with this wall. Wall's bright green, too green, not a good colour, too much blue in it, colour's too cold. Textured with something, not a nice effect at all, completely wrong, evil-looking satanic
Stop it stop it. Want some balance, will perish without it. Must get it whatever the cost.

Here is a window
a portal to punch through
Like so.
Now, with this clear sword that clarifies
This slither of sharp reality
I will cut through the lies in my veins my flesh and
carve
out
the
truth.

Like so.

'Gone.'

'What do you mean, Gone? Gone where?'

'He's gone, for good. Brian told us first thing. He said he'd spoken to him and he isn't coming back. Said he's going on a college course and he sent his regards to all of us.'

I glanced at Tony's desk. It looked abandoned and forlorn. Like us it had imagined his absence was temporary. Tony hadn't been in for a week; the last time I had seen him had been the night he came round to my flat. I hadn't told anyone about his visit.

I wanted to go and see Brian straight away, try and find out if he knew any more. But I was two hours late and needed to get to my desk and behave as though I had been there all morning. I got up on time but then when I went to leave the flat I couldn't find my keys. After about half an hour of going through all my pockets, my coat, bag, the kitchen drawers, I thought I might go mad. It sapped all of my energy. I sat down to try and think clearly about the situation. I had never bothered to have a spare set cut, and it was likely I would have put them somewhere I wouldn't be able to remember, anyway.

How easily the will to live is dented. Never mind being forced at gunpoint onto a windowless cattle train and sent off to certain death in a concentration camp. Hide my keys. I looked at my watch and an hour had passed. I went cold with anxiety. I was already late for work; even if I found them right now, if they appeared next to me on the sofa, I would still be nearly an hour and a half late. Every second from now compounded the misery. I could see a cartoon mouse with a giant hammer tapping my tack-shaped head into the ground. Tap tap tap. I jumped up and went through everything again. This was not possible. There were only so many places a set of keys, used a matter of hours earlier, the previous evening, could be. And then it came to me. I walked to the front door and opened it slowly and reached around it without looking. I pulled the keys from the lock. They were cold from the night air. I swallowed hard and tried not to think of what might have happened if they had been taken by some passing psychopath.

I stayed at my desk until lunchtime and then waited for Brian to leave. He was a creature of habit. Brian had a daily routine of going to a café in Soho that none of the others ever used. Then he would make his way to a pub called The Greyhound that was in such an obscure passageway he obviously didn't want anyone at work to know he had a lunchtime drink. I knew because I had followed him before, a number of times.

I ate in one of the sandwich shops and then made my way to The Greyhound. There are pubs and bars at every turn in central London. A lot of them are places where you might arrange to meet friends regularly, or ones you might only pop into briefly if you are going to see a film or have a meal. And then there are the ones that you would never enter, not if you passed them every day for a lifetime. Pubs you aren't even aware exist, they are so run-down and miserable looking. The

Greyhound was one of these. An unmarked door was the only evidence of its existence, the glass in its tiny window yellow and knobbly like old-fashioned pint glasses, the ones with the huge handles that men of a certain age and type complain they miss. I pushed the door open and went in.

There was a smell like an overflowing ashtray sprayed with cheap perfume. Two men in tracksuits sat at the bar, transfixed by a horserace on a portable television. A young woman slouched at a small table, smoking languidly and staring into space. There might as well have been a card placed in front of her saying Prostitute, Resting. The whole scene was like something from another age. I had stepped out of the late twentieth century, a world in the turbulent years of the millennium's last decade, and into the Soho of fifty years before.

I walked over to the bar. It was so small I had to stand sideways to avoid pressing against the two perched on their stools. No one was behind the bar. I waited for a minute or two and then a man I hadn't noticed sitting by the door put his paper down and went through the gap in the counter. I ordered a pint of Guinness.

'Guinness is off,' he said, a cigarette still dangling from his mouth.

I looked again. Another remarkable achievement of pubs like The Greyhound is the stalwart resistance to modern drinking trends. They resolutely refuse to stock drinks found everywhere else. Beers you might be unaware are even brewed any longer are the brands these dumps still champion. I checked the fridge to one side of him.

'I'll have a Beck's please,' I said.

The barman bent down and pulled a bottle out of an open cardboard box.

'Do you think I could have a cold one, from the fridge?' I asked.

He looked at me and I tried not to stare at the cigarette reduced to a filter that was still attached to his face.

'Only put them in a minute ago,' he said.

I paid for the warm bottle, took my change and went to the empty table where the barman had been. As I sat down he came around the bar. He scowled at me, picked up his paper and took it back to the counter.

I had timed this visit well. A couple of sips of my tepid drink later the door opened and I saw the back of Brian as he moved to the bar. It was odd, seeing him in this new context. At work he was a slightly sad figure, struggling to remain vaguely contemporary at an age when he would rather not bother. He wore tinted glasses and suits that looked as though they had been altered at least a couple of times, as fashion declared his lapels too wide and his trousers too flared and then changed its mind yet again and said the turn-ups would have to go, too. His hair was always neatly cut but a bit too much so; it was too easy to picture him in the same local barber's chair every other Saturday morning. But here in The Greyhound he blended in perfectly. A man in his natural habitat.

Brian paid for his drink and remained at the bar. He exchanged a few words with our friendly bartender and kept glancing at the screen in the corner. A betting man, possibly? I didn't want him to feel I was spying on him so I waited for the race to finish and then called his name. Brian twitched and turned around. He gulped when he saw me, frowned and forced a smile.

'Well. Fancy seeing you here. Funny little place this, isn't it?' I said as he put his pint of bitter down opposite me and pulled back the low stool. Brian glanced around the fake wood panelled room as if seeing it for the first time.

'Yes, it is, isn't it. I was heading back from Regent Street and I found myself by the market. I haven't been around here for years.'

I smiled and nodded. 'Me too. I mean, I'm round this way quite often, but I just came down to see a friend who works on Berwick Street, and thought I'd grab a swift one.' I said this in a slightly lowered tone and Brian visibly relaxed at my hint of sneaky camaraderie.

We spoke for a few minutes about a new contract and then I let him carry on at length about a company he had just found that was developing revolutionary new materials for surfacing playgrounds. I listened with a look of gravity appropriate to the subject of protecting fragile young skulls. I didn't mind; the theme was sombre enough for me to reach my line of questioning in a minute. Brian was rambling. I wondered what else he might have to be worried about anyone knowing, as though my intrusion into this fairly innocent lunchtime activity threatened to expose other more private vices. I hadn't intended to make Brian nervous, or pry into his personal business. Perhaps he thought I'd chosen this haunt of his to confront him with evidence of his nasty ways and ensnare him in a spiral of blackmail. Personally I couldn't have cared less what he was into. Whatever it might be it would still have Brian involved in it and was therefore implicitly dull. I'd just wanted to see him somewhere other than the office, somewhere private where he would be comfortable. He stopped talking and looked at his watch.

'Brian, I wanted to ask you something. About Tony,' I said. Brian eyes batted around behind his brown-fogged specs.

'Tony? What about Tony?'

'Well, I mean, he's at work one day, then he's away for a week, and then he's gone for good. It just seems strange.'

Brian stared at his glass. He looked drained and sad. I wondered what could be the real reason for this. He wasn't close to Tony; I knew they had never once been out socially during the eight years Tony worked with him.

'It's as I said in the office, to you all this morning.'

To us all. That was kind of him. No mention of my late arrival that morning. I knew we had an unspoken agreement.

'He called me last Friday night and said he's going to be starting a college course in, in computing, I think he said. I told

146

him we wouldn't be able to give him enough time off to do the course and he said I shouldn't worry because it was full-time. He said his father's lending him the money.'

I watched Brian closely. I decided he was telling the truth.

'Why? What did you think had happened?'

I drained the last of my flat beer. 'I thought he might be dead.'

Brian leant back on his stool and turned away as though I had gently slapped him.

'Dead? *Dead*?'

'Yes. I had a feeling he'd killed himself.'

'Killed himself? Bloody hell. I mean, he was unhappy, and his work had gone to pot, but *suicide*? No way. I'll tell you this; the bugger is very much alive. He was very very rude to me. He said he holds me responsible for his lack of promotion. Me! Like *I* have *anything* to do with *anyone's* bloody promotion these days.'

The implication didn't escape me.

'I told him, I said, Tony, I've known you a *very* long time and I resent you swearing at me and blaming *me* for your *own* shortcomings. I had to put a lid on your management training for your own good, that's what I said. But he wouldn't have it and he got more and more angry. Honestly, the things he called me. It left me shaken, I don't mind telling you. I hardly slept. My Maureen was very worried.'

Maureen was Brian's devoted wife who was known to all at work only as a figure in a framed ten by eight photo taken on their wedding day, which had appeared on Brian's desk shortly after the Mutiny of the Shells. If she had walked into the office wearing anything other than a seventies wedding dress no one would have had a clue who she might be. But we did from time to time hear about His Maureen and her devotion to him and her keen sense of values. She was an enigma, existing on a moral plane beyond our reach. An angel, ageless in her horrible dated white gown. I wondered what His Maureen would say if she knew that His Job might be on the line.

'Well, that's a relief. A shame he had to take it out on you though, Brian… He didn't happen to mention me at all? He didn't have a message or anything to pass on to me?'

Brian was confused. 'A message for you? No, no he didn't. He didn't mention anyone.'

I felt relieved and a bit disappointed.

'Thanks. I think we'd better get back, don't you?' I said.

He grunted. 'Yes, yes. Come on.'

Brian wasn't happy. The conversation had run just outside the field of his own troubles but close enough to stir the subject in his mind. He'd only come out for a pint of bitter and I had gone and spoilt it. I felt a bit guilty.

'I don't know about you but I think once was enough, in that place,' I said. Brian glanced across at me and we walked on in silence.

But that night in the middle of wretched sleep I'm back there again.

I'm sitting at a table with Brian and Tony. We are all sipping at long straws that stick out of our cocktails. I am angry with Tony. He looks very pleased with himself. He is holding his oversized drink as though it's a small sherry, pinkie finger extended, and he's admiring the lime umbrella that protrudes at a rakish angle from the glass. I want to ask him what the fuck is going on, why didn't he call me, the one person who's put up with him for so long and listened to his pathetic problems? I can't because my straw is stuck to my bottom lip and I can't get rid of it.

The bar is packed with people from work. They are all watching a horse race on a screen that fills one wall. It keeps distracting me because the race has been on for ages and doesn't seem any closer to finishing. It's reached a feverish climax and held it, the commentator raging and bellowing without end. Brian is looking at me like it's all my fault, like I'm to blame for all our colleagues being here, ruining his pub. We are sitting close to the enormous plate glass window facing the street. Crowds of people edge past peering in, and for a moment I'm unsure whether The Greyhound is actually on a canal in Amsterdam's red light district. Our table keeps wobbling and my stool is unstable. The sticky carpet has been replaced with a thick coating of tiny rubber granules embedded in the floor. I pull the straw away from my mouth and grip the edge of the Formica table, complaining that I can't put up with the way it's moving about. Tony says that he agrees with Brian on this one and that if the flooring prevents any serious head injuries then it's for the best.

I'm about to reply when I look across the room and see a woman sitting alone, smoking nonchalantly and staring at me. I pick up my drink and start walking towards her. My feet sink deeper with each step and then I'm moonwalking, taking huge strides that get me almost nowhere. Eventually I sit down exhausted.

'Sally! I can't believe this. It must be fifteen years, surely?' I say.

Sally nods slowly and takes another long drag on her cigarette. She has streaky blonde hair and is wearing a lot of make-up. But her face is very young, even child-like. It makes me uneasy. I am glad to see her but I have a sense of foreboding. She puts her cigarette in the ashtray and yawns deeply. I am captivated by her glistening gullet, the soft flesh of her inner mouth. It is grotesque and compelling. I am about to reach towards it when she closes her mouth and picks up her cigarette again.

I woke up with a start and lay very still. Sally was my best friend when I was young. She was one of those children that have an innate sense of purpose in life, a calling that is eerily indisputable from an almost indecently early age. With Sally, it was animals. We would wander around the back garden as if we were exploring a vast wilderness. Sally would root about with her nose pushed close to the earth and the plants, searching for anything moving. She was always picking up ants and spiders, scrutinising them and carefully putting them back. But the slug was the limit. I spotted it first, moving sluggishly across the patio. Exuding slug. I saw it and made a sound like someone being sick and then watched in horror as she plucked it from its weary course and sat it across the open palm of her hand. She raised it to her line of sight, looked it squarely in its slug tentacle eyes, and kissed it gently, her eyes half closed. I thought I might pass out. Then she opened her mouth and in it went. She closed her eyes and mouth as if tasting something wonderful and held the slug's soft body gently pressed between her tongue and the roof of her mouth. Her lips formed a circle and she eased it forwards with her tongue. Out it came. I remember gasping for air and my legs wobbling as each of the stalks on its head popped out and it squirmed back onto her hand.

It was two days before I ate a thing and a week before I would go near the garden or Sally. I really think it changed me. The image is as clear today as it was then. A wave of revulsion went through me and left a permanent mark. I would wake up at night for months afterwards in a cold sweat. At first I saw the events as they had happened, though painted in the mellow colours of the dream world's palette. Later the dream morphed and the roles shifted. I was the one inserting the fat slug. And a year or so later I was there again, and I was the slug Sally was offering up to her open mouth. My revulsion had changed to pleasure, confused and fundamental.

Head's very sore. Hungover. Not just drink, though. Always hurts, afterwards. Exciting, though. Shaking like I've been on a rollercoaster. Which I have, in a way. Still there, I know it, but I can use my body now, take control of myself. Feel a bit calmer. Air in my lungs, my chest goes up, and it goes down. Arm seems to work fine, another scar won't make any difference now. Amazing how much blood comes from the smallest head wound, nearly always looks a lot worse than it is. Rub my hands. That's better. But I do need to sleep. That makes it worse, always. Might manage it, now. Where though? So hard in the morning. All the good spots still taken. I know, I've got it. Underpass, that one the other side of Soho. So tired. Really want to sit down, but won't be able to get up again. Wish I wasn't in town. Too much when I'm recovering, getting my senses back.

Lucky, no one down here. Timed it well. Just going to sit still for a bit, tuck myself in a corner. Get some sleep, let the day go. Start working again tonight. Where's my map?! Got it, got it, it's fine.

Oh god that's better. I'll just curl up here for a while.

Hmm? What's that? What's that noise? Shit. Is he taking the piss? That can't be what I think it is?
And held loosely by his side,
yesterday's paper telling yesterday's news
How can you tell me you're lonely
It is, it's that fucking song. He's asking for it. Must stay calm.
Let me take you by the hand
And lead you through the streets of London
I'll show you something to make you change your mind
Just look at him. Young twat. Can't be a Londoner, he wouldn't fucking DARE. Commuters liable to tear him to bits, I would have thought. Jesus, the money in his case. Got to be tourists throwing away their money like that, surely. The wanker.
Dirt in her hair and her clothes in rags
She's no time for talkin, she just keeps right on walkin
Right, that's it.
– SHUT IT YOU BASTARD
He's not listening. I've got rights, I don't have to be put through this.
– Oi! I said, stop playing that FUCKING CRAP
In the all night café at a quarter past eleven
Same old man sitting there on his own
Looking at the world over the rim of his teacup
Each tea lasts an hour and he goes home alone
Have you seen the old man outside the seaman's mission
Memory fading like the ribbons that he wears
I'll kill him. I'll walk up casually and stick a busted bottle in his neck. I'll ram it right in 'til his eyes pop out. I'll kill the fucker and do a dance in his blood. What do you think of that? Got a tune for me to jig in your guts to? Oh what's the point. Just curl up. Get under my jacket. Can't see the cunt now, can't see anyone.
For one more forgotten hero in a world that doesn't care
I'll just sit here with my jacket tented over my head and knees. I'll

do my disappearing act for a while. That's better. Calmer now. Not enough oxygen in here; good, I might just sleep. Might get some of the rest I need so badly.

At three in the morning I was sitting in the kitchen drinking my third mug of herbal tea. Every time I relaxed my eyes I saw it again, a bizarre amalgam of Tony, the girl, my cubicle, a contractor I was having some trouble with. But mainly it was just her. It didn't make sense, the way she left so quickly. Why had she changed so much since our first night? Where did she have to go? In my addled state I started to wonder if she was real. Perhaps I had imagined the whole thing, it would explain a lot. No, she was real. But something wasn't making sense.

My insomnia had returned with a vengeance. I can fall asleep without much difficulty but a dream sequence will start that is so real I wake up and hours then slip by in which it replays over and over without losing its force, while I pretend to be sleeping. The constant wrangling with my own subconscious leaves me tattered. That night was the same stupefying scenario and by the morning I felt demented. Birds whistled madly in the trees and sunlight glared off the pavement. My eyes were hot from not sleeping and my legs felt heavy. Even now the dream was turning over behind my eyes, and she flitted back and forth between her appearances like a quick-change artist.

I turned onto another street and saw her. I had glanced across the road just as a figure left one of the houses. I knew it was her but I blinked and squinted. I crossed over to catch up and then stopped. What was she doing here? She said she didn't live locally. But then if she didn't, why did she use that pub? My mind raced back over our conversations, her reluctance to tell me anything about herself. And the man. The man I used to see her with, in the pub. I grimaced at the conclusions spinning inside my head. She was already out of sight and I couldn't be late for work so I made a mental note of the door number and carried on.

That evening I drank a bottle of wine and walked three times around the block where the house was. I passed closer by the door and spent a little longer looking at it each time. I wanted to walk right up and look through the window. I wanted to see them rolling around on the floor. I felt sick inside and I didn't know why. I felt terrible with the need to know more. After another loop the alcohol had taken hold. A light was now on in an upstairs window. I stood under a tree directly opposite. I wanted him to appear at the window. I wanted to see her standing next to him.

The light went off and I tensed. I heard the latch on the door open and then she stepped out. She had a large bag over one shoulder, which she struggled to manoeuvre to the front gate. I crossed the road and walked up to her.

'Hello.'

She jumped and then dropped the bag. She stared at me.

'What are you doing here?'

Her voice was flat and hard.

'I was passing. Like you were, when you walked past mine.' I looked at the house. 'Nice little place. I thought you didn't live around here?'

She huffed and stared at the ground. She shut her eyes tightly.

'It's none of your business, but I don't. I can't believe you would follow me.'

'I didn't follow you. I saw you leave here this morning, when I was walking to the station. I'm sorry, I didn't mean to freak you out, but I don't understand why you have to be so secretive.'

She let out a scornful laugh that shook me.

'Where is he?' I said.

Her face creased and her eyes bulged with anger. She swung around and hit me on the side of my head with an open palm. My ear pulsed violently and I stumbled backwards, my reactions dulled by the wine. She stood rigid, rubbing her fingers inside her clenched hand to ease the tingling.

'Who do you think you are? I've met you twice, TWICE, and you think I'm going to tell you about my life?' she screamed.

'No. But I can't see why you would lie about living here and make such a fuss about not telling me anything at all. And why you ran off like that and it was a big mystery where you had to go. It meant a lot to me, meeting you. I thought you were single. I thought we got on and we might get to know each other properly but you just wanted it to be a game.'

She sat down on the bag which sighed and ran fingers across the crown of her stubbled head. I stood over her rubbing my cheek. She was shaking.

'It wasn't a game. I don't live here. And I am *single*.'

'Look, I used to see you, you and him, in the pub. Then he stopped going and I thought you had split up or something. If you're still seeing him and I've got this all wrong just tell me.'

And then tears made small black spots on the pavement in front of her.

'He's dead.'

My hand stopped moving. She shifted and ran her sleeve across her nose.

'He was my husband. We split up a couple of years ago and he moved here. We started talking about getting back together, once the air had cleared. Then he found out he had cancer. The doctor told him he had two years at the most and then a specialist said it was more like one year. I came to look after him. And then he died. He lasted nine months. I've been at my parents for a few weeks and then I came back to look after the house and arrange to sell it, clear his mortgage, all of that.'

She looked up at me and all I could see were two sparkling pools where her dark eyes were.

'When I walked out of the pub last time I had to meet his parents here to go through his things and decide what to do with it all.'

I didn't know what to say. I looked back at the house. I thought they were splitting up when they were trying hard to pretend he hadn't been told his life was nearly over and their reconciliation doomed.

She eased herself off her bag and faced me.

'I'm really sorry I shouted and hit you, it's not your fault, you've been great. I've tried to be normal and seeing you helped but my heart isn't in living again, yet. I've tried really hard, tried to move on, even kept changing my image to see if I could be someone else for a while, but it's all just left me feeling crazy, and coming back here makes it worse.'

I gave her arm a squeeze. I wanted to tell her that I would look after her and we would be alright and she should bring her bag round to mine right now.

'It's pointless me saying sorry. I hope it starts getting easier for you soon. Really.'

'Oh I'm sure it will. Now I've done the hard part. I'm thinking of moving abroad, France, maybe. You'd be amazed what these houses go for now.'

She smiled wetly at me and I hugged her. I scribbled my phone number on a scrap of paper knowing she'd never use it.

She thanked me and gave me another hug. I picked her bag up and walked her as far as the main road where she stopped a cab and got in. I closed the door for her and as the cab moved away from the kerb she lowered the window.

'Sophia,' she said, and waved.

I waved back and shouted my name but I don't think she heard me over the traffic.

Now I've seen them and started thinking about the problem again, I'm getting more and more annoyed. Something must be done about this. There are so many of them and only one of me. Others might not have the same problems with it; it might well be that I'm sensitive in this respect. I know I'm getting increasingly fragile but again, that is their fault. The barrage has worn me down. I've had to resort to heavy drinking to drown them out too often. I need to say something. I want to complain about the lack of consideration.

I walk into the police station and up to the main desk. A middle-aged policeman looks up from the paperwork in front of him smiling. His eyebrows drop again as he takes me in. Then he carries on reading. I cough a couple of times and eventually he looks up again.
– I've come to make a complaint.
He nods slowly, not saying anything. He swivels his head around and looks at the clock behind him that says two forty.

– Right. If you'd like to take a seat over there and wait, a young officer will be out shortly to see you.

He smiles falsely and carries on scrutinising his forms.

I sit on the bench for a long time. I don't know why, there isn't anyone else here waiting. The policeman glances at me then the clock once or twice smiling to himself. I've read the posters on the walls several times and all I've learnt is that it is very dangerous out there and we should all be very careful. I wonder if there might be a job going, doing these posters. I could write and warn people about far worse than bag snatching or vandalism, things that happen just as often. But I don't want to confuse the issue, not while I have it firmly grasped in my mind. I'm here to complain and that's what I'm going to do. They know this already, of course. That's why they've left me here. They've been forwarded a signal and told to just let me cool off for while. They're hoping I'll get bored and wander off again. Fat chance. Not this time. I've had enough.

The clock makes a small clicking sound as the hands pass to three o'clock. Without looking at the time or me the policeman walks away from the desk and through a door behind it. I'm left alone with two CCTV cameras for a few minutes. This is the quietest police station I've ever been in; where is everybody? I can hear the muffled sound of keyboards being pressed, telephones ringing, but there are no actual signs of life, criminal or otherwise. Then it comes to me – this is a decoy station. Of course! I shake my head smiling. How could I be so thick? The signal was sent ahead and I've been re-routed to a dummy location, a stage set. They will probably keep me waiting here indefinitely, while they decide how to handle me. I'm feeling pleased with the way my mind is working when there is a sudden burst of activity. A tall, young policeman with straw coloured hair appears through the door behind the desk just as several more come marching in from the street, all talking and joking, a clunking noisy mass of dark blue and black, boots going clomp clomp and belts rattling with police paraphernalia. The thought of this lot running, giving chase to someone makes me giggle. They stop and stare at me, look at each other and then carry one through a door marked No Unauthorised Admittance. I've seen a lot of those doors before.

As they move past the young officer behind the desk looks up and sees me. He looks back down, muttering under his breath.

– *Ohferfuck'ssake*

I fix my eyes on him. He won't get rid of me with simple rudeness. He sighs and shuts the logbook in front of him.

– Yes. *Sir*. What can I do for you?

I get up and walk over to the desk. I stand as close to it as possible and look up at him. I think the other side must be slightly higher, a raised platform of some kind.

– I wish to make a complaint.

He nods and takes a piece of paper from a drawer and picks up his pen.

– Concerning?

– Concerning the operators.

He looks at me through his hair and puts the pen back down.

– The what?

He must think I'm stupid.

– The operators. There are too many of them, and they are making me very confused. I want to report the problem.

He stares at me for a moment. The door behind me opens again and another procession of Plods goes past towards the entrance. He gives them a despairing look over my shoulder. I move slightly to my left to block his view.

– I want to make a detailed report of the current situation because it can't go on; someone will get hurt if it does.

He gives me a harder look.

– Will they, now. I see. Well that is serious, isn't it? Why don't we check if there's an interview room available and I will get someone to have a proper chat with you about it?

He seems pleased at this idea of his.

– I think that would be the thing to do.

He looks at the time and checks another file on the desk. He smiles at me.

– I think you're in luck. There's a room free and I know just the officer for the job, someone who will take very good care of you.

I thank him and he lifts up the desktop, stepping around me. There is a slight lip between the two floor levels but he is a lot taller than I am, anyway. He opens the door and with a wave of his arm authorises my admittance. I walk ahead of him through a corridor with a number of doors leading off it. He guides me through one of them into a very small room with a low suspended ceiling, strip lights set into it. The walls are textured and grey, perforated with small holes, some kind of soundproofing. There is no window and it is quite stuffy. He pulls back a plastic chair from one side of the table that fills the space and invites me to sit down.

– Now I'll just go and get the officer who will be handling your complaint; would you like a glass of water or anything?

I shake my head and he closes the door behind him. I sit still, resisting the temptation to get up and examine the room closer. They will be recording already and I don't want to give them the satisfaction of seeing me trying to find the equipment.

The door opens noisily and the older policeman who kept me waiting for so long walks in with a file under one arm. He looks very annoyed. I return the expression; if he had dealt with me in the first place we would both be doing something else by now.

He goes around to the other side of the table and sits down without a word. He opens the file and takes a pen from the breast pocket of his shirt. He sniffs the air; he's obviously noticed it's very close in here. He gives me another unpleasant look. He then grumbles a few questions and scribbles my answers along several dotted lines.

– Right, tell me what you've got to say about the person you intend to hurt.

I stare at him.

– Intend to hurt?
– Yes. You said something to the desk duty officer about intending to hurt someone.

I'm feeling very calm, I know this is another of their tricks.

– I didn't say that. I said someone would get hurt if things carry on as they are. I'm the one who'll get hurt, by them.
– Them?
– The operators.
– And who are The Operators? Can you give me any names? Are they a street gang, or something?

Oh very good. His face is a picture of innocent curiosity. As if he's asking a serious question, and not just toying with me. I take a couple of deep breaths, trying to decide how best to deal with this. I'm going to put a stop to his playacting.

– I can dictate this for you, if you like, and you can write it all down.
– You do that. Fire away.

It's very hot in the room by the time I've finished. The policeman looks tired and harassed, beads of sweat cover his bald pate and we sit in silence while he reads through the four sheets of notes. I've definitely shaken him.

– This is bollocks.

I lean forwards, trying to see if he wrote down what I said.

– What do you mean, bollocks?
– None of this makes any sense. I still have no idea who these operators are, or what they do that affects you.
– An operator is a person who makes the calls, puts out the transmissions. And there are too many of them.

He looks quite annoyed. My understanding is unsettling him.

– Right. I'm going to read one paragraph out loud, if that's alright.

I nod and he skims along with his finger to a bit that makes him frown.

– *There aren't any blocks in place, and none of them seem to be able*

to get a hook on the others, leading to too much confusion. Each must
be lining through many dummies but for someone like me, with more
latticework and not much board cover, it means their unshielded flexing
often paralyses me. I am being weakened by the crowding and unless
there is a rest period I feel I won't be able to work much longer.

He stops and looks up at me.

— What the hell is all that about?

I open my mouth to go through it line by line but he cuts me off.

— Look, let's agree on one thing. You hear voices, in your head, yes?

— No.

— No?

— No. I never said anything about voices in my head. Why would I hear voices? I'm not a madman. I can't explain the type of transmissions I get because they're very sophisticated; in fact now you read it back to me, I think I may have oversimplified it.

— Well I'd say you're full of crap, son, and I'm buggered if I'm going to waste any more time listening to it.

He puts the top on his pen and drops it on the desk defiantly.

I've no choice but to push further, reveal more of what I know. I gesture for him to lean closer. He contemplates me for a moment and then bends one ear forwards. I lower my voice.

— Listen, you do know that you can be phased at any time? I can sit here all day and wait, but I don't think you can.

He sits back and stares at me. He's gone quite red, his eyes are burning into me. He rocks backwards and forwards with his arms folded, his lips tightly pursed as if in deep thought.

— I won't even say what I'd like to do about people like you.

I wave his silly threat aside.

— You have no power, you're here to serve. I'm not interested in what you might want to do about me. What I want to know is, what are you going to do about this?

I place a finger on his paperwork.

We've been here for a long time, and the conviction of my speech has worn him down. His expression changes. He runs a hankie over his head and gathers the sheets of paper together.

– I will type this up and hand it to the… Main Operator.

– You will? Really? I can't believe it.

He nods, wearily, defeated.

– Yes. It's a serious matter. I will make sure it's dealt with at the highest level.

I'm thrilled that this has been so successful. I was worried I'd get shown the door and would have to try again.

– Thank you very much. That's a relief. I must say I'm surprised I'm the only one who has been in to complain.

– Oh, you aren't.

– No?

– Oh no. You'd be surprised how many come in here to complain, all the time. Not always in quite as much… detail, but yes, there are a lot of people out there who share your… views.

– Well, there you are then. It's a problem, isn't it.

– It is, it is. Anyway, thanks very much. I'll just show you out.

We leave the room and walk back to reception. Then it occurs to me that he might be trying to fob me off; I have no way of knowing whether he will really deal with this matter properly. We walk past the blond policeman who smirks and he opens the door for me.

– Actually, perhaps I should go along there myself, to wherever you send the reports, just to let them know it's coming. Where does the main broadcast come from?

He rolls his eyes. My candid question has disarmed him.

– Broadcasting House.

The other one laughs.

– Where?

– Broadcasting House. Just past Oxford Circus, Portland Place. Can't miss it. Go on, go there now. They'll be pleased to see you.

I run along Regent Street weaving in and out of the traffic trying to think of the quickest route there, to lessen the chance of it slipping from my mind. Now he's told me, it seems obvious; so obvious it's ingenious, and typical of their methods. The building is a landmark – there's even a radio mast on the roof, an emblem so proudly visible I never even thought about it before. I glance up at the rooftops and everywhere I look I see them, they're all over town now. The huge aerials they use are partially concealed on all sorts of different buildings; there are more and more of them all the time. So many operators all over central London, so many conflicting signals it completely confuses me. Why are there so many? Can the population have swelled so much in recent years? It must have, there's no other reason. But there are too many. So often as I walk around I can feel the transmissions overlapping, blending into gibberish that makes my skull hurt. It's like having a radio inside that is constantly tuning through the wavebands. They should be more careful, there should be a better system than this. I set off with something in mind and then something else entirely different, even contradictory, comes across, butting in and taking over. It's very confusing. At its worst it prevents me moving at all. I get trapped in the crossed wavelengths, a dozen frantic signals battling for control, dominance of my mind. The pain can be overwhelming, I have to scream sometimes to try and block them out and get some peace. I've thought a number of times how much I would like to go up in that big wheel, the London Eye, down by the river, but then I get scared at the thought of being able to see them all so clearly from the top. The effect could tip me over the edge, seeing with my own eyes the scale of the problem, finally knowing for sure that they have the whole city covered. I was very lucky, the one time it got really bad. I found a big sheet of metal leaning against a wall somewhere round Vauxhall, and crawled under it for hours. I could hear the transmissions bouncing off the surface above me like bullets. That piece of tin may have saved my life.

Lungs hurt now. Got to keep going. Got to. Before words get harder to find before they put out a signal that gags my thoughts

and stops me from
saying he can't go on, he
needs a rest
he wants them to stop
wants to stop

Stop. Get breath back. Where are we? Oxford Street. Why?
Don't know. Had to tell someone but it's gone again, it's no good.
Have to wait. Head pulsing hard, painful across the forehead.
What should we do? Got to get away from here, got to find
somewhere higher up, above the streets and the aerials and the
operators and their constant demands.

The stillness says the heat can't go on. It's intense and all-consuming but the dead air of the last few days tells me that it's a spent force, it's been overstretching itself and will collapse in tears any time now. It can't happen too soon. Everyone in town has been on edge. It's as though war has been looming and we have all been waiting for the threat to dissipate. Fights break out on the tube, people get stabbed outside pubs. Bizarre accidents happen. People wake up with others they don't know. The tension is still as palpable as body odour on the underground.

But it will end, and I think it will be today. When I got up this morning I could taste a change in the humidity and when I went out onto the balcony a vast plane of angry dense cloud was visible far out to the East. It will roll over town soon. It's a Saturday and I want to go up to the Heath. Sarah had mentioned it recently at work in that casual way that suggests everyone knows about it, goes strolling there all the time.

'Is it good?' I said.

She gave me a funny look. 'What, you've never been there?'

I shrugged. 'No. Why, have I been missing something?'

'It's nice. That's all. It's the only proper open space in London, really peaceful. It's very popular. You can see the whole of central London, all the buildings, from the top.'

I wasn't interested in popular wide-open spaces. How could it be peaceful if everybody else was up there with you? Surely that was an ideal moment to be in town? But her comment about the view intrigued me. It was something I needed to see.

I pack a few things into a rucksack and plan my route. I consider momentarily the idea of walking all the way. This strikes me as overambitious and counter-productive; I want to have plenty of energy left when I finally get there, and I might want to stay for some time. I don't often walk around London. Before I moved here it would never have occurred to me to walk anywhere without a reason, for pleasure. To me the city was described in its totality by the underground map. A network of tube stations with some buses between them. I'm a lazy person essentially and I associated walking with work. I don't know why, but walking for its own sake seems more logical living here. The first time I visited East London was completely unintentional.

I came out of a house and I had no idea at all where I was. I'd gone back there the night before with a girl I met at a party. I was wired from a hangover that hadn't had a chance to start and I felt seedily good from a night that was already slipping into the distant past. But I hadn't a clue where I might be. I walked to the corner and saw a sign saying Brick Lane. I'd heard of it because of the curry houses and the market but I'd never been there. I was living in Ladbroke Grove at the time and anywhere east of Tottenham Court Road was a mystery. It's funny now, because I know the area well whereas Portobello is another world to me. People in London get very good at mentally deleting huge chunks of the city, I think.

I'd only intended to walk as far as the nearest tube, but it must have been much earlier than I thought and I hadn't seen anyone to ask where it was. The sun was coming up and everything seemed totally alien. I passed three huge slabs of metal jutting out of the ground behind Broadgate. I stopped as people emerged from a club that others were queuing to get into. I went by an Italian church with an ornately decorated entrance. How I managed to weave through such a large area of London and miss every station along the way I don't know. Eventually I came to a place I recognised, Angel. It was still too early for the station to be open so I let my legs carry me down the hill slowly to Kings Cross. It was a long walk and my legs ached for days afterwards, but I enjoyed seeing London as if for the first time, abandoned in the early hours. Not that I did it again. There always seemed to be something better to do than wander round town at dawn like a homeless person.

I come out of the underground and a steady drizzle is falling. I'm surprised it's reached here so quickly. A procession of people is coming down the steep road ahead of me and I push past them in the opposite direction. Water is already trickling fast in the gutter and once I'm off the road I stop to pull my anorak from my bag. The rain gets annoyed and falls harder. I have no idea which way to go so I zip up my waterproof and pull the cord on my hood tightly. I'm left with a glimpse of footpath seen through a red Gore-Tex sphincter. I keep my head down and let my feet decide which route to take.

The path keeps rising so I know I must be going the right way. I can feel my calves throbbing and my chest is getting tight. The fast steady tempo on my hood stops and when I look up I'm under trees. The rain doesn't quite penetrate the canopy but huge drops gather and fall on my head now and then. When I come out again onto open heath I can see the summit just ahead. As I break cover the weather sees me and goes into a rage. The summer shower gives way to a storm. I don't think I've been out in weather like this since I was a teenager. The feeling of being vulnerable and exposed to the elements makes me elated and scared. I run to the top and laugh out loud as the unexpected panorama bobs into view. I've never seen the city like this before. London is reduced to a toy. My own hand, a single finger, is bigger than any building in the city.

The rain is now a solid sheet that holds me up, bends and twists me. I'm soaked through and there's no point running for cover. Hailstones begin cascading all around, fall so hard they hurt my head. I push back my hood and blink at the city down below. White veins of lightning fidget nervously over it. I watch as the battle rages just above the buildings. Everything looks clean and sharply defined against the churning black backdrop. The air cracks and I throw back my head, my mouth riveted with sharp needles. Trees sway all around. I gasp at the broad streaks of light that rent the sky and feel the pulse inside me as the tail-end of each sonic clap flicks the heath. I shut my eyes tightly and count to five but when I open them the architect's model below me is still there. My legs are shaking and my arms flail around. I feel charged by the electricity in the air. I see and hear the next bolt at almost the same moment and as I look up a blinding flash pops directly overhead.

I start running down the hill but the grass is a slippery green sheet and I slide and stumble. I find myself on another path and jog along it. My lungs hurt and I'm sore inside my sodden clothes. My ears are ringing and when I blink I see white. I keep heading downhill until I'm back on the road I started on; the trickling gutter is now a fast flowing stream that bubbles and froths around each drain.

A large puddle surrounds me and my seat is darker than the ones on either side. The tube is quiet and the few dry passengers are interspersed with other drowning victims, each sitting in their own puddle. Gradually the train fills and there are more of them than us. The storm must be passing.

Warm air greets me when I climb above ground again. I'm still soaked through and the light breeze is as intense as an upturned hand dryer in a public toilet. I can't believe it. The street is completely dry, bright sunshine bounces off buildings and cars. How can the storm have completely missed my own neighbourhood? People are looking at me in surprise and amusement. Everyone is in t-shirts and shorts. Everyone's nice and dry. My trainers suck and fart as I walk along leaving a trail of dark footsteps behind me. The skin on my face feels tight and my hair is tangled and matted. I walk as quickly as I can through the estate, past children who point and whistle. I keep my head up and pointed ahead as though there is nothing unusual to look at.

– Are you listening?

– Hmm?

– What's that mean, hmm? That's no answer. I'm talking to you.

– What?

– I was saying. Nice, here, isn't it? I was asking if you knew that was parliament, down there.

– Oh. Yes, it is isn't it.

– Not exactly a chatterbox, are you?

– Sorry, I just don't want to talk, that's all.

– Really? I could have sworn I heard you just now, as I was walking along. But your friend doesn't seem to be here now. Don't mind if I sit down, do you?

– Look, I don't mean to be rude but fuck off, mate.

– Charming. Lovely language. Only trying to be friendly. Comes to something, doesn't it, when you can't even make conversation.

– Look, we're knackered. It's hot. We came up here for a rest, to get away from town, to be alone. So drop it. Just because you're old, that doesn't mean anything, alright?

— There's no need to be so offensive, I'm done in myself, I've come up here for a rest too. Walked all the way from West Finchley today, I have. Miles. Miles and miles. From right over there.

— Yes I know, I know where West Finchley is, thanks and it's a long walk back so if you get going now, you'll make it before dark, maybe.

— What would I do that for? What's the point of that? I've come up here looking for a bit of company and hoping to get away from all my troubles, people pushing you about, no respect for me at my age.

— Just shut it, alright? If you're not going to move, if you're not going to take advantage of the huge fucking green open space, then at least shut up. We've had a long walk here too, and it was to get away, OK? Jesus, thought we were the only ones bothered to do this.

— Why d'you talk like that?

— What?

— Why d'you keep saying 'we'?

— Do I?

— Yes, you do. 'We' this and 'we' that. On your own, as far as I can see. No sign of your 'friend'.

— I don't know. Habit. None of your fucking business either way what we — I — do or say, is it.

— Been on your own too long, talked to yourself too much, that's what I think. Could use some company yourself, by the sound of it.

— Right that's it, I'm off. You can talk to the trees for all I care. I have come here to see a friend, if you must know. A mate who lives just over there. He's not in yet and — I'm waiting for him to come back, that's all. So I'm not like you at all, am I, you silly old cunt.

— How dare you! I don't see why you have to be so abusive. Look at you! Got a lot of mates living in Hampstead, have we? I don't know who you think you are, talking to me like that. You're all alike these days. Alkies and junkies the lot of you. I've been walking up here for thirty years, and I haven't ever been spoken to like that, ever.

— I'm not interested. I don't want to talk you, and I don't care how long you've been on the street.

— You're the one on the street, my friend. Look at the state of your clothes! You don't fool me. I've got a nice house, I live there, don't I, just past West Finchley. How dare you, especially when you're the tramp! I can't get over the nerve. Here I am, being friendly and sociable, even willing to talk to someone like you, a down and out, and all I get is lip about being a tramp! To think I imagined we might get on. There was a time when I could talk to people like you, but not now, you're all so aggressive, I wish you wouldn't come here.

— What the fuck are you on about? I don't believe this. Walked miles just to get some air, get out of town, and all I get is some nutter trying it on! If that's what I was after I'd stay down there and charge for it, wouldn't I? You silly old fucker.

— You cheeky sod. Who'd want anything to do with you, free of charge or otherwise? What're you doing here anyway, eh? Answer me that.

— I told you, I'm waiting for my mate. Who happens, while we're on the subject, to be a policeman. And if you really want to know, I am too. I'm undercover and I'm up here looking for twisted pervs like you. What do you think of that?

— I think you're a bit touched in the head, either that or you've been out in this sun too long. I'm off anyway. A pleasure talking to you, I'm sure.

— Likewise.

It's been weeks since Tony left work, and if the idea of sleep is so clearly unacceptable to my brain, I might as well stay in town of an evening and drink on my own. I've realised I prefer it this way and I do it often. Now that the frustrated whine has been removed from my ear I can concentrate fully on the spectacles around me. Though it is more difficult to really scrutinise people without the subterfuge of a companion's conversation. Once or twice recently I've had to pull out my mobile and pretend to be engaged in cheerful banter because someone has spotted me staring at them.

Another night in a busy smelly pub on St Martins Lane draws to an end and I plod along through the traffic of theatreland. I pass through the alleyways behind Wardour Street. It's very quiet just here, and as I come out of the dark passageway I spot a small figure just ahead. A woman appears to be trying to hug a shop window. As I go by I'm amazed to see that it's Sarah. She looks very upset; her forehead is resting against the plate glass and her shoulders move up and down rapidly.

I'm not sure what to do.

'Sarah, hello?'

She swivels her head round and glares at me.

'What do you want?'

'I don't want anything, I wondered if you were all right, that's all. Fine, I'll leave you alone. See you tomorrow.' I reach the next street corner and hear her call my name. I stop but don't turn around. I could walk away from this. I really don't want to get caught up in Sarah's world, and I'm sure she doesn't want me to either. So why call me back? I hear her again, closer.

'Please, I'm sorry. I didn't expect to see anyone I know.'

She catches up and steps around me, putting a hand on my shoulder. Everything I've ever known about her makes me flinch. She senses it and recoils slightly too. 'I'm sorry, this isn't your problem. I thought I was alright, but I saw Gavin earlier and. And.'

Her lips tremble and her shoulders start doing their Tommy Cooper impression again. My face must be a picture of drunken confusion because she stops snivelling.

'Gavin – my ex-fiancée? He asked me to meet him for a drink. I don't know why I agreed. When I got there, he was with that little bitch he's screwing. He wanted the three of us to meet and *get on*. God, men do such bloody *stupid* and *cruel* things.'

She stops to catch her breath. I'm not really sure what to say. Yes, men can do all sorts of bad things. No, I never knew anything about you two splitting up or his new relationship, honest. But I needn't worry; in her slightly drunken distress she doesn't seem to remember that she's never talked about it before.

'Look Sarah, you're obviously very upset. But you shouldn't be walking round here on your own, not in this state. There's a bar just along here that's open late. Why don't we get a drink?'

What am I doing? I hate this woman. She steals my pens,

177

deletes my files. She might even have tried to poison Judy. But I'm drunk. I want more. Who doesn't? Who really appreciates the clanging of the bell at the end of a night's drinking? And perhaps I'm curious. This is the very first time Sarah has shown anything other than a cold unpleasant nature towards me. Could she really be human? Will she buy a round?

She dries her eyes. I can see she's thinking it over. 'I'm not sure. I'd like to, but there's a lot to do tomorrow, isn't there. Isn't there?'

I pull a theatrical face and extend the crook I've made with my elbow. She smiles gratefully and links her arm through mine, and we stagger towards the dimly lit entrance ahead.

'But don't you see, don't you *see* how horrible he's been? He's completely taken advantage of me. How could I respect myself if I *didn't* want him gone for good?'

Sarah takes a long gulp of her second large vodka and tonic and looks at me sternly, wanting immediate back up on this. I lean on one arm and realise how tired I am. I'm very confused. I'm not sure at what point we stopped discussing the behaviour of her ex, and moved on to Brian. It's my own fault. In my desire to find out whether she has been sabotaging workmates I made a few barbed comments about the atmosphere in the office and set her off on a tangent I hadn't anticipated. Sarah hates Brian. She thinks he's chauvinistic and past it. She thinks they should kick him out and let her run the office. I could have sworn that less than an hour ago I found her in tears in the street, a vulnerable lonely soul.

'I'm not sure, Sarah, to be honest. I mean, Brian isn't very good at his job, but why would you want to do what he has to?' Her expression tells me I'm sliding dangerously off track. 'What I mean is, wouldn't you do much better somewhere else?'

We are back on course.

'Oh I know you're right. I often think I've wasted far too much time there. Surrounded by *idiots*.'

I stare at her but she seems not to recall who I am. She stops examining the melting ice in her glass and looks at me.

'I mean, it's a terrible place to work, isn't it? They're all useless. Wasters. Don't you think?'

Clever Sarah. My ruse is being cunningly inverted. Through the boozy fog of her miserable evening she's still managing to navigate a devious course; *she* is mining *me* for information. She wants a full confession. Something she can put away and use later if necessary.

'I wouldn't go that far. I quite like some of them.'

She gives me a sideways look, almost affectionate. 'You are funny aren't you?'

'Funny? What's funny about me?'

'Oh don't take it the wrong way. I just mean that you hardly say anything in the office; you seem very…self contained. Private.'

I'm not comfortable with this line of questioning. 'Am I? I don't think I am, no more so than anyone else. I like to get on with my work, that's all.'

She raises an eyebrow, knowingly. 'Oh *come on*. You don't enjoy the work anymore than anyone else. Less, I imagine. You're more of a thinker than the others, more…cerebral. You always seem far away in your thoughts, like you're thinking hard about something else entirely. Some grand plan.'

She stops and looks into her glass again. I feel my insides turn over. She's looked at my files. Prattling on with superficial compliments she's let it slip. I have to pretend I don't know.

'No, really, I like the others, I'm not any cleverer or deeper than they are. Tony and I used to regularly meet for a drink.'

She looks exhausted and disappointed. She pushes her empty glass away.

'Oh yes, that's right. You and *Tony*. Your *boys' nights out*.'

We sit in silence, neither of us quite sure how we ended up here together. I'm having some trouble keeping my eyes open; her final cheap dig has sealed our conversation tightly shut and

I really can't be bothered to prise it open again.

I stand up and offer her her jacket. 'Come on, Sarah. Time to go.'

She sighs and stands and we push past the gaggle of late night drinkers at the bar. Once outside I notice how drunk I am. The air pings in my head and fills my empty stomach. I'm very drunk. I want to get away as quickly as possible and find something to eat. An empty cab miraculously appears and I flag it down.

'Good night then. See you tomorrow.'

Sarah just stands there. I hold the door open wider and make a small waving gesture towards it. Your carriage awaits, ma'am.

'Oh, you stopped it for *me*? That's. Considerate. Thanks.'

I'm too far gone to acknowledge her awkward gratitude. I nod and slam the door after her and set off towards a kebab shop I know will still be open.

The kebab shop is closed. The only other one I can remember is way up Tottenham Court Road. I shove my hands in my jacket pockets and notice I don't have my wallet. I'm flustered until I remember that I didn't pick it up off the kitchen table this morning. I grabbed the pile of coins and couple of notes next to it. Why? Why leave it there? I have no idea. I quickly rummage through all of my pockets and find I have a total of twenty-two pence. It doesn't make sense, I know I had at least twenty pounds cash this morning. But I've been out until late, and Sarah didn't buy any drinks.

I find myself walking towards the river. I'm too exhausted to go on much longer and very hungry, but still my legs pull me further from my route home. They pump away, twitch as busily as a divining rod. I'm too drunk to protest; perhaps they know of somewhere to get food? Now I'm wobbling along the metal walkway on Hungerford Bridge that seems more precarious and narrower than usual. What am I doing?

I stop; I can feel eyes on me. A girl is crouched in a corner of the railings, a dog beside her and a polystyrene cup at her feet. Her hair hangs in huge matted dreadlocks around her shoulders and the light glints on the rings in her nose and the centre of her bottom lip.

'Spare some change?'

I look down into the cup. There are quite a few coins in it.

'I know this is going to sound really strange, but I was going to ask you the same thing.'

I smile but she frowns and gives the sleeping pile of fur next to her a nudge. There is a murmur but no movement.

'Don't take the piss, mate.'

I'm too drunk to feel embarrassed. 'I'm not! I wouldn't! I've got twenty-two pence in the world, I swear, and I really need to get home, and eat.'

She looks at my suit. 'That's your problem, isn't it. Shouldn't have spent it all in the pub.'

I consider this for a moment. She does have a point. But I am very very tired. And I must eat.

'Yes. Well, would you mind if I just sit here?' before she can say anything I slump in the opposite corner. I glance down and see the dark water churning violently far below through the grating. A new chapter of my drunkenness opens dizzily and I look up again. I've already thought better of this; I'll be useless at begging. But my legs refuse to work and I don't seem able to reach the railings. My eyes join the strike.

She's saying something about

...a wanker.

get lost you...

...dog.

Then something else, just as I doze off.

I wake in an explosion of light and noise. Feet are treading all around me. The pounding goes through me, shattering me into bits. I cower from the early morning brightness and wince at how painful every movement is. The full horror of my situation becomes clear to me when I sit up. Hundreds of people are walking past in both directions, everyone hurrying to work. No one is looking at me, which is the only consolation. I'm numb with shock. I could have been killed, anything could have happened to me. The girl and her dog have gone.

So have my shoes.

I let out a howl, unable to stop myself. A couple of commuters glare down at me in annoyance.

'I'm, I'm not.' I start to say. 'I. I've lost my shoes.'

The words sound so awful, so pitiful. I shut my mouth tightly. I have to get a grip, this could happen to anyone. I have to deal with it. I have to shut out the world and behave calmly, ignore the state I'm in. Ignore my pathetic blue socks. I grope desperately in my pockets and make a tight fist around my keys. A miracle, I'm saved. I have somewhere to live, a home, a safe place I can recover inside. This will all be put right once I've had something to eat, a hot shower and gone to bed. If I can just survive the journey I will be alright. I have to get off the bridge.

I crawl slowly to my feet under a barrage of abuse from my brain and mingle with the crowd. I run up Villiers Street, trying not to think about how odd the ground feels through my socks, or the satanic rumbling of acid in my stomach. I jog slowly around to the front of Charing Cross station and join the short line for a taxi, keeping my eyes on the floor. When I get to the front I take off my jacket and hold it very low in front of me, almost touching the ground. A cab pulls forwards and I jump in. I give the driver my address and lean back. I can still hear the menacing roar of the river in my ears. The relief at being delivered to the safety of home makes me want to cry.

The driver looks at me in his rear view mirror, frowning. 'You alright, chum?'

It takes a second to realise he's talking to me. 'Yes, yes, fine. I'm just. I'm fine. When we get there I'll need to go in and get my wallet, my cards. Is that OK?'

He shrugs. 'All the same to me.' He clicks off the intercom but gives me another odd look in the mirror.

I study my reflection in the glass behind his head. Crusts of saliva have formed around my mouth, my eyes look sunken and bruised, and my hair is standing on end at an angle. I try to run my fingers through it but they get jammed in the front. I smell my hand and the odour makes me gasp. I screw my eyes shut and try hard to block out any thought of what might have happened as I lay on that bridge, comatose.

I need a new pen. Find them all the time, and they often work, but I want a red one, with a fine felt tip, preferably. It will confuse me if I use any other colour. My system is worked out and long standing, so it won't do to change now. A small pair of scissors would be useful too. To snip the top corner off pages I've done and to cut out newspaper articles. Quicker then. Have to be quick, especially with the A-Z and with the keys. People get the wrong idea, have to be very careful not to let anyone see me trying them. A lot of doors I don't have to go near, it's clear they're wrong. All the keys are either too big for most locks or much too small. Let's see. Got to go back up Poland Street, missed a few last night when a police car passed. Got the numbers written right here, on the map. Good.

Terrible dream again last night. Horrible. Woke up screaming. Hospital one again. So real. Tied down, blood everywhere, people shouting, tubes all over me. Wish it would fade, but it's always so vivid. Had pills for it a long time ago, can't get them now. Worries me, sometimes means I'm heading for another bad patch. But I'm alright today, and been much better lately. Thoughts come slower, one at a time. Food tastes right. I can feel my body when I touch it. Days last a day's length. Good that I know the signs, know what to watch for.

No.

No.

No.

No… hang on.

No.

No. Colour it in. Where to now. Turn the page.

OK, walk down as far as the river, do along by Aldwych. Won't do too much though. Stay there tonight and then carry on along towards the city tomorrow night. Maybe get as far as Blackfriars Bridge. Saw a man jump there once. So strange. I could see this figure struggling to stand on the ledge. I only noticed him because he was wearing a big rucksack. It was very heavy and he was having trouble staying upright. And then he just stood there, motionless, as if he was admiring the night skyline. Like a climber struggling to the summit and then standing proudly at the top. It was very late and no one was about. Then he turned, like he had thought better of it and would head back to base camp. Then he slid backwards, the bag pulling him over, and he toppled off. I could hear this faint surprised yelp as he hit the water, upside down. I was on the other side and quite far away but nothing came bobbing up. I watched for a minute or so and then went to sleep.

My leg's been itching again today. I don't know why, I took the bandages off ages ago, it's been healing well. I think it must be the heat, and possibly the fabric of my trousers rubbing against it. If I can, if it's possible, I'll find somewhere tonight that I can sleep without them on. Hostel would be the obvious choice. But I hate them and they hate me. I'm banned from most. Not my fault though. People always picking on me, causing trouble. Or trying to steal my map, or keys. I'd rather be outdoors, anyway. I can't ever sleep properly in summer under a roof.

Where am I now? Amazing how hot it can be at night in town. As soon as you get even a mile out, it's noticeably cooler. But I've got to keep working, working is what helps me, I'm sure of it. No point to it otherwise, a futile gesture. But it matters to me and a sense of purpose is very important I think. I'll wait for an hour or so before starting again. It will be cooler and quieter too. So hard not to drink when it's this warm. But got to keep off it, keep away from booze for as long as I can. Definitely makes me worse, brings it on.

Regarding the completed works to Tottenham Court Road underground passage:
Can I just take this opportunity to say Well Done to all those involved on a sterling piece of work. I used the underpass for the first time today since the hoarding was removed, and the ingenuity of the solution left me simply stunned. Aesthetically accomplished and a contribution to humanity, it is a cause for celebration.

There was an email from Brian waiting for me next morning.

thank you for your email expressing your opinion of the work done on underground passageway, which i see you sent at 12.30am. london undergound and camden council are more than happy with the results and while i have no objection to staff expressing their opinion i would prefer it if you to keep this within the company and not cc your sarcarstic conments to the clients and contractors, all of whom have written to me this morning. please see me to dicsuss this when you arrive.

I closed it and sighed. His miserable lazy use of language depressed me. And why had he felt it necessary to adopt the childlike tendency to write emails in lowercase? I knew why. Because a girl who had been hired recently to sort our network out did it. I put the email over the trash icon and went to find Brian. He would only come and sit on the corner of my desk like a schoolteacher trying to be cool otherwise.

It was a small job that had dragged on for months. An ugly passageway habitually used by junkies, it had become an eyesore and a health hazard. At night a lot of people slept there and it could be a terribly sad sight in the morning. It was nothing to do with me, really, but I used the underpass every day like a lot of the others at work. So when our firm was asked to resolve the problem I'd taken an interest. I hated seeing the pathetic bundled sleeping bags each day. There weren't many sheltered spots in that part of town and it was quickly turning into another Cardboard City. What must have finally spurred the authorities into action was the burgeoning drug trade at street level. Over the following weeks I overheard various discussions about it, and would occasionally ask Tony how it was going. It was the usual headache; make the area cleaner and safer without spending anything, with the added complication of how to prevent homeless people from sleeping there and junkies shooting up.

The solution was pitiful. A sloping ledge began at waist height, protruded about two feet out along the full length of each wall and ran down to a few inches above floor level. Try sleeping on that, you fuckers, it said. For some bizarre reason the structure was inverted and repeated on the ceiling. The whole thing had been painted bright pink. It had become a vaguely sci-fi wind tunnel designed to give you a headache. The cheap film set stayed in my mind all day. That night I got drunk and then returned to the office to send my congratulatory message.

It is a thin line, he considers, between what is and what isn't, between what is seen and therefore exists, and what isn't and therefore doesn't. And it is quite shocking to him, when he really thinks about it, that it is *things* which dictate this. Possessions make the difference. It isn't necessarily the case that the more you have, the more certainly you exist. But he believes that the less you have, the less stable your tenure in the visible world. Not everywhere, perhaps, but in the majority of places, and certainly everywhere he has ever been.

This simple understanding hit him quite hard when he first had it. It upset him and liberated him at the same time. He undressed and went about naked. If he already had so little that he had crossed the divide, why bother with anything, even clothes? This didn't last long. It was a cold morning and people would be using the park soon so he returned to the spot where he had left his things and got dressed again.

But it had changed him, and for some time after he lived quite happily. He didn't want anything, or anybody. Love, ambition, even physical desire, had left him completely. He considered it a fact that the sexual urge was in some way linked to the lust for money, that at every level, the fundamental need for currency dominated and controlled everyone's desires. He didn't have the one, so he shook off the other. And what was more, the invisibility that the lack of things imposed on him felt like a blessing. He understood and sympathised with the shocking sensation of no longer existing, which could be so hard to bear for those newly acquainted with it, but it was beneath him to experience it himself. He had sunk to the very bottom of the pile, and in his own estimation risen to the top. The life sentence passed without judge or jury was to him a special dispensation. He walked with the air of a king, the serene disposition of a Buddha. A thin, thirty-two year old London Buddha.

This suited him well. With a mind uncluttered by the mundane concerns of everyone else he could concentrate on what mattered. He came up with a plan which he followed through with great discipline. Every other day he would beg all over town, starting at dawn around mainline stations, spending hours asking people in train and underground carriages and ending late at night by the entrance to Leicester Square tube. He begged with zeal. He had a sign, a polite but pleading manner, he had stories to suit each situation, each face. He dealt in used travelcards, checked every Returned Coin slot he passed. The following morning he would take all the money to a bank on Charing Cross Road and spend a long time bagging it correctly. The cashier always gave him a disdainful look as she weighed the bags and exchanged the coins for notes. He always thanked her, folded the money and took it to the graveyard behind St Giles-in-the-Fields. Once he was sure no one was around he sat on a tomb and carefully wrote his name on each of the banknotes.

The rest of the day was spent dispersing the signatured money. One note would be used to buy some food and whatever small supplies he might need. A few would be passed into the hands of other beggars, slipped into charity boxes and donation envelopes. But it was the third method which gave him the most pleasure. He would sit and wait until he saw a passer-by he felt suited his purpose, catch up with them, tap them on the shoulder to gain their attention and before they could tell him they didn't have anything to give, present them with a five or ten pound note, telling them they must have dropped it. They were usually too shocked or bemused to say anything.

He followed this routine for several weeks, until he decided that even handling currency was having a detrimental influence on him. He returned to an existence religious in its intensity. He ate, drank and wore only what came to him, without any desire or determination on his part.

And then, after a while, he wanted a few things. Only small things: a better pair of shoes, a haircut, a blanket to sleep under at night. He found a pair of shoes, he got his hair cropped in a hostel, he found a good blanket on the street. But then he felt his trousers were too ragged to keep wearing, and the blanket was warm but he really needed a sleeping bag. And he would need some kind of rucksack or shoulder bag to keep his new sleeping bag in. And when the weather got worse he felt that he should find a permanent spot, somewhere out of town, that he could use as a base, somewhere he could leave his things and come back to every night, a skip or a shed or something. And so the desire for things was back again, even though an interest in money wasn't.

He spent that winter in a disused garage between Tufnell Park and Archway. Once he had moved in, he began seeing things every day that he felt would be useful, and he would take them back with him. He started using a shopping trolley to gather these things, because he was finding more and more and couldn't carry them all. By the following spring, the garage was bursting with old bicycles, televisions, scraps of wood and metal, chairs, a fridge, all sorts of things discarded by others. He had a bed, a real bed he had found dumped on a street corner. He even had a radio that worked, and he would steal batteries for it whenever he could, because the things he heard talked about on it made him curious and had reconnected him with the world.

One day he came back late and the garage was on fire. It had been burning for a while and not much of it was still standing. A group of kids were watching the flames, shouting and laughing. He really didn't mind. He felt relieved to be released from the obligation of ownership. Once again, the lightness of owning nothing and being nothing entered him and he walked away without looking back.

Transcript of an Edifying Exchange

He. So thank you for your email. Evidently the changes made to the underpass are not to your liking.

Me. I'm not sure 'liking' is the right word but no, I think it looks rubbish, and is morally reprehensible.

He. Morally reprehensible. We are talking about the same thing, aren't we? We are discussing the underpass at Tottenham Court Road?

Me. We are, yes.

He. And you think what amounts to a minor refurbishment can accurately be described as morally reprehensible.

Me. Yes. And it looks rubbish…

He. Alright, alright, let's leave aside issues of taste for one moment. I've asked to see you because I'm confused as to the point of your comments. You obviously feel you would have had some invaluable input on the job and as it has been some time since you expressed much real enthusiasm for anything here, I wanted to find out what it was about this that piqued your interest.

Me. I'll keep to the subject, Brian, if that's OK, and not digress in order to respond to your comments about my general attitude. I, like most of us here, use that underpass everyday. I saw it deteriorate over time and I know how unpleasant it got. Not only were a lot of homeless people sleeping there but the area around the far exit was a place to score drugs. The police allowed the dealers to remain there because each time they disrupted their trade, arrested people and moved others on, the activity dispersed all along Oxford Street and around Covent Garden which caused problems with tourists and shoppers. I think the underpass deteriorated further when the council closed the public lavatories. It was only then that we saw people lying in the passageway with needles hanging out their arms; that's when the council started getting complaints all the time.

He. OK, let's suppose for a moment that that is a fair assessment of the problem. What would you do about it?

Me. The only real solution I can see would be to change the law, legalise the supervised use of heroin obtained from authorised sources and provide proper treatment for those addicted and seeking help. And either turn the passageway into a night refuge for the homeless or provide free accommodation elsewhere.

Silence, papers being rustled

He. I'm sorry, I could have sworn we were talking about something involving the work of this company, not the restructuring of society.

Me. You wanted to put the issue of aesthetics to one side, Brian, so as far as I can see that leaves us with the socio-political consequences of our work, particularly in a case like this. I'm simply identifying root causes. It's clearly a classic pyramid problem, isn't it. The sale of heroin is legislated against and therefore so are those who buy and use it. The illegality has no effect on the demand other than possibly to increase it, and drastically affects the supply. Thus a thriving black market is created that has its own infrastructure and requirements for distribution. Its point of sale is by necessity a) within easy reach by public transport and near a place the drug can be taken immediately, if necessary, and b) somewhere from which any police activity can easily be monitored and escape from whom is relatively assured. In other words, somewhere like that busy junction. Then combine this with the fact that the drug is highly addictive and is often a contributory factor to people losing their livelihoods and ending up on the street and that passageway becomes just about ideal for all involved.

He. And that would be your considered response to the client's brief, would it?

Me. Yes.

He. I am going to ignore the fact that I think you are taking the piss and ask you why you think the scheme that was implemented 'looks rubbish'.

Me. I think the sloping panels at floor and ceiling level are ugly, pointless and counterproductive. Whether you sleep in a right angle corner or against the lip of a slope makes little difference, if homeless and desperate. These additions make the space even more claustrophobic than it was and increase the air pressure, creating an unpleasant draught. The colour puts commuters off using the passageway altogether and combined with the new strip lighting could cause nausea and migraine symptoms. I presume this is intentional and designed again to deter people from sleeping there.

Silence, long

He. Have you finished?

Me. Yes.

He. Good. Now, I'm being patient, and I'm taking note of your comments, so please, tell me WHAT WOULD YOU HAVE DONE.

Me. I don't know.

He. You don't know.

Me. No. The answer I'd like to stick with is the first one I gave you. If that's too idealistic then I would have to say given the brief and the budget I would have refused to tender a proposal.

Another long silence

He. I like to encourage open debate here but at the start of a project, not once it's finished, and not with the client, and not when it isn't your bloody job to begin with. I hope you've enjoyed this chance to be pointlessly cynical about one of our projects. It's the last one you'll get. If you ever come into this office at night drunk again and write sarcastic emails you will be in big trouble.

Me. Sorry, Brian. It's unfortunate that I wrote that so late at night. But in my defence I would have to say that I've never witnessed anything approaching open debate in this office.

He. Who do you think you're talking to? *Why aren't you listening?* What is it that has turned you into a bloody anarchist?

Me. I wouldn't say I was an anarchist by any stretch, Brian, but I would say, if you're asking, that I probably do share many of the concerns of those who take direct action against an increasingly globalised economy and consumerist society.

He. There is no need to raise your voice.

Me. I am not raising my voice I am perfectly calm thank you.

He. OK, let's just end it there. You're behaving totally unlike yourself. I've never known you to be so... vocal. What's wrong with you? I mean, it is very nice to hear you talk so passionately for once but really, I don't know where you get the nerve to sit there talking to me like that. And you seem, I don't know, you look odd.

Me. What do you mean, odd?

He. Well, you're a bit pale, and if you don't mind me saying so, your clothing has become... inappropriate.

Me. Inappropriate? Brian, what are you on about? Did you call me in here to get my views or did you just want to have a go about my attitude and dress sense? What's wrong with what I'm wearing? I'm wearing what I always wear to work.

He. You're doing it again! You're raising your voice and again I find myself having to remind you who you are talking to! Alright, I'll tell you. You turn up late, you leave slightly early. You more often than not arrive hungover, you say almost nothing all day. Your hair needs washing and cutting and your shirts all have buttons missing or need replacing altogether. In short, I don't know if you want to be with us any longer.

Me. I do.

He. You do what?

Me. Want to be here.

He. Really?

Me. Really.

He. Well please show me some indication of that on a daily basis.

Me. I'm sorry Brian. I hadn't really intended to say anything about the underpass, but then I wrote that email and you called me in here and it all came out. I do feel a bit, I don't know. Overwrought, or something. I haven't slept well in ages. I think the business with Tony got to me.

He. I'm going to go home and relax this weekend and try to forget all about this and I very much suggest you do the same. You've been behaving increasingly erratically over recent weeks; I want to see a marked improvement on Monday.

Me. You will, you certainly will.

He. Yes well let's just start again next week. And go easy on the overactive social conscience.

He sits halfway up the steps, watching.

Up above at street level the living dead huddle together, bartering, woozily relaying their mindless never-ending sagas, arguing over nothing, sometimes setting about each other with their crutches and sticks. They play out a patient pantomime of waiting, oblivious to the tourists and commuters around them. Oblivious to everything, even their own existence once the man has arrived. Once one or other of the dealers is in view all comradely congeniality ceases, the junkie's antenna finely tuned to the presence of their imminent fix. They jostle for key position, elbowing each other out of the way. Those with the cash move swiftly, those without hover behind, half-baked begging stories forming in their feverish minds, urged on by forlorn hopefulness and desperate need. The dealers turn constantly, keeping their backs to them while a stream of transactions take place. The cashless circle around uncertainly, latching on to those who've scored as they peel away and walk off quickly. They clutch at their arms and attempt to remind them of past favours and friendships while their eyes stay locked on the other's hands, hands that cradle the fix.

They pass him without looking.

Down below the fix is consumed. In a slight recess a junkie rests on his haunches and flicks gently at the syringe, ignoring the endless patter of another who squats at a respectful distance and runs a hand up and down a sparrowy arm in futile expectation. The tiled walls are decorated with thin tracks of arterial spray, the floor a mess of foil, cans and needles. And bodies; like the aftermath of a disaster, the scene of a mass murder, there are randomly spaced blankets and sleeping bags with a single arm or leg poking out from each one. None stir. A terrible place. The diseased mouth of a central London underground station. People stumble off the tube, trying to get their bearings, searching for non-existent signs. They leave the banks of ticket barriers, turn a corner and enter the piss stinking wind tunnel with its unconscious community. They hold their breath and tread cautiously, tiptoeing over the fords of urine. Dazed by the filth and squalor, for a moment they wonder if they've accidentally travelled the wrong way on the tube and ended up in some desolate outer city zone.

They climb the grimy steps without seeing him, their heads tipped back hopefully to the light and sucking in the leaded air gratefully.

When the phone rang last night, I thought it was her. Calling to see how I am, tell me what she's up to, sounding much better and happy, then cracking a little, lost for the right words, then finally asking if there is some way, any chance, we could meet and talk properly.

I was getting ready for bed when it rang. I hadn't heard its urgent trill for a while. I stared at the phone for a few seconds and then lifted the receiver.

'Hello?' I said.

'I know you. I know where you live. I'm gonna burn you.'

The voice was deep, very flat and filled with violence. My brain didn't process the words straight away and it was a moment before I could respond.

'What? Who is this?'

The voice was more insistent. 'I said I'm gonna burn you.'

I heard every word this time. I held out the receiver and stared at it. My mind raced through the possibilities, mad thoughts about people I might have bumped into on the tube or someone in a pub I might have looked at for a second too long.

'Look, I don't know who you want, but they're not here. You've got a wrong number.'

I could hear him shifting about, the heavy rasping breath of a lifetime's smoking. A picture was forming involuntarily in my mind of my would-be murderer. Not *my* murderer but someone's. A huge thick set man, older and very hard. A real nightmare. Determined and certain in the way stupid people can be. Eyes bulging with simmering rage showing the yellowy whites around his clouded pupils. I snapped out of it. He was laughing.

'OK, OK, bye.'

And then –

'I know you.'

Click.

I woke up and the phone was ringing. I fumbled for the handset. Before I could raise it to my ear it stopped ringing. I fell back and didn't wake until morning.

– You.

– What?

– Been wonderin where you were.

– Who's that? Kenny? That you Kenny?

– Sorry, did I wake you up? See me now?

– Oh. Mikey. Alright, Mikey. No, I was just dozing off, really. What're you doing here?

– I was goin to ask you the same thing. Ain't seen you in a long while. You been hidin from me?

– From you? What would I do that for?

– Take a guess.

– What? I don't know what you mean.

– Take a guess I said.

– Who's that behind you? Oh hello Tadpole, you alright?

– Tad's not speakin to you. Are you, Tad?

Tad steps into the light and I see him clearly.

– Fuck, Tad, what happened to you?

Tad looks at his feet and then at Mikey. Mikey gives his hair a rub and grins.

— Poor old Tad, eh, would you believe it? Healin up though, ain't it, Tad. Yeah. It'll be alright in a bit. Hossie say he'll be able to see out of it again, probably. Didn't they, Tad?

Tad smiles sheepishly and nods.

— But what happened? Were you attacked?

Tad frowns and looks at Mikey. Mikey grips his arm.

— Attacked? No. Not really. Wouldn't call it that. I had to teach him a lesson. I had to teach him not to fuck with other people's stuff, didn't I?

— What, you did it? Jesus, Mikey, what you do that for?

I'm fully awake now. My trousers and jacket are under my back folded up, and I grip the thin blanket covering me.

— I just told you. But I did apologise to Tad after and I made it up to him. Do you know why?

— No. Why?

— Because Tad here was the victim of a practical joke.

Tad is looking down at me now, he's glaring at me under my blanket.

— And so was I. Someone did something that made me think Tad had betrayed my trust in him. So after I'd punished him and then found out he was innocent, I made it up to him. Didn't I?

Tad nods keenly. His fists are bunched up. I wish I were wearing my trousers. I wish I were on my feet.

— Look, Mikey, Tad, I'm sorry to hear all this, but what's it got to do with me? Why are you telling me?

Mikey kneels down and I lean back.

— I'm givin you a clue what it's got to do with you. Can you see it?

I don't know what he means. I'm scared. Tad's looking around and Mikey is moving slowly towards my face, smiling. He raises his hand and I flinch.

He points at his hat. The stupid dirty red bobble hat he always wears. I notice for the first time it says MAN. UNITED in white letters around the rim. Not a very appropriate statement for

Mikey. Not an accurate description of his sentiments at all. Stop it, I've got to focus, this is serious.

– This is the last time I'm goin to say it. Do you not get the clue I'm givin you?

I try to smile at him and Tad. My legs are hurting because Mikey is leaning on them. Mikey looks up at Tad.

– I told you didn't I? I told you the cunt would deny it. I said he'd say it wasn't him.

– Look, Mikey, for fuck's sake, I'm sorry, I don't know what you're talking about, I really don't. I've not been too well and my memory's a bit fucked, but I know I haven't done anything to you.

– Are you callin me a liar? Is that what you're sayin?

– No! No I'm not, I wouldn't, I just don't know what you mean, I'm sorry.

Mikey laughs.

– It's not me you should be sayin sorry to is it? It's poor Tad here who deserves your apology. Tad suffered as a result of you insultin me, you fuckin with my hat. Not that he's goin to accept an apology, are you Tad?

Mikey pushes himself back up off my legs and I want to shout with the pain. Tadpole swaps places with him and stands over me, straddling the blanket. I try to wriggle backwards but he grips my body with his legs. His face is a mess of fresh scars and stupid anger. I still don't know what's happening, why they think I've done something. I want to ask Mikey when and what I'm supposed to have done, tell him again that my memory gets bad, often fails me from time to time, but that if he's right, I'll make it up, to both of them.

But then the fists start raining down on me.

Something else.
Sharp.
In my guts.
– NO

– Don't scream you fucker
Won't scream. Sorry.
– Teach you
It will. Yes. Sorry.
– Don't you fuckin dare curl up. Don't you fuckin DARE.
Sorry. Hurts so much.
– Tad, Tad, his trousers and jacket, look. Chuck them in the water.
My jacket, my trousers. THE KEYS, MY MAP
– What, you want them back? Want your stuff? Get off me, don't get your fuckin blood on me. You tosser, look at the blood on my sleeve. Tad, give us a hand. If you want your clothes, go and get them. Grab his legs. Not there, by his ankles. Come on, Tad... Jesus, bastard's heavier than I thought. Lift him back up... Not again... Let's leave it, he's too heavy, someone could come by. Just drop him here.

...

...

So cold. Freezing cold. Can't feel
anything. Just want sleep. Stay still and
rest. So peaceful. Can hear
my body slowing. Sound of
the river passing by
peacefully.
It's
so
cold

I was walking along minding my own business when the arm appeared in front of me and wrapped itself around my neck, pulling me backwards and to the floor.

I look up and see a big face upside down. Stay there, it says. You just stay down 'til they get here. I feel the weight of a leg on my chest.

Can I just stand up? I say. I don't get a reply but the leg moves and suddenly I'm on my feet again. I'm lifted over to a parked car and twisted around. He's a big black guy, wearing a Pret A Manger uniform. All I can think is, Pret A Manger aren't open all night, are they? I want to ask him but he has a lapel of my coat in a fist that is somewhere above my head.

'What the fuck you think you're doing,' he says. 'Turn my back for one second, man.'

I'm not sure what he means. He sees my puzzled face and it makes him angry. I'm off again, dragged sideways this time. My legs flick about trying to find the pavement. We turn a corner and he lets go and pushes me forward, up to the cab door of a large van. Pret A Manger it says on the side. The door is open and I look in. It seems familiar.

'Come on, you cunt, before I hurt you. What did you want in my van?'

His van? I don't know what you mean, I say. Then I'm in the air again and I'm delivered over to another car. He pushes my face up to the passenger window. I look in and see an old man who is staring at me and recoiling. This him? Says Mr Pret A Manger. The old man nods quickly and starts his engine. I'm yanked backwards and find myself once again looking in the side door of the van. I wasn't, I didn't, I say.

'You're fucked mate. Law's on its way. You were seen, in my cab.'

Oh. It's coming to me now. But it seems like something from further back than a few minutes ago, tonight. I'm still not one hundred percent about it but I do have some snapshots in my head of me sitting at the wheel. I'm sat there holding it like I'm driving and I'm looking out of the window.

He is very angry, I think, considering I wasn't stealing anything. The door was open and I hadn't ever sat in a big van before. I should tell him so. Look, can I just tell you. I stop because he has me by the front of my coat again. This time I hear a nasty ripping sound in the lining. He puts his big hands in my pockets and fumbles about violently. He pulls them out again. Another tearing sound. He examines his find and laughs. He slams my keys onto the seat of the van.

'So what the fuck are all these?' he says.

I look at them. There are three sets, all on one big metal band. I put them on it recently because I was sick and tired of misplacing one or the other set and thought they might be unmissable if they formed one huge jingling mass. One loop holds the keys to my flat, another big bundle are to the office and another are an assortment connected to buildings we are working on. There are a lot of keys. I can explain all of them, I say. I can tell you what every one of those is for. I'm feeling a bit more sober now. He gets angry again and puts one hand all the way around my throat. My eyes flick about and settle on the keys.

I can see a thin coiled ribbon of paint on one of them and my memory fills in the gaps. I would like to get away from here before the police arrive, or the owner of one of the cars gets back. I flinch as I think what would be happening if he had seen me thirty seconds earlier. He has his free hand pulled back and clenches it and I hear a voice behind him say 'Leave him, for Christ's sake. It's nothing, he's not worth it. Come on, we're running late.' He stops for a moment and relaxes his grip. There is some grappling and I'm pushed hard. I stumble away from the cab onto the kerb and my keys land next to me. I look back and see the van move off. When they reach the end of the street I give them a wave. The lights turn red at the junction and the van stops sharply so I grab my keys and run like mad back past the parked cars.

As I turn onto Bond Street a car slows alongside me. I stumble to a walking pace and keep my eyes on my feet. The car pulls in ahead of me and I look up as two policeman get out. I think about turning and walking back but one of them is speaking to me.

'Just a second, sir. Can we have a word?'

I stroll towards them. 'Hi,' I say. 'Just on my way home.'

'Can you come and stand over here for a moment sir, where I can see you?'

I nod enthusiastically and step into the circle of light. My right hand is deep in my coat pocket, gripping my keys so tightly it hurts. I can hear the confused staccato of a police radio.

'Can you tell me your name sir?'

'David. David Armstrong,' I say. I don't know why I've lied. I haven't thought about David Armstrong for one second since college. The policemen look at me and then at each other.

'Well David what was all that about?'

'What was what about? Oh, that. Don't know.'

I feel a surge of unpleasant warmth as I realise they'd been watching. I wonder how much they saw.

'Really? You have no idea why you got pushed about by a delivery man in the middle of the night? Bit odd, don't you think?'

I don't want this to go on. He might have really called the police; there could be another car on its way right now, or a call on the radio telling them to look out for kids vandalising cars. Or someone could walk up at any moment saying 'excuse me officers but all the cars down there have got a dirty great scratch running along them.' And then they might look in my pockets and take out the keys and there it would be, my front door key with paint all over it and then they would look in my wallet and see I was lying about my name.

'Look I'll be honest, I'm drunk, and I walked past him and I made a bit of a joke and he got nasty.'

'Really. Well, he can only be as far as the Pret A Manger on Oxford Street by now. Would you like us to go and get him? Were you injured in any way? You might wish to press charges.'

'No, no. Really, no, thank you.'

'No. I didn't think so. Perhaps next time you're drunk and out late you might think twice before 'joking' with someone twice your size. I'd get a cab or a bus and go home straight away if I were you sir, before he changes his mind and comes back again.'

'Good point, officer. Thanks.'

They seem satisfied and I take a small step backwards. The one doing all the talking turns to listen to a storm of static on his shoulder but the other one is looking at my hand, bulging in the bottom of my pocket. I bite my lip and freeze. He opens his mouth but the other one says something into his radio and touches his arm.

'Come on, back up needed in Broadwick Street. Go on now sir, off home with you.'

I'm already walking and I don't wave as they go past.

I'm standing on the corner of St Giles High Street and Denmark Street shivering and watching the snow fall onto the roof of the church when a dark grey Mercedes people-carrier with mirrored windows pulls up alongside me. I see my scruffy double in the driver's shiny metallic door. The window purrs and I'm chopped in half. A smartly groomed man about my own age turns to look at me.

– Excuse me, if I carry on along here, can I get to the Strand?
– Yes, but you can't turn left at the end, I'm afraid.

My face reappears as the window rises again. The passenger door clicks open and I get in.

I sit down and the vehicle pulls away quickly. I shake hands with a man in his fifties seated opposite me with his back to the driver. He is wearing a blue herringbone double-breasted suit, a striped gentleman's club tie and black handmade brogues that shine brightly. We haven't met before and we don't introduce ourselves. He passes me an empty black canvas gripbag and I strip out of my stinking rags. I struggle with the custom made thermal bodysuit underneath and put all my things inside the bag before zipping it shut and passing it back to him. He exchanges it for a grey cashmere sweater, a pair of loose woollen trousers and slip on shoes. The clothes have been waiting for me next to the car heater and they are very warm. I thank him for this and he smiles.

– Least I could do. How are you?

– Good, thanks. It's been going well lately.

– I thought so. We haven't heard from you for a while; I presumed you must be taking care of yourself.

– I have been. I seem to have blended in completely now.

– Splendid. We'll be there in about forty minutes. If everything goes according to plan this evening, and I see no reason why it shouldn't, I'll be able to let you go in the morning. I'm sorry this means you won't be able to have a proper wash or shave but it is essential that you continue as soon as possible. You'll need a rest after our session, and a doctor will be coming over once we're through to check you over and give you your jabs.

I groan theatrically and he laughs.

– Yes yes, I know. But better a few injections once in a blue moon than run the risk of catching some medieval disease, wouldn't you say?

He gazes out of the window next to him.

– God only knows what some of them out there are carrying.

We sit in silence for the rest of the journey. The van passes through West London and then joins the M4. Eventually we pull into a very ordinary street somewhere near Heston. The driver opens my door. I climb out and we walk up the gravel path of a semi-detached house. It's as normal inside as out. A family home with all the signs of daily life one would expect to find. I congratulate him on this.

– Yes, it is rather good isn't it? It's almost at the end of its run and I only hope the next is as convincing.

I know there is one room somewhere here that is far from normal and the thought makes me shiver.

– I say, would you like tea, and something to eat? You must be very hungry.

I thank him and he goes into the kitchen and picks up a phone. He speaks quietly into it and then comes back into the lounge.

– Won't be a moment.

We chat about the house and its decoration until there is a knock at the back door. He excuses himself and walks back into the kitchen. He reappears with a silver tray, which he places carefully on the coffee table in front of me. A silver pot of Earl Grey tea stands brewing next to a china cup and saucer, a small jug of milk, a plate of salmon sandwiches and another with a selection of pastries. He watches me closely as I eat all the sandwiches and most of the pastries, drinking three cups of tea to wash it all down.

– Well, I'd say you needed that.

He says pleasantly.

– Don't get too many salmon sandwiches out there.

I reply bluntly.

He brushes his leg and nods gravely.

– Quiet so, quite so.

The phone rings and he hurries through to answer it. He's gone for at least a couple of minutes and when he returns his tense smile tells me that it's time. I get up before he says anything.

– Let's get on with it, then.

He relaxes slightly.

– Yes, lets.

He places a hand gently on my shoulder and guides me through the lounge door and up the stairs. I walk ahead of him along a narrow corridor until we reach the end door. I open it and walk in.

I lie on the sofa with my eyes gently closed, rubbing my left arm where it stings and taking deep breaths. I can hear him saying goodnight to the doctor at the front door. He comes back in and sits on one arm of the chair opposite. I force the corners of my mouth up and he smiles back, warmly.

– How's that arm of yours?

I glance down at the neat row of puncture marks.

– OK. He was a lot gentler than the last one.

He laughs.

– Ah, yes. I seem to remember hearing he could be a little... brusque.

I sit up and feel hot shooting pains in my temples, a terrible tightness in my stomach.

– You must rest as much as possible. A car will be here in an hour or so to take you to the place you'll be staying tonight. I'm pleased to be able to tell you that it went very, very well this evening, far better than I could have hoped. I will be sure to mention this in my report. We are all very grateful. If you're strong enough in the morning I would appreciate it if you would continue immediately.

– I'll be fine by tomorrow. You should make all the arrangements tonight. I'll be ready to be put in place first thing.

He grips my shoulder firmly.

– Good chap. You're doing tremendous work.

I grin and reach for my sweater and pull it slowly over my head.

– Well I am, quite literally, your man on the street, aren't I.

I sat reading the paper on my balcony. There was an article that I couldn't get out of my mind. In Tokyo, authorities are urging people to take caution when out in the street due to the danger of crows attacking them. Apparently the crows are huge, some with a wingspan of over a metre. They have grown so big because of the heat generated by the city; it is built almost entirely of concrete, and the dense urban development produces a permanently tropical atmosphere above the city that the crows thrive in. Because of the strict refuse laws and the rules on recycling, the crows have gradually lost their natural fear of humans and are inclined to swoop down and attack them. They have been known to kill small dogs and cats. Older people have already become accustomed to carrying umbrellas at all times.

I looked up from my paper and out across the park and buildings. The sun was disappearing behind the flats opposite, but shimmering heat was still rising from the buckled and patched asphalt below. Imagine that. Huge black crows swooping down, dive-bombing the feeble and elderly. Picking off pets. Paragliding on thermals before pointing their shiny black beaks at their target and dropping from the sky like ebony kamikazes, clipping the branches of cherry blossom trees, sending a flurry of pink confetti into the air before *Aaaeeeeiiiiiii!!!* Another old, so very very old dear tumbles to the heat-softened tarmac, her tattered parasol clattering down beside her, flecks of blood across her silk summer jacket.

I tugged on the bottle of beer that had been warming gently on the balcony ledge and contemplated the possibility of a Giant Crows Scenario here. It didn't seem very likely. It wasn't warm enough, probably not quite densely populated enough. I gazed down at the trees across the road, the swaying boughs heavy with sparrows and pigeons. Christ. Monster crows. I stared out across the park. The area might be untidy, rough, even, but the balcony made all the difference. I loved coming home each evening and throwing open the doors to my two metre by one metre kingdom. I would sit for hours and survey the comings and goings of the neighbouring serfs. The benches directly below me each occupied by young couples necking, dissolute men staring into space, and drunks, napping or arguing. On the other side of the park, Asian kids smoked weed and occasionally torched a car. And in the middle, along the scrappy barely visible footpaths, mothers pushing prams and dragging toddlers on walking straps. This vista of everyday life made me feel rather serene; all stages of life portrayed, like in those Buddhist tableaux of the seven ages of man. Not exactly, obviously. I doubt teenage delinquency, underage pregnancy, middle-age alcoholism and premature decrepitude feature strongly in the Buddhist version. But then Buddhism isn't a particularly dominant force where I live. It is a very different, unnamed religion that's followed around here. Its symbol is the black satellite dish and the symbol covers every building in sight. I looked at them all now. Too many to count, far easier to make out the homes of non-believers.

I sighed contentedly and finished my beer. My chair was surrounded by a bulk of papers I'd brought home from the office and hadn't even looked at yet. An unexpected breeze came by. I watched in amazement as the whole pile rose, moved to the edge of the balcony, and stopped. I leapt up and put a foot out to pin them down, and as I did so, a stronger wind whipped along the wall and swept the whole lot into the air. I stood with one foot out and gawped at the nightmare unfolding in front of me. I'd been so relaxed seconds earlier, drifting in a warm reverie, and now here I was, in hell. I moved to the rail and peered over.

The pages looked painfully white, exposed and vulnerable as they fluttered over the road below and the park beyond. I tried for a second to remember what the document was about. All I could recall was that I had brought two sets of paperwork home with me. One was important, and had to be completed for a client meeting in the morning. The other was for another junior who'd asked me to go over a brief as a favour. I closed my eyes and tried very hard to think which I'd taken out of my case and onto the balcony. I didn't want to go back inside and look. I didn't need to, I knew already. I'd lazily grabbed the whole lot. I winced and looked again. A small group of kids had assembled in the street and were grinning up at me. I jumped back out of sight. I waited a couple of minutes and looked again. They were still there, laughing now and kicking at the pages as they fluttered around. There was no way I was going down there. I stood and watched, hoping they'd think I was just a nosy neighbour, gloating at someone else's misfortune like them.

I went back inside and collapsed on the sofa. What was I going to do? The scene at the meeting tomorrow morning was forming clearly in my mind. Oh God. Things hadn't been going well lately and this was all I needed. Brian would go mad if I screwed up again. I rolled the empty beer bottle on my thigh and breathed deeply. I closed my eyes and tried to think of a plan. I hated this job. Hated it. So, why go in tomorrow? Why not just leave, never go back? I could do that, I could just walk away from it all. I opened my eyes. No I couldn't. The rent was due in a week, I had no savings and I was a coward and there was no way I was losing this job. I got up, put my jacket on and went downstairs.

I walked around the park for a while, nonchalantly glancing at the hundreds of sheets of A4 paper that had mysteriously appeared everywhere. I wanted to wait until the last few kids had gone in for their tea. But then I glanced down and saw my own name staring back at me from the head of a solitary page and I couldn't stand it any longer. I ran frantically around grabbing as much as I could, stuffing them into my jacket pockets in great fistfuls. A couple of people stopped to watch. My arms and my pockets were completely full. I wanted to gather the rest of the pages, but I'd nowhere left to put them. I kept my head down and scurried back to the flat.

I was breathing hard by the time I got indoors. I dropped the sheets I was holding and emptied my pockets on the kitchen table. I tried to scrape the clumps of dirt and grass stains off them. That was OK, no need to worry about the state of them. I just had to be able to read them, tonight. No one need ever know. I started trying to order them, then remembered they were two completely different documents. Christ, this could take hours, and then I'd have to start the actual job of correcting them. My lips were trembling and sweat was gathering around the neck of my T-shirt. I eventually got them into two separate piles, and then into sequence. I took a sheet of plain paper and began writing down all the missing page numbers. I hadn't got very far when I slumped and dropped my pen. At least half weren't there, easily. Half. There was no way, no way at all, that I could decipher these notes. I picked the lot up and threw them across the kitchen. They lay strewn across the floor in a small impersonation of the scene outside. I took another beer from the fridge and opened it. I sat there for the rest of the evening, drinking and contemplating the mess.

It's so cold when I wake up that I don't have a body. I move my limbs slowly but there's no feeling at all from the waist down. I punch my legs and a tingling sensation returns. My head hurts so much I have to crawl to my feet. Stabbing sensations shoot across my stomach. I look around me at the expanse of white, the trees all crowned with it, weighing them down. I recognise this place but I have no idea how I got here. What am I doing in Finsbury Park? Dark red empty cans are scattered around in the snow like clots of dried blood on a bandage. I grimace at them but my face is too tight. I grope about in the short beard around my mouth and chin, and pick out hard clumps of something that smells of chemicals. Glue. I swear out loud and stomp in a circle. I haven't touched the evil stuff in years, I've seen what it does too often. Where the fuck did I get that from? And where's the inhaler, the plastic shopping bag, all shrivelled and yellow? I have no memory of getting hold of some glue yesterday, but then I can't remember much at all – did I really drink that many cans? Where did I get them? The thought of the glue makes me sad and angry that I could have been so stupid, even though I know deep down that in truth I have a penchant for one of the cheapest nastiest highs going, only one up from drinking metal polish. But on a very very cold night, and if I'm very very drunk, it can be as appealing as a final snifter of single malt in front of a roaring open fire. No wonder my head feels battered and bruised, my insides all twisted in knots. A dog starts barking somewhere in the park and I gather my things together. I shout my name as loudly as possible shattering the unearthly silence, and walk away from the debris of my evening that insults the virginal whiteness around it.

'I think we're all here now. I'd just like to say a few words on behalf of, well on behalf of us all, I think. We hung onto you as long as we could, but the day has finally come, as I always knew it would, and you've been made an offer you'd be mad to turn down. So I have to say warmest congratulations, and it is very much our loss, and their gain. I'm sure I speak for everyone when I say how inspiring it has been to have you here. I would personally like to add that as your boss it has been something of an honour to work so closely and profitably with you. That Oslo job was just one example of your skill and judgement, and your comments and concerns about the underground passageway have radically shifted the philosophy of the whole company. We had a bit of a collection, and I must say everyone's generosity illustrated the warm regard you are held in. Well, here it is. And I have to say, you fully deserve it. The very best of luck in the future, and if things should by some miracle not work out, you are welcome back here anytime!'

Raucous cheering and clapping erupts and continues as Brian hands me the giftwrapped present and steps back into the gathering. I stand there and wave my arms up and down, imploring them to let me speak. Everyone is smiling and laughing and I try to take it all in and look as casual, but grateful, as possible.

'I don't know what to say. I am so thrilled. You're a great bunch. I mean it. I've worked in some terrible places' (I pause as a wave of giggling goes round the room) 'but as soon as I started here I thought, this is different! You're going to really get on with this lot! And I have. With all of you.'

I carefully remove the very tasteful silver paper. Wow, it's a Sony minidisc player, the latest model. I take it out of its box and hold it in the palm of my hand for everyone to admire. There's a lot of cooing, it looks so lovely and new. Mrs Crabtree mutters 'what is it?' to one of the younger members of staff and everyone laughs. I beam at them all, my colleagues, my pals. I open my arms and they all come and give me a hug.

'I'd like a word in my office. Now, please.'

I turned from the window just in time to catch Brian's back disappearing behind the partition. I turned off my tape player, chucked the headphones on the desk and followed him. What now? What have I done, or not done? I tried to smile as I sat in a chair. I caught his expression and stood up again, as if I was just testing it. Brian leafed through some papers on his desk. I looked down and saw they were slightly damp, with streaks of dirt across them.

Oh fuck.

Brian carefully organised them, tapping the edges against the desktop until they made a slightly pathetic bundle.

'Do you know what this is?' he said, pointing his fat finger at the pile. 'This, is a problem. A big problem. This lot were found yesterday. One of our regular contractors was out on a job and saw these lying in a gutter and thought they might be important. Luckily, they were on our headed paper.'

He paused, letting 'luckily' sink in. He crossed his arms on the desk and stared at me. I didn't know what to do. I couldn't believe that anyone would bother to do something so... thoughtful. I looked out the window behind him and then back at the papers, like they were unfamiliar to me.

'Don't. Don't even pretend, for one second, that this has nothing to do with you. If you pretend, I will fire you.'

I gulped and my palms were slimy with sweat. I ran them slowly along the sides of my trousers.

'I. I think I can explain this, Brian. It's funny, actually. I mean, it's not funny, but it's true, yes, they're mine. I was walking home, and my bag must have been open because when I got in, and looked, the papers I intended to work on weren't there, and I thought, maybe I left them here, in the office. But when I came in the next day, they weren't here.' I stopped to catch my breath.

Brian was nodding, but he was nodding into his hands which were clutching his downturned head.

'That's all very well. I accept these things may happen. But one thing bothers me.' He looked up at me.

'And that is, you didn't come in the next day. In fact you took three days off. You were away, on sick leave, until the clients had flown out again. Weren't you?'

I took another deep breath. He was absolutely right, I was, I did. I couldn't face turning up for the meeting without the document and called in sick. I remembered Janine, the receptionist, sighing heavily on the phone, as if I was a schoolboy always trying to get out of doing games. I cleared my throat.

'Yes. Now I think about it, that did happen. I wasn't very well, at all. I got that summer flu bug that's been going round. But it's all true, and as you yourself say, it could, could happen to anyone, really.'

I looked at him hopefully.

Brian straightened up and turned to look out the window, breaking eye contact.

'Things haven't been going very well, have they. This is about the fourth time recently you've seriously jeopardised a contract. I know we had our chat not long ago but it's just not working out. There's a lull in work at the moment, and we're overstaffed as it is. I want you' – he looked at me then, to demonstrate his resolve – 'I want you to take some time off. To think about your commitments. I don't want to hear from you until you've sorted yourself out.'

He was looking at my shirt, the ink stain around my breast pocket.

I automatically passed a hand over it.

'Understand? Have a rest and a think, and call me. You were getting on really well for years, and it would be a shame for it to end like this.' He smiled weakly.

My audience was over. I nodded vaguely and wandered out. What did he mean, commitments? Not working out? End like this? It was like getting chucked by a girlfriend.

Two or three of the others were hovering by the photocopier. They all looked at me.

'Hi,' I said. 'Bit of a head to head with Brian. Interesting, actually. Wants me to work on something new. From home.'

They looked at each other and moved back to their desks. I switched my computer off and put my walkman and tapes in my bag. I walked away from my cubicle, and then went back to it. My collection of pebbles and shells. If I took them with me that might look bad. Brian did say I would be coming back, didn't he. But then if I didn't go back, never set foot in the place again, I'd have lost my pebbles and shells. All those memories and associations. I grabbed them as quickly as I could from my desk and threw them in my bag. A couple didn't make it and went clattering across the floor. I chased after them, swearing. I could feel the blood rush to my head as I bent down. When I got back up everyone was watching me.

'My shells.'

Margaret gave me a sympathetic smile. 'See you soon.'

I grinned at her and marched out. I kept up a brisk pace until I was out of the building and then jogged as far as the tube.

Oh god oh god oh god what was I going to do.

Up on the bridge I look at the view. On the bridge, on the ledge, I stand, admiring the lights. Thousands and thousands of them. It never gets dark here, never truly a black sky. What colour is it now? White. No, hot red. No, no, wrong, it is white. With streaks of red. Is that possible? Well it is so it is. A white night sky shot through with ribbons of burning hot red. A deathly silent night that keeps bursting with noise and dying again. What am I doing up here? Why am I standing here?

I'm not standing, I'm lying down. Floating and drifting on my back.

Put my fingers in my throat. My own fingers? In my throat? Not entirely sure. I have more limbs than before. I'm a multi-limbed creature whipping hands all around myself.

Up again, high into the air, moving at fantastic speed. The air is getting colder. London disappears into a flickering speck of condensed brightness. The whole country a patchwork of light and dark. Now the curve of the earth is visible below me. All of inhumanity down there.

Where am I going? So dark now, not a thing in sight. Total freezing blackness.

Plunged back to earth in spasms of unbearable hot and cold then down further, sucked right down into the poisonous Thames. Deep under the water. Total darkness all around me, complete nothingness.

It's so fucking cold. Terrible pain.

My tongue is jammed to one side. It hurts.

What's happening?

The bridge is pushing in hard, it's scraping my insides, hurting me. The bridge is in my throat. Is it the bridge? It feels like it. Traffic starts running along the bridge into me. No, the brightly lit cars, all the little warm cosy mobile houses, they're all around me. Here's a nice one, bigger than the others, it looks nice and inviting. It wants me.

I'll use these limbs, I'll offer myself up. I'm going inside it, I'm floating into a bright white mouth, I'm swallowed whole, a modern-day Jonah.

What will I live on? How will I survive?

Maybe Brian was right. Maybe I do, as he said, need a little time off, some time to think about my future. I've not been feeling right lately, and a break might be just what I need. I will take maybe a week or so, then call. I really don't want to have to start trekking around looking for another job. It's the only one my degree could realistically lead to and all companies would be much the same. I have spent five long years in that cubicle. But whenever I think about retraining or going back to university I get palpitations.

I make some tea and sit on the balcony. It's a glorious day. Who in their right mind would want to be stuck in an office on a day like today, anyway? There isn't a cloud in the sky. Sunlight bleaches everything, cleans the park and the road and the flats opposite. I sip my tea and watch people below hurrying towards the tube. Go on, don't be late.

I wonder what I should do. It's day one, after all. Day one of my Big Think. Maybe I should take it really slowly. There are five books sitting on the shelf in my bedroom that I haven't even started. I haven't had the time to read, lately. OK, I'm going to pick one, and read it, today. A day of reading, for pleasure. How civilised. I go into the bedroom and look at the shelf. I pick up each book, read the blurb on the back and put it down. By the time I'm looking at the fifth, I realise none of them are quite right, not quite 'today'. I could read them anytime, really. I want to make the most of this new-found freedom, this chance to forget all about the world of work for a while. It's a beautiful day, a real summer heatwave. I should get out, go for a swim, or something.

I go back into the living room and flick through the TV guide. Daytime television doesn't seem to have changed so much, since I was small. Children's programmes, news updates, regional affairs, an old film at lunchtime. Yes, it's all very familiar to me. I switch the TV on, press the mute button and catch the end of a programme about dentures. It must be about dentures because a white haired woman is talking in a funny way, opening her mouth wide and drawing a circle in the air around it with a finger. She holds the upper set of a pair of false teeth – not the ones belonging in her head, thank god, but some others – up for us to see and the camera goes in. Ah, these must be the teeth in question, the faulty fangs. They do look a bit misshapen, warped, like they hadn't set completely. If false teeth do 'set'. They shine brightly under the studio lights, the enamel glinting like a packshot in an advert for some sort of kitchen cleaner. They look like they've been given a good going over with Flash or Vim. The camera pulls back and the woman is now sitting next to a man in a white coat. The shot changes and we see the studio audience. They're mainly older people, retired. They look quite stern. They are very concerned about these teeth. It could happen to anyone, whatever it is that has happened to her, and her teeth.

I watch for another couple of minutes and then switch the TV off. It pops and sighs. Yes, I quite agree. It's eleven in the morning and I'm already bored. I stretch out on the couch and stare at the ceiling. Maybe I should call someone. I've been so busy I haven't really seen anyone for ages. But who? I've lost touch with everyone I was at university with, and the only people I've met since have been those at work. I go back out onto the balcony and gaze around. The park is now scattered with bodies, people enjoying the sunshine. I imagine the scene as if whizzing forwards in time ninety years or so. The whole park knee deep in human slime and bones, skulls floating about. Every last one of them long since dead, reduced to effluence. I shiver at the thought. That does it, I'm going out.

I stroll across the grass, negotiating limbs and towels, and find a quieter spot. I sit down quickly – it always feels a bit odd, the sitting down part, for some reason – and pull the legs of my shorts up to expose more of my pathetically pale skin. If the weather stays like this I'll be going back to work looking like I've been abroad. That would really get to them. I lie back and close my eyes. I can hear people all around, talking, laughing, playing games and sunbathing. The sun is wonderfully warm on my face. I can feel myself relaxing, really calming down for the first time in ages. I slip my feet out of my sandals and feel the coarse grass with my toes.

I hear the amplified sound of footsteps near me. Something is obscuring the light; someone is standing over me. I open my eyes and sit up. Two kids, boys about fifteen, are standing looking at me. They move from side to side, and I have to shield my eyes to see them properly. Two blue figures in a blue landscape. I blink and rub my eyes and the colours develop properly. One white, one black. Both in trainers and jeans, wearing puffa jackets and baseball caps. They must be hot, I think to myself.

They're both smiling. I notice that some change has fallen out of the pocket of my shorts. My wallet is next to the small pile of coins, for some reason. The two boys are looking at me, and the wallet and coins. I look around. I must have dozed off for hours, because the park is deserted. The sun has moved completely to one side of me. I suddenly feel exposed and vulnerable. The black kid steps forward.

'Alright?' he says.

I start to put my sandals on. 'Yes. Just lying here. You know.' They both laugh like I've told a joke, said something funny.
I feel my whole body go rigid. Adrenaline floods my limbs; I'm tingling all over. They're both standing too close for me to be able to get up quickly without touching them.

'I live just over there,' I point at my building. It seems much further away than I thought. I notice my hand is shaking and bring it down sharply.

They both look vaguely in the direction I pointed, and then cast their eyes around the park. There isn't a soul here now. It has reverted to the patch of scrub it really is. I can't stay down on the grass any longer. This is going to get difficult. I launch myself up onto my feet. I'm still on my haunches when one of them moves his leg forward, catching my shoulder and knocking me off balance. I fall back down onto one of my hands.

It all happens very quickly then. I've made a move, I've upped the ante. Maybe they would have just left me alone, moved on, if I'd joked along with them, kept it under control. But how can you keep anything under control, when it isn't yours to keep? The one who moved his leg shifts his foot again, stamps on my wallet, hiding it, like it's already his. I reach out with my free hand and he leans forwards and grabs it. He twists my hand hard and I feel a jolt of pain shoot up from my fingers to my shoulder.

'Lissen,' he hisses. 'You be more fuckin careful, man. Got to keep your eyes open.'

I'm drenched in sweat, the pain is unbearable. How does he know how to do that? How many times has he done it before?

He throws my hand away, discards it like he's touched something dirty. He cusses, sucks air in through his teeth. He moves his foot and picks up my wallet. His wallet. He stands up and joins his friend, who's been keeping lookout, I realise. They seem very relaxed, like they've been chatting to me. He slips my wallet into his back pocket without looking at it. Definitely his, now.

'Keep the change,' he says. The other one laughs as they slowly walk away. 'Bumboy,' he says, over his shoulder.

Ah. The reason, a validation.

I sit very still. My breathing takes a couple of minutes to calm down. I'm shaking all over. I'm excited, I'm in a state of nervous excitement. I open my mouth to get more oxygen and it starts trembling. I run a hand over my face and it's wet with sweat. I look around. The park is empty, apart from an elderly man with a dog. They're on the far south side of the park, they must have just entered the gate. He's standing still, looking in my direction, I think. He looks at the backs of the two boys who are just leaving the north gate. I jump to my feet and grab my things, my jacket, my sunglasses, my change. But not my wallet. My wallet. My mind is racing, trying to see clearly what has happened, understand this bizarre scenario. I try to focus on my wallet, what was in it. Thirty odd quid cash. A couple of cards with phone numbers on. Shit, my Tesco clubcard. How do I get that back? Credit cards. A cashpoint card. The card number! No, no, not even I'm stupid enough to write it down, not in my wallet. His wallet. I'll have to call, get them all cancelled. Do it now. Do it before those bastards start spending.

I walk quickly out of the park, avoiding looking at the man. I jog across the road towards the flats. I've got something important to do, I've got to get on with it. I race through the carpark and run up the stairs. Was my address in there? Do they know where I live? No, they don't have my address. But they were local, I might see them again. What then? 'Hi, remember me? Mugged me, in the park. It was a while ago…'

It takes ages to get my key in the lock, my hand dancing around the keyhole. I grunt and stab it in, slamming the door behind me. I get the phone book out and start flicking frantically through it. I grab a biro to circle a number but as I press on the paper pain pulses up my arm. I throw the pen away angrily and hold my hand up, compare it to the other one. It's very red and quite a bit bigger. I flex my fingers like I'm putting them into a rubber glove. Maybe I should get it checked out, go to hospital. What first? I've got to cancel the cards before those bastards use them. I pick the pen up off the floor and try to use it again but the pain is even worse this time. I've go to get this checked out, got to go to casualty. I take my jacket off the back of the door and put it on. I go to do up the buttons, but my hands are shaking badly and my right one is too sore to use at all. I drop them to my sides and crumple onto the couch. I hold a cushion over my face and start crying.

Light very soothing against the eyes. Nice warm colour, seen through all the tiny capillaries. Veins of blood making a map of me, describing the shape I'm in. A canal system with valves for lockgates. All my badness loaded on barges moving slowly but surely towards their destination on a bright day.

Wonder when they opened the curtains. Or were they open all night and the day has just begun?

So quiet in hear right now. Here. Or hear.

The last thing he heard was
grab his legs. Not there, by his ankles.
Pull the bastard back up

My hand feels a lot better already. Nothing broken, just some bruising. All the soreness has shifted inside me. They were kids, for fuck's sake. They didn't say anything, or at least nothing I can remember. Whenever I lie down and try to sleep it plays out over and over behind my eyelids, like a film with vital scenes spliced out. Why didn't I hear them sooner? Why was all my stuff lying around? Why didn't I get up? Because nothing like that had ever happened to me before, when sober. Because I'm over-sensitive and weak. I'm a victim of crime. A victim of my own upbringing.

I shake the self-pity away and flex my hand, focus on how much more I can move it than a couple of days ago, or even this morning. I feel glad that I don't have to call work, tell them what's happened. They wouldn't believe me anyway. I concentrate on how lucky I am. I can relax, sit tight and think things through. I'll mark the calendar a week from now, that's when I'll call Brian.

There are things to be done anyway. A mountain of washing,

almost everything I own, is sitting on the kitchen floor, its peak above the worksurface. I use my arm like a claw and scoop clothes into the washing machine until it's full. I gently press the controls, wincing pathetically. It occurs to me that I could use my other hand, and this thought depresses me. It's like my brain has been given a twist as well.

I sit in the lounge and read the paper while the machine starts laboriously turning. I go through all the main stories until I come to a tiny item that I read several times.

LOVE GRENADE

A man and a woman arguing outside a St Petersburg restaurant were killed yesterday when a grenade he was holding exploded.

And then I lie back, letting the paper drift to the floor.

They had met in the spring of the year before. He worked in a factory on the outskirts of the town and lived alone. He had been married, but it hadn't worked out, for one reason or another. His wife had moved back to her elderly mother's flat. There had been no children, which made it easier. In the first few months after she left, he had drunk heavily. He only really controlled it when he got a warning at work. It would not be a good time to lose his job, with so many people unemployed and desperate. So, he had stopped drinking.

Winter was giving way to spring when they first met. He had woken up late for work, and was running along the street when he accidentally bumped into her.

No, that's not right.

He had arrived at work late that morning, and had sheepishly gone to the foreman's office to apologise. When he entered the room, the foreman wasn't there, but a young woman was filing documents in the metal cabinet. He had never seen her before. She told him that she had started that day, as secretary to the director. They spoke slightly awkwardly and he left quickly, anxious to get on with his job as the foreman was late himself. After that they found they ran into each often, perhaps more often than was necessary.

One day in mid conversation he asked her if she would like to go for a coffee, and to his surprise she agreed. After that first meeting away from the noise and confusion of the factory, they met regularly. He found that he was happier than he could remember being, ever. Each day they smiled politely at each other and then in the evenings they would laugh and enjoy each other's company in one or another of the local bars. She was considerably younger than himself, and he knew some of the other workers at the factory had started gossiping, but the happiness he felt whenever he saw her made it worthwhile.

Then one day she didn't arrive at work. He didn't say anything as he knew the others were keeping an eye on him. When she wasn't there again the next day he went to the foreman, but all he could tell him was that she had handed in her notice. He found it very difficult to work after that. He went to her flat but a neighbour told him she hadn't seen her for a while. Each night he went to one or other of the bars they had frequented but she was never there. He would sit and drink, in hope to begin with and out of desperate despair by the end of the night. One day he was called into the foreman's office, and was told he would have to leave. There had been complaints that he was always late and the foreman himself had seen him taking a drink from a bottle. He didn't protest at all; he was relieved not to have to continue working in a place full of painful memories.

He was walking through the town centre to a bar one day when he stopped suddenly outside a fancy restaurant. There she was, in a smart uniform, serving at tables. She was smiling at a customer and laughing and carrying a tray over her shoulder. He pushed the heavy glass door open and went in. People turned to look at him but he went straight up to her.

When she turned and saw him her smile vanished. She asked him what he wanted. He was confused; he had rehearsed this scene, the moment he would find her, a thousand times. But now he couldn't think of a thing to say. He started to ask her where she had been and why she had left without saying anything but she cut him off in mid-sentence and said he would have to leave if he didn't want a table. The manager came over to ask if everything was all right. He stared around him at the people looking back at him. He wanted to say yes, he would like a table, but he knew he didn't have enough to eat in a place like this. He left and went to the bar and got drunk.

Over the next few weeks he would pass every day and look in. Sometimes she would see him and turn away quickly. He thought about waiting for her at night when she left but was afraid she would be as cold as she had been the day he first saw her there. He really didn't think his heart could take that. His drinking got worse and worse. His savings dwindled but he no longer cared what might happen, and looking for work was beyond him. His routine most days was to get up in the clothes he had passed out in, go to a bar via the restaurant and drink until the torment had eased.

One day months later she saw him. She had long since stopped noticing him outside, his decline matching her tapering awareness. But she saw him now and he looked different. He was better dressed, the way he had been when they first met. His hair was cut and parted neatly, the beard that he had allowed to grow had been shaved off and his moustache trimmed. He stood directly in front of the doors instead of peering around the edge of the plate glass window. She could feel the heat of his eyes on her. A froth of anger and hatred rose in her and she slammed the empty tray she was holding down on the counter. She marched towards the doors, straightening her skirt and keeping both eyes fixed on him.

As she pushed the door he took a step back into the street, and put on the felt hat he had been holding, adjusting the brim.

She screamed and shouted in his face, told him exactly what she thought of him. After so much silence, so much time, her own vehemence surprised her. He told her how much he loved her. She slapped his face, knocking his hat to a comical angle. His shocked expression and the hat resting on the back of his head made her laugh out loud. He twisted and held his coat down as he freed his clenched fist from his pocket and held it up to her stunned silent face.

There is a high whirring sound that is wrong and I jump up and run into the kitchen. Hot foamy water sits an inch deep across the whole floor. I curse and tip toe to the machine. There's a red sock hanging half in and half out of the door like a tongue. A tongue as wet as my feet now are. I swear out loud and switch the machine off.

There is a very bright light speaking. It keeps asking him things, saying hello.

Hello, can you hear me? Can you tell me your name?

He doesn't want to talk to the light. The light is annoying him. It bobs around and then goes out. It keeps talking though.

He's not responding, but his pupils are OK. And the scan is fine. What did they say about these scars?

Some of them are fairly recent, others go back maybe four or five years, and they weren't dealt with here, that's for sure. Not by any hospital, judging by the state of them. Anyway, it's not really relevant is it?

No, but it might help explain this if there's a history of severe mental health problems.

I would say that was a given, looking at him.

Yes, well, we'll have to keep him sedated for a while until the wounds have had a chance to heal a bit and find out more when he wakes up.

What do they mean, wake up? Not asleep, he's chosen not to speak, that's all. Doesn't feel like it. So nice and still, here. Clean, warm. Sound of rain against the window. How long has he been here? Not bothered really. He wants to sit up but knows he can't. Knows the sitting-up skills aren't there. And he doesn't want to speak, so he lies still and listens.

The horizon quivers and swells. A broad expanse of featureless white framed all around by black. I peer sideways as the distant mountains jig into view and then out again. Everything echoes in my helmet, a detailed soundscape to a featureless panorama. I listen intently. Every plate of my armour rubs against the edge of another, a rhythmic cacophony of sheet metal. In a lower key is the hollow clatter of my mount. I glance down at the bleached bones of the horse skeleton I'm riding. The huge white skull nods and the dry wind rushes through the scoops of its eye sockets. We rattle and clatter together as we pass through the shimmering silence of the desert.

My mouth is so dry it wakes me. I throw back the sheet that is wet with perspiration and clamber out of bed. I feel for the bottle of water that I know is here, on the chest of drawers. I pick it up, remove the top which isn't on, and gulp down huge mouthfuls of warm water. I can't remember it ever being so hot at night, not here, in London. I don't want to turn on the light, once a light's on that means the end of sleep, for me. I take another long pull on the bottle and feel the wetness travel down my parched insides. I go over to the window and open it fully.

A thick plume of toxic perfume fills my lungs and I step back, gagging. I look out and see a car in flames below. Something inside it catches and the fire swells, the windows pop and the metal frame flexes and groans. The paint blisters and a rash moves from the roof to the side doors, flakes of black skin peel free and rise up on the heat, then sail towards me on the night's own warmth. I'm transfixed by the sight, I feel I'm still dreaming; I'm watching myself, a metaphor for the state I'm in. There's a gasp as the tyres ignite and the whole car sings and sinks. A small pool of black is fizzing around each wheel, like tar released from a dead smoker's lungs. I'm distracted by the comical whine of a fire engine's siren. I see the bouncing blue ball of light on the tops of the terraced houses several streets away before the engine appears. Once it sees its destination it slows to a casual pace, almost dawdling around the park before pulling up under my window. The crew jump out and the conversation they were halfway through echoes off the quiet buildings. I watch as they drench the fierce and beautiful thing.

The air turns sicklier and only now really reminds me of something burning. Without its orange puffball the car looks awful. A blackened corpse surrounded by wet ash and puddles of resolidified plastic. I lean back in and turn around. Something brushes my face and I instinctively reach for the light and switch it on. For a second I'm sure there are dots in front of my eyes. There's a black snowfall in my room. The bed, every surface, is covered in delicate burnt flakes. I catch one between my fingers and it disintegrates, leaving a dark smudge on my fingertips. Watching the moving pattern is making me feel sleepy and I'm grateful. I lie down and switch off the light. I close my eyes as the tiny petals keep falling.

Small bubbles of information keep rising up to the surface from the last few months that I don't know what to do with, don't know if I can even trust. They don't seem quite right to me, like scenes from a familiar film run through a strange coloured filter. They're not details I truly remember, too specific and unconnected to the next to be of any use.

OOOOO That man with the orange juice and the sore stomach, how funny. What a fool. Death by Sunny Delight, or whatever his chosen brand was. Gentlemen, choose your weapons. Tropicana? Smooth Style or with bits? An excellent decision, sir OOOOO 'Look in here.' I don't want to. 'Look, look at my mate, swinging from a cord. Look at the state of her. I did it, I drove her to this. I put her in this wardrobe, this upright coffin.' Get off me, leave me alone, I don't want to talk to you, don't want to look OOOOO Got an arrow in ma leg frum a darn injun. Had to snap it off un pull it out. Hurt like hell, am tellin yoo. Got some good sippin whisky from a liddle lady and poured it on ma wound. Healed real good, as good as new OOOOO Held up the paperweight and looked at the world through it. Saw it more clearly than before. Saw through its beautiful colours and the tiny people scurrying around inside, filing and typing and talking and worrying and crying and laughing and saw the city beyond it clearly. Clearly beyond me.

Night falls like a dropped knife. There is a clatter of reflected bronze, a sudden shift in colour as the sun's last rays cut their way through the buildings. I lie on my bed staring up at the ceiling, and let these last fingers of light play across my face. I'm so tired I can't think straight. When I move my head from side to side it feels like a video camera on steady shot. So I lie very very still, and move my eyes around in their sockets. It's useless, it feels just as bad. Three days now without sleep, and I wish I could just drift off for twelve straight hours. I close my eyes and the last of the sun's warmth rests them.

When I open them again it's very dark. I'm scared for a moment until I realise I must have been asleep for hours. I sit up, turn on my bedside light and look at the clock. It's gone midnight. Amazing, I've been out cold for nearly six hours. I get up to go to the toilet. I left the light on earlier and I must have opened the window, because there is a huge moth circling the bulb. I stare as it crashes into it, the thin shade swinging violently. There is a puff of dust each time the moth's plump body collides with the bulb. Wild shadows dance across the walls. I rub my eyes; I want it to fly out of the window without my involvement. I'm too tired and disorientated for this. I go back through the bedroom and into the living room. I switch on the TV and lie on the sofa. A programme is on about teenage rape victims that makes me feel uncomfortable and I turn over. The next one's about nuclear energy versus solar power. I remember that I didn't turn the light out so I go back into the bathroom. The moth has disappeared. I stand under the bulb and look up. It's covered with blotches of brown powder, as if dusted for forensic evidence. I turn off the light and go back to watch television.

I've just realised, apart from the background of pain, my sore wounded body, I feel better. Clearer, again. As though concentrating on hearing and not seeing is making me think more lucidly. Is that good? Don't know. I don't want to think too much. It upsets me. Think too much and then start remembering things, things that can't help me, or anyone else. My memory is a pack of cards. Some days it's like playing patience; cards get moved around, reordered, some fall into place and make a pattern. Others find vague connections but remain fragments, hang around homeless like me, unable to make a proper link, find their place. Like me. Other days it's constant shuffling and then others they just get chucked in the air. What do? Cards. Cards? Ah yes, memory, my memory.

What am I doing here? Where am I? I'm so far inside myself but now and then there is something else, something from the external world, not a place I like or would recommend. Sounds, sensations. Flickers of sharpness when I get nudged or a tube is adjusted. Wish these tubes weren't here, wish I could just sit up and start chatting, have a nice cup of tea, meet my family, apologise to all concerned for being such a bother, discuss the weather, what I've missed. No relatives. No need to apologise. I've missed nothing. Everything important is happening in here, inside.

Such a noisy place. No, that's not quite right. It's so quiet I hear everything too clearly. The beeps and blips of machines. The steady wheeze of something else, respirators, I think. I'm aware of the presence of several others, in various states of consciousness, at different degrees of dead or aliveness. Some won't make it, no chance. Others are so close to going home I can almost sense their expectation, the nervousness brought on by the anticipation of leaving this room and by the hard knock their ego has been given by the experience.

There is life here, but it comes from outside. It pays a visit but only when entirely necessary. The occasional flurry of activity, a moment of drama, somewhere in here. Somebody waking up or dying, I imagine. Very tempting to open my eyes and watch when there's a full-scale emergency going on, the room suddenly packed with nurses and doctors shouting. Usually followed by relatives wailing and screaming, a sound that slips into a steady weeping as the facts sink in and have their full impact. Confirmation of death and one's own mortality making a rhythm with all the equipment supporting life.

It's funny. I think I know what everyone looks like, all the nurses. Interesting how much sounds tell you. Nurse Richards. Early twenties, probably a bit overweight. Pleasant face, nice smile, I should think. Another nurse with a funny accent, from Somerset, or somewhere like that. A smoker, I would say. Good throaty laugh, really husky. Bit older than her friend. Those are the main two that deal with me. Lucky I suppose; I'm used to being treated roughly in these places. Usually handled by male nurses, men who behave like they're the ones who should be in here. Burly bastards on the whole, pissed off with their jobs and utterly indifferent to the plight of their charges. Unless one of them charges, and then they're very particular indeed.

These two are OK though.

The cashpoint won't give me any money. It won't give me any money because there isn't any in my account. There isn't any in my account because I haven't earned any, because I haven't been working. This is all so simple, but the logic doesn't prevent my palms getting wet or my face flushing when the machine laconically reminds me of the insufficient funds to complete the transaction and spits the card back, its urgent bleep demanding I take it and move along. I want to try it again, but there is a queue of people waiting and I know that there isn't anything left.

I go home and empty my pockets on the table. I look through the desk drawer, upturn the change pot in the kitchen. Thirty-three pounds, twenty eight pence. That's it, then, the lot. The sum total of my worth. OK, not my worth, let's not get carried away. It seems odd. I don't think I've ever been here before. I'm going to have to make some decisions. Get down the housing benefit office and register. How long does that take? No idea. There is a week until the rent is due.

My head empties again. I make a cup of tea and watch television. I'm a pauper, a destitute, surrounded by the luxuries of home. It'll be alright, something will give. I even manage a smile. I tap my leg to some music in my head, nod my foot that hangs off the edge of the sofa. A holiday. That's what I really need, that's what would get me going again. My foot stops nodding. Holidays cost money. OK, a daytrip then. A nice day out, get away from this flat for a few hours. Sea air, that will get the brain cells buzzing. I picture myself on a deserted shore. My shoes dangle by their laces from my fingers, cool seawater foams and spurts through my toes. My shirt hangs open and a light breeze wraps around my waist like fond arms. The sun dips below distant orange clouds, sends the whole sky shocking pink.

The weather has been slipping and sliding and cooler dirty days are taking hold. I think I am probably the only person on the train travelling with the intention of taking the sea air. I feel very Victorian. I never realised so many people commuted from the South Coast. It just never occurred to me, because if I lived by the sea I don't think I would have the will each day to travel into the choked gut of London.

Why haven't I done this before? I look out as the edge of the city is pulled away by brownfield industrial sites. I turn away to change the tape in my cassette player and when I look back, fields have the advantage and we're almost there, or so it seems. But then a proper suburb arrives, and another and another, each one looking less and less like civilisation. We pull into a station in a blot of grey that shows no signs of life at all. A carriage door clunks loudly opposite and there is some silent commotion as everyone shifts to let a man and a woman sit down. I watch the grey surrender to green. My tape has finished again and it would take too much effort to reach up for my bag and get another so I sit with the headphones on, woozy from the warmth of the heaters under the seats and the lack of oxygen.

'Bridges. No Bridges. Want them, want bridges.'

'Now, John, there will be bridges, any moment now.'

'Where? Where are they? COME ON.'

The man is bouncing on the edge of the seat opposite while the woman, who is sitting next to me, strokes his knees. He's in his late thirties, and quite a large man. He's handsome but his skin is ravaged by ancient acne. His walled eyes roll around and the way he holds his head tilted slightly back gives him the air of a majestic seal. I feel myself go hot with embarrassment as his excitement mounts.

'COME ON. BRIDGE! COME ON!'

The woman continues talking to him in a reasonable, reassuring tone, her voice a pleasant slightly posh treacle.

'Any moment John, now don't get too worked up. I know there's a bridge any time now.'

We go over a bridge. John is beside himself with joy.

'A BRIDGE! A BRIDGE!'

I find myself smiling; my face must be burning up. A rictus has formed on the faces of all the other passengers. My emotions are so mixed I have to concentrate on my breathing. I'm frightened and withdrawn, I feel as though there has been an intrusion. This retarded man has broken the spell hanging over us all with his lack of adult reserve. His immense and simple happiness makes me happy too. But I pray desperately that he won't start speaking to me and give silent thanks that I'm wearing my headphones. I look around the carriage at the other passengers whose mortification has frozen them in casual pretence that nothing untoward is happening at all.

Another bridge.

'BRIDGE BRIDGE BRIDGE.'

Spittle flies from his mouth, which the woman catches expertly in a tissue. Her composure is compelling to watch.

'That's right John. It was big, wasn't it?'

John nods at the whole carriage. 'Big bridge. Very good.'

He seems to settle down and notice all of us for the first time. My heart is leaping.

'Where you going?'

My eyes are locked to the view and my breath fogs the window. I realise he's looking the other way. I relax and turn to watch.

A young man in city uniform folds his paper. 'I'm going to Brighton.'

He smiles genuinely at John, who is satisfied with this answer and plays with the buttons on his jacket.

'And where are *you* going?'

I can't believe this. The city worker has asked John a question. He has invited conversation with this poor imbecile.

John carries on playing with his buttons. The woman smiles warmly. 'John, the man asked you a question. Where are you going?'

John looks up at the man and his eyes flutter thoughtfully. 'London Bridge.'

I swear I hear someone titter.

'No, John, we've *been* to London Bridge, and it was very good, wasn't it. And then we went to visit your friend Malcolm and now we are on the way back home, aren't we.'

John sighs and his wistful melancholy makes my eyes sting. In repose his face is almost beatific.

'Well it sounds like you've had a pretty good day so far, John.'

The suit is very relaxed and friendly, not condescending at all. He is confident and sympathetic and he makes me feel ashamed. He and the woman lean in to each other and I catch only a fragment of their grown-up conversation. 'His birthday today.' 'Oh I see. A real treat then, if he likes bridges.' 'Yes he *adores* bridges, even pictures of them, it's the one thing that really excites him.' 'Well, nothing wrong with that is there. It must be good for him to have a chance to see them for real, and the travelling probably helps too.' 'Oh you're absolutely right, it does, enormously.'

Why couldn't I do that? Why does this overgrown child threaten me, and most of the others? It makes me feel weak, selfish and uncaring. I should try to be nicer. I'll strike up my own conversation with him. I'll ask him where he got his jacket, what did he do at London Bridge, did he see the big battleship? Would he like to listen to some music? I can see this revised scenario and its consequences very clearly. The woman, who is probably in her late forties and quite attractive, notices me for the first time and is touched by my interest. She develops certain feelings for me during the rest of the journey, and when we pull into their station I help them off the train. I give John a friendly slap on the back and she hugs me and writes her number on my hand, and the two of them stand there on the platform waving to me as the train pulls away and I wave back while the rest of the passengers hang their heads in shame.

The train jolts to a halt. They get off and after a while we arrive in Brighton.

The season must have finished some time ago. It's colder here and only a few souls wander along the beach. I'm hungry so I lean against the chipped railings and eat the sandwiches I made this morning with the last of a jar of pickles and some crisps. They taste much better than I thought they would, perhaps because of the sea air. That's often the case. I really feel like having a drink but I don't want to sit in a smoky pub in the afternoon, especially not here. I march briskly along the front. The old pier is just ahead and I want to see if any more of it has disappeared into the water since I was last here years ago. By the time I get to the pier a belt of rain has pushed in from the sea. I can't stay out in the open so I run across the road and into the first pub I see.

I didn't buy anything on the train so I have enough for a couple of drinks. A puddle grows on the bar while I sort through my change. There's no one else in here but a television up on a bracket blares out satellite news indifferently. I buy a pint of bitter because I don't recognise the name and sit by a window. The rain is moving horizontally, the wind letting it dash the road and then pulling it up again. I haven't brought a proper waterproof with me and I wonder how long I can make my money last in here. I open my bag and take out the letter that arrived yesterday. The handwriting is Aunty Beth's, but I haven't opened it yet. Her reassuringly elegant style is now a shaky scrawl that says Bad News Within, the grief so clearly encapsulated. I hold it up to the light but nothing is revealed. I will have to open it for the sadness to escape.

I read it as quickly as possible, gathering the essential information and editing out the rest. Uncle Graham died suddenly three weeks ago. Very difficult time. Things he wanted me to have. His medal collection and war memorabilia, small amount of money. Moving away shortly, will write when new address available. Love.

Uncle Graham was nice. He tried hard to be a dad but Aunty Beth was never ever a mom. He must have felt a sense of sibling duty, which she didn't share biologically or prescribe to emotionally. I didn't mind. I hadn't wanted a new mom anyway. She was always kind in the way an older aunt should be and we both felt that was sufficient. Uncle Graham was too old to really be mistaken for my father and too young to play the gruff and distant grandfather, a role happily played by my real granddad until he died, but he had tried to provide some sense of family and belonging. I hadn't seen either of them for years though he always stayed in touch; her contribution was to initial the bottom of a card or letter and write the address on the envelope. I feel sorry for Aunty Beth. Even now the last connection is severed she's obliged to play her surrogate role, one last time. I feel like a puppet hanging by a single thread that has been finally snipped. I am in every sense on my own now. No blood ties to bind me, nothing to hold onto.

The freakish weather has subsided so I drain my glass and head back towards the sea. A light drizzle mists the air, but the sky is much brighter. The shingle is wet and noisy underfoot as I weave my way across its undulations to the water. I take the letter out of my pocket, roll it carefully into a tube and put it in the empty Lucozade bottle that's been sitting at the bottom of my bag for months. I wait for the next wave to turn and throw it into the air.

The rain attempts another comeback so I sit in a decrepit shelter up above the seawall. Could this place possibly look much better in mid-summer sunshine? I stare out at the grey water and the leaden sky that sits on it and my lips start trembling. I can't help it, I'm so done in. What is going on? What am I doing here? My eyes are filling with tears. I'm looking at the salty sea under a rainy sky through salty water.

'See Shells She Sells on the Seesaw.' I start to laugh, then a bubble of self-pity rises and I sob into my hands.

'Are you alright?'

I jump and move my hands. A couple with a small girl are in front of me, looking very concerned, a bit apprehensive. A family out for the day, not really expecting to see grown men talking to themselves and crying. I don't want them to bother me.

'I'm fine, thank you,' I say. The parents look at each other.

'I'm here with her,' I nod my head at an elderly lady who is propped up on a pair of sticks, looking out to sea, a bit further along the promenade.

'My grandmother. She isn't well. This may be her, her last outing, if you know what I mean.'

They both look at the old lady and back at me, nodding sympathetically. The woman gently cups the little girl's head and holds it against her side.

'We're just down for the day. She has to be back at the hospital tonight. I'm giving her a moment on her own, right now. We're OK, though, thanks.'

It does the trick. They wish me all the best and move away. I watch them walk along, all three holding hands. They pass the old dear and must give her a nod and a smile. I can see her smiling back at them, slightly confused. They walk a bit further and the couple turn back to look at me. I nod and smile, give them a little wave. They smile back and carry on walking. I watch until they disappear out of sight, then pick up my bag and walk back towards the station. When I reach the top of the street I turn back for a last look at the sea. I can just make out the shape of the old lady, still standing there, perched on her sticks at the edge of the world.

OOooo 'Let me take you by the hand and lead you through the streets of London' tra la la lala. What rubbish. Maudlin bollocks. The pathos of the human condition, and other great hairy testes. Always hated that song. Even before...
before.
Something else is coming through now, though. Something much older, what is it? What has this reminded me of?
Another song. The only good song about being skint and sick in London that I know of. Do I? Yes.

I like to walk in the summer breeze
Down Dalling Road by the dead old trees
And drink with my friends
In the Hammersmith Broadway
Dear dirty delightful old drunken old days

Can remember, almost remember, first hearing it. Where though? Where was I? Can't...

last year of school. It was, it was the last year of school...

Then the winter came down and I loved it so dearly
The pubs and the bookies where you'd spend all your time
And the old men that were singing
When the roses bloom again
And turn like the leaves
To a new summertime

...between school, and... somewhere. College. Did I? Yes, yes I did. College. No, must have already been there, must have been a year later. Maybe.

Now the winter comes down
I can't stand the chill
That comes to the streets around Christmas time
And I'm buggered to damnation
And I haven't got a penny
To wander the dark streets of London

Amazing. All the words are there, recalled without effort, the whole song, I think. But where exactly, and when, that's a mystery. Who was I with? I have a rough idea of when, but what year though? When was it and what was I doing? Don't know. That time's lost to me. No. Not quite lost. It's there, on the edge, it's shimmering on the horizon of my memory.

Every time that I look on the first day of summer
Takes me back to the place where they gave ECT
And the drugged up psychos
With death in their eyes
And how all of this really
Means nothing to me

Five young men stand in a tight group. They appear to be on a hill, perhaps in mountains somewhere. They are all very tanned, all unshaven. They look as though they have been there a while. They all wear the same uniform, though some are in better condition than others are and there is some variation in the tunics and trousers. They seem quite relaxed. Three have rifles slung over their shoulders, two are holding theirs in front of them, as if to show that they are ready. In front of the group rests a wooden box. It looks like a small crate, and it's leaning towards the camera. Its lid stands against one side. Inside are three heads. The heads of three young men. They fill the whole box. They're each at a slightly different angle, their faces pointing in different directions like three bowling balls. They look quite comfortable, very familiar with each other. Their eyes are closed, their mouths slightly open. They seem peaceful. They look like they might be singing a hymn. A chorus of the unspeakable violence meted out to them, unsung. Unheard.

I double click on the printer icon. I don't know why, but I have to make it real, get in on paper, not just stare at it on my screen. I want to own it, be able to refer to it. The printer bleeps and hums, its ink jets whizzing across the paper, making a picture, making sense. It releases it and I pick it up from the tray. I push a pin through each corner and stick it on the small notice board over the fridge. I stand back to see how it looks. The only other picture on the board is a very old photo of mom on holiday, eating a huge lobster. She's laughing and pointing at the lobster; it's far too big for her. In itself it's a nice photo, taken long before I was born. She's young, she looks very happy and it's one of the very few I have, that's why I stuck it there. It looks wrong now, with its new boardmate. I frown and try moving them further apart, but it's no use. I get a beer out of the fridge and look at the board again. No, the juxtaposition is all wrong. It looks ironic, too clever. It's not fair on mom, not fair on the heads. I take down the photo of mom and go back into the living room.

A beautiful summer's day, a real surprise as it hasn't been a good summer, quite gloomy, in fact. We're all laughing like mad, it's so funny. A nice relaxed little trip up the river in a couple of boats, which almost straight away turns into a competition to soak the other's occupants. No danger, really, it's a very shallow stretch, and not at all fast flowing. It starts with a bit of splashing and name-calling and then descends into a pitched battle, a proper water fight. We're all laughing so hard, everyone's absolutely drenched, we tip over. The other lot see this and get so carried away cheering they tip over too. We all roll around in the water, giggling and splashing, everything made hilarious and silly by the lunchtime drinking and a couple of spliffs.

I can't find my sunglasses, what have I done with them? I'm really annoyed, I only got them recently. I start thrashing about trying to find them, shouting to everyone to do the same. Two of them... Jan. Jan and Dave, that's it, they're pointing at me and laughing, everyone else looks and laughs too. I want to know what's so funny, what is it, can't they help me find my glasses? Jan wades over and holds my face close to hers and for a moment I think she's going to kiss me, I close my eyes in anticipation, and feel her gently lift my sunglasses from my forehead and place them on my nose. I blink through the watery yellow lenses and smile and we all clamber to the bank. We sit there, still giggling, strip off our clothes and ring them out. Jan tugs at a dripping wet sock and then swings it at my head. 'Sock it to me, pal,' she says. Later at the house, the small wooden shack on the river used at weekends by. By someone's parents; they've gone abroad. Everyone is tired and sore from the effort of getting back, it took so long to rescue the boats and row them up the river. The sun's edging towards the ground and we all listlessly watch the unbelievably fiery ball. A potent whiff of hot knives, a throbbing tongue swollen with Jack Daniels or Jim Beam. Face muscles ache from all the smiling. Jan leans back between my legs. I look nervously at Dave, I don't want him to think I like her; they're my friends, they love each other. I don't want her to feel the erection I can't do anything about. I edge her forwards by drawing my knees slightly together. Someone sets the small stereo up on the decking and we listen to the John Peel show. It's the usual eclectic mix that we all appreciate but the songs are starting to mess with the total tranquility I'm experiencing. Then something comes on, something I've not heard before. 'What's this?' I ask. Dave gives me a look that says oh come on, it's old, you must know it, it's a classic. I ask again. Pogues is all I get back. Pogues?

Then the winter came down and I loved it so dearly
The pubs and the bookies where you'd spend all your time

I follow the rest of it more carefully, the way the raucous tune mixes with the words, slips into something else, darker. Something I don't fully appreciate. But something that I comprehend intuitively, that goes into me, permanently. Like a marker, a note from the future. Life's calling card. Not then, of course; I don't have a moment of premonition, exactly. I like the song and it makes the hairs on my neck bristle. We all laugh as Dave clambers to his feet and does a drunken jig. For the first time that day I think about the future, about how desperate I am to get away, away even from this perfect moment and this lovely place, and be in London. My next big step. I have to get the grades. I'm not concerned. The exams are done, that's why we're here. The results aren't out for another couple of weeks, but I know I've done it. I'll be leaving for good and starting a new life in London soon.

I decided to go for a walk. The fresh air would do me some good, and it was definitely cooler than it had been for a while. I hadn't really left the flat in weeks. I opened a cupboard in the kitchen and noticed the calendar. A date was circled in red pen and underneath it said 'Call Brian'. I had a vague memory of writing it but not much. I had to get out. I got dressed and brushed my teeth. I ran a comb through my hair and found an old bottle of talc which I thought smelled nice. I sprinkled some under my armpits and on my T-shirt and went outside.

I decided to walk in the opposite direction to the one I used to go in every day. It was a long time since I'd done that. I think it would have been shortly after I moved in, and had that urge to 'know the area', that I had gone across the main road and into the hinterland of the canals and derelict buildings. The spirit of adventure hadn't lasted long. Today seemed as good a day as any to strike out and see my neighbourhood properly.

After a few minutes I looked up and realised I didn't know where I was. Nothing seemed recognisable. I was sure I hadn't deviated from the route I'd taken before, but I found myself standing in a courtyard facing a large galvanised metal gate. I retraced my steps to the road. Where I remembered a long wire fence and a broad patch of stubbly grass surrounding a tumbledown warehouse building there was now a block of apartments. I stared at the neatly rendered grey walls and the rows of balconies. I was amazed and slightly scared. I didn't like this at all, the way this whole structure could just appear out of thin air, envelope the skeleton that was there before and give it a new, false identity. An imposter, imposing itself on me.

I looked at an enormous billboard that I must have passed without seeing a moment earlier. A young woman leaning against a balcony half-turned towards me, as if she was torn between taking in the Panoramic View and admiring her Open Plan Living Space. She had curly straw coloured hair that the breeze wrapped around her neck. The huge smile on her huge face made me feel awful. She was grimacing, begging me to help. Why me? What could I do? The building was bearing down on me, its sinister presence made me weak. I turned and ran back to the main road and kept running until I found myself under a low bridge on the canal towpath.

I stopped and crouched down. I couldn't remember what turning I'd taken or how I got there. A family of ducks paddled past close by. The parents took the lead followed closely by a line of ducklings, the smallest trailing at the end. Each created a slipstream for the smaller one behind. They looked like an amphibious Russian doll.

'Quack quack,' I said.

I got up and felt better. I decided I'd carry on along the safety of the towpath and see where it brought me.

I hadn't ever walked along a towpath in London before, and I was surprised each time I came to a bridge to recognise buildings and roads overhead. I had no idea there was even a canal here. I carried on until I came to open ground. This must be the marsh that someone had told me about when I first moved to the area. It seemed strangely familiar. A train suddenly appeared on a raised line next to me and I realised I had been here before, I'd seen this land from a train cutting through it like this one, going to Stansted. It's a strange sight from above. The city becomes East End tenements, blocks and small warehouses, until these part and you see the odd wilderness of the marshes. There is the immediate sensation that London is definitely behind you. I watched the train disappear and carried on walking.

I cut through the tall reeds and found myself on a narrow tarmaced road. On my left I could see vast reservoirs going off into the distance. It must have been some kind of nature reserve as well; the air was thick with birds of all different types, and I could see a small island some way out in the water, the trees covering it weighed down with dark clumps of nests. I carried on until I saw a fenced off compound on my right that looked like a small old-fashioned airport. A glass control tower faced an expanse of filter beds, with other small buildings dotted around. There was a sign at the entrance saying 'Cornmill advanced water filtration works'. I wondered whether any of my water was there right now, having its me-ness filtered and removed. Or whether I had any of its freshly cleansed water in me. The thought made me queasy and I turned to head back. I'd been walking for a long time and I noticed how tired my legs were now that I had stopped. The light was starting to slip away, another sign that the summer's energy was fading and the nights were perceptibly shortening. I went back the way I came, darting off the road and into the still lush foliage that concealed the wooden walkway over the marsh.

Looking back I can see my reaction made it worse, but at the time, I couldn't control that; it happened too quickly.

I hear a sound in front of me and expect to meet someone but we take each other by surprise. We both jump. The dog jolts back, its two front legs straight and its head lowered, with its body hitched up behind. I let out a spontaneous yelp.

The dog begins to growl. It's a large mongrel, with a fair-sized portion of Alsatian. I step backwards and it growls louder, its courage returning. I can feel sweat gathering around my collar and my hands are clammy. I put another foot backwards. I'm not wearing the right footwear and my heel slips on the wet timber decking. My ankle buckles and I kneel down hard, the palm of my hand slapping against the rungs. I let out a howl and the dog lurches forwards, barking wildly. My body falls sideways from the raised walkway into the dense reeds. I land on my back with my arms and legs above me. I can feel water instantly absorbed through my clothing and seeping against my skin. I think of adverts on TV for pantyliners and the thought strikes me as inappropriate. The dog stays on the walkway and barks down at my half-concealed body.

And then everything goes quiet. The dog stops barking and all I can hear is my own breathing, the dog's panting and somewhere further away birds singing. That is all. I lie quite still, looking up through the tops of the reeds at the dogs grizzled muzzle and the sky above it. A tiny jet plane launches itself from the dog's head and I follow the trajectory of its vapour trail. I feel strangely restful, more so than I can remember. I'm lounging on the soft mush beneath me and seeing the world as I haven't before. There is something very basic about this experience. It's a primal scene, like a diorama you might see in a museum case. A waxwork of primitive man hiding in a swamp while a pack of stuffed wild dogs search angrily above, frozen in time. Then I feel cold and uncomfortable and I'm frightened, frightened of everything. This dog, now protecting the public path. The marsh. The changing light. I think about how far I am from home and how it will be dark long before I get back. I wonder what to do. I lean up on my elbows and water wraps around the joints.

'Go away, dog,' I whisper.

The dog cocks its head to one side and looks at me. I can see one of its eyes through the grass, a big beautiful brown eye.

And then it vanishes as quickly as it appeared. I can hear its body whipping through the undergrowth, the delicate patter of its paws on the decking. I crawl to my feet and lever myself onto the walkway. I empty the green water from my trainers but it doesn't make much difference. I want to run, run as fast as I can but I'm worried the dog might be just ahead and I will catch up with it and we will have to re-enact the whole ridiculous scene again.

I came to open land and I was amazed to see houses, and some kids cycling along the footpath opposite. There was a pub with people standing outside, called The Anchor and Hope. I didn't want to dwell on the name. I'd passed this way earlier but it still surprised me to see signs of the modern world. My perilous brush with nature had happened within a few feet of civilisation. It didn't reassure me. I felt pathetic, and still scared. It was miles back and my clothes were heavy with water. I thought about finding a main road and getting a bus but I didn't want anyone to see me like this. I found the towpath and started back along it under a badly bruised sky.

I'm burning up. it's so hot I've got to cool off. I'm going to stay in the water. I splash about, the water feels nice.

Jan, I say, Jan, over here, I love you, Jan. I'm Your Man, Jan.

Then I go under

Can you hear me? Hello, hello, can you hear me? I need you to open your eyes, come on

I can't see her: Jan! Jan! I thrash about. I look up and I can just make out the boat, I can see faces peering over the edge.

I don't know who

He's not responding. Call the crash team

I can't breathe, my lungs are filling with water

Why can't I move?

Someone's holding me under

OK, stand back everybody

They take their hand off my head, I bob up, fight for the surface, but they draw back a huge fist and

…

punch

to the
Solar
Plexus
…
…

Out of the water, into the air. Lungs swell like balloons, I'm
flying. Over the boat. Look down: they're all looking up at me.
I'm coming down. Where? On the other side. In the water? No.
On the bank onto the soft grass land on my stomach so sore
That did it, there's a reading. He's back again
Back?
From where?
I haven't been anywhere.

We're both standing there looking at the thing, the thing on the floor, the thing on the floor in front of us.

'What is it?' I ask.

'Don't know,' she says. 'Touch it.'

I don't want to touch it; I don't know what it is. I poke it with my foot. Nothing happens.

'Nothing happened,' I say. What is it what is it.

'Do it again,' she says.

I do it again. Oh shit, it moves, it's alive, it's a real thing, a living thing.

I don't like it.

'Me neither,' she says.

It makes a noise, a horrible sound, low and rumbling, not a sound I like.

'Oh god, what was that?' I say.

'Let's kill it,' she says.

'How?' I say. 'How the fuck are we going to kill it? We don't even know what it is.'

'Use your foot. Stamp on it,' she says.

'Stamp on it?' I say. 'You stamp on it. I'm not stamping on it. No way.'

She closes her eyes and goes

Stamp   Stamp   Stamp.

Oh no, this is terrible, I can barely look. She's stuck, she can't move her legs, she's sort of running on the spot in slow motion, and she's screaming her head off, and I don't know if it's because she's scared or because it's hurting her or what.

'Help!' she screams. 'Get me out of this!'

I don't know what to do, it's getting worse and worse, my legs are shaking and I'm sweating and I feel like I might fall over if it carries on. Now it's getting bigger it's growing and rising up it's covering her to the waist and I'm shouting 'No! no!' but that doesn't do anything and there's a bad smell like burning rubber I feel sick oh fuck I feel really sick like some terrible evil has gone into me something that can't be undone it's too late it's too late it's smothering me

I'm

going

und

I didn't see any of them again. I did the proverbial runner, from my own past. I didn't mean to, it just happened that way. I got to university, got to London, and got on with it. New people new things to do. It's funny that people you know so well for your entire childhood, throughout all those formative years, can just disappear, become an irrelevance at nineteen or so. Some people hold on, they stay close forever. They stay where they were born. They marry each other's brothers and sisters and live next door for the rest of their lives. How does that sound? Sounds weird. A bit creepy. Keep me from that. What was that film? Deliverance. Deliver me from that.

I bet they all stayed in touch though. I imagine they meet regularly for a drink, a bite to eat. Discuss kitchens, cars. Kids. Me? I doubt it. I doubt I ever appear on the duty roster of cosy conversation. Why would I after so long? I wish I'd stayed in touch though, with Jan, Dave. Sally. A few of the others.

I got a letter once. Years ago now. After university. After I'd stopped seeing any of those people either. So unexpected;

I couldn't remember the last time I'd got a letter with that postmark. 'Home' it said, mockingly. Home indeed. I tore it open and it was from Jan. Asking me how I was doing, bet I didn't expect to hear from her, did I still look the same, did I remember? Remember the boats, and the soaking? The sunset? It was like reading about someone else's memories. Sentimental nonsense. I kept it for ages and even started a reply once or twice, but the words wouldn't come, it always felt phoney. I'd moved on, several times over. That was all behind me, what was ahead?

Dear dirty old drunken
Delightful old days

'The lounge area is as you can see extremely generous for an apartment of this size. The open plan layout allows a lot of natural light to fall everywhere. The fittings are all stainless steel, and the flooring is real wood laminate throughout. Would you be looking to live here yourself, or would it be a buy-to-let? Sir?'

'What was that? Sorry.'

'I was asking whether you might be intending to buy the property with a view to renting it out; we do specialise in rental management.'

'Renting it out. Oh, no, no. I would be living here. Can you tell me, is this the same apartment as the one in the picture?'

'The picture?'

'Yes, the photo on the sign outside.'

'Oh, that. I don't know, sir. All the apartments are much the same in terms of size and layout.'

'Yes, but the view looks different, from this balcony. I think she, sorry that apartment, is a bit higher up.'

'I'm sorry I really don't know. The balconies do all face in the same direction.'

'I appreciate that, but I did say on the phone that I really wanted to see that one, the one in the picture.'

'I can check when I get back to the office, sir, but given the amount of interest we've had in this development I would say there's every chance it will already have been sold, especially if it's on the floor above. I'd suggest that while it isn't the one you had in mind, a quick decision will be vital if you want to secure any flat here.'

'Really. I wonder, would it be possible just to quickly look inside the flats upstairs? If I could just check whether the photo was taken from one of those, I would feel more...certain.'

'I'm sorry sir, I only have the keys to the three apartments you've seen, and most of those above are already occupied anyway.'

'Are they? So soon? Wow. But the woman, in the photo, she doesn't live here, does she?'

'No, of course not sir, she's a model, I presume.'

'Yes, of course. A model. I thought so, but then when you said... anyway.'

'Would you like to see the secure parking area?'

'Parking? No, no, that won't be necessary. Thank you.'

– Right lads, what'll you have, what'll it be? Come on now, I'm not joking, what can I get you?

Blank faces. Like I've interrupted a Mensa meeting. Great minds locked so deeply in intellectual combat a simple question throws them completely.

– Go on with you now, fock off.

I expected worse. I'll win them round.

– Oh, come on, you're not going to tell me not one of you fancies a drink? I can't believe that for a moment. Look, here's the money, the cash, I have it right here. Off license is just there. What can I get you?

Five pairs of disbelieving eyes stare out of five dirty faces. The mention of drink has done it. It's a cool brisk morning and I'm flying. I'm out of it, totally on autopilot. This is such a great idea. I was walking along when I saw this lot crouched here behind the station. Freshly awoken, though that's hardly the right word. They definitely weren't fresh and they didn't look happy, so I thought I'd make them happy.

– Look, tell you what, I'll decide, I'll do the honours, OK?

I smile at them but there's no reply. One or two make as if to struggle to their feet. Maybe to give me a thrashing, maybe to give me a hand, who knows.

I jog over to Booze 4 Less. A very good name, I think. Concise, erudite, informative. Even the numerical abbreviation makes sense; no time for bothering with the niceties of language, they have booze to sell, and 4 less, no less. I buy two four-litre bottles of strong cider, a bottle of Bells, six cans of extra strong lager and twenty Rothmans.

Oh their faces as I walk back across the road, my arms laden with delights. I place the bags carefully on the floor in the middle of them. They slowly nose around each one like cats investigating shopping, eyeing me cautiously. Yes, my friends, it's all for you, it's real, enjoy. I'll have to get them started. I crack the seal on the Bells and take a hard tug. The foul sweet liquor sends a wave of pleasurable warmth through me. I flush brightly and hand it over. I watch as each of them grips the bottle with both hands. Feeding time for the little piggy wiggies. They gaze heavenwards as they gulp repeatedly, gratefully. It takes a while before the bottle comes around again. By the time it is handed back to me, it seems as though they have forgotten who I am, that I am their mystery benefactor. Wasn't I there all along? Hadn't I slept right there, next to them? I mimic their drinking action this time and turn my eyes up to the clouds as I swallow. The top of a red bus clips my view and I see stupid staring faces looking down at me.

I went to a cemetery today. I didn't intend to. I didn't set out for my walk full of morbid reflection. I didn't even know it was there. But I passed and it was open so I went in. It was huge. I was surprised that I had never seen it before or heard about it. No one else was there. I felt as though I was walking through a fragile eco-system. All the graves were very old and the whole place had descended into chaos. Nature had won it back. Huge bushes revealed themselves on closer inspection to be monuments entirely consumed by ivy. When I bent down to see why the ground was so uneven I found it was covered with fragments of gravestones, layer upon layer. The further I went the more odd it became. I saw a queue of at least twenty ancient gravestones stacked neatly like half fallen dominoes. Why would that be?

Later I came out of dense trees onto a clearing. The ground was crowded with small stubs of stone. When I looked closer they were all blank with age. Children's graves, I realised. It gave me the creeps. I was hungry and it was getting dark so

I left and found somewhere cheap to eat. When I got back home I thought about how surreal the cemetery had been, and began to worry that I might have imagined the whole thing. But when I looked at the A-Z, there it was. A big square of pale green set in a muddle of streets. I drew a circle around it.

They must be reducing my medication. Trying to draw me up to the surface. I can't move, it hurts so much. My guts are in agony, my head too. I didn't hurt like this before.

Are the places I know still there, even though I'm here? Would the things I recognise, my familiars, recognise me, even though I've given up on the business of seeing at all, decided it's more trouble than it is worth? Has the dirty patch I spent years creating on the side of that building on New Oxford Street by leaning there every day lost its sheen? Most of them in here must miss their own beds. Their homes, their cars and their own clothes. The stuff that makes them who they are. They're numb without their numbers. In here, the cult of codes is worthless. The tyranny of numbers they all survive by remembering is exposed for what it is: a cage in the head with the lock on the inside. No wonder they're all so vulnerable. National insurance, credit cards, bank accounts or phone – the numbers don't add up to anything, they have no application, count for nothing. An abstraction that makes them fretful, the cage door swinging open while they edge to the back of it. I am the only free man here. I stepped out of my cell and out of my cage. I don't suffer from that illusion.

My memory is making me a man, again. The man I am, my own man, a man made of London. I live right there on the pavement. I'm not a resident of the hinterland, a dweller of doss houses and hostels, habitué of soup kitchens, drying-out clinics and psychiatric wards. I leave those places to the semi-professionals in training for the career ahead of them whether they like it or not. Fallers on hard times, with harder ones yet to fall to. I fell hard, and stayed there, and that's just the way it should be. A one-man organic recycling machine, thriving on the shit of the city and the dirt in the air. I spilt my blood on the street a long time ago and made a solemn bond. It chose me and I responded, willingly. Its secret is safe with me, it's encoded in my DNA. This is not a romantic notion. Or a mad delusion brought on by a lack of human warmth. I understand my position perfectly. Nothing and no one is waiting for me. Everything and everyone is. London can't operate without me. Nothing's happened out there since I came in here. So nothing gets written up reported edited or printed. No news is good news, good news for me. The city has been frozen in mid flow and won't be released again until I'm there to witness it. Well London will have to wait a while. I'm otherwise engaged presently. I'm busy organising and filing a few previous experiences. When did I ever have the opportunity to travel so far inside? Such a luxury.

I know who I am, even if they don't. My retreat bothers them. They want to know who, why, where and when. I'm not telling. Let them sweat it out. I'm safe here, and I'm safe there, out there on the street. But in between is the danger zone. In the conscious space between, there is the risk of exposure. Questions, answers, more questions, drugs, treatment, observation, restriction. A whole world of meddling intrusion between me and where I want to be. As soon as I stir, it will start. So perhaps I'll run the risk of remembering and stay in here longer.

She reminded me of someone. It's odd that it's only just occurred to me, that it never crossed my mind when I saw her. Well, I only met Sophia three times, so perhaps it's not so surprising. And it was quite a few years ago that I knew

Who?

Who did I know? What was her name?

Ah, yes, got it. Sophia.

NO, that's HER name, not my old girlfriend's. That's mad. I went out with her for months, why can't I think of her name? Why, when I make the shape with my lips, doesn't the word simply pop out? This is getting to me now. I'm upset. What are the early signs of Alzheimer's? That's it, that's what I've got, oh God, what am I going to do? It explains everything, the not sleeping and the nightmares when I do, the drinking, the problems at work, why I'm here and not there. Oh shit, I use aluminium pans, don't I. I've only got myself to blame. How could I be so stupid?

Calm down. Don't be ridiculous. You're too young, and you're just having some bother placing an old girlfriend. You've been drinking a bit too much lately, not getting enough sleep.

But I *can* place her. I can remember that time very well, because we went away on holiday together, and while she was shopping one day I walked for a long time up the mountain with spectacular views of the island and had a Beautiful Place. A good one too, a real special moment.

What was it? *Where* was it?

This is getting silly. Take a few deep breaths and try to slot this all together. We have the fact it was an island. That we left her shopping and sightseeing in town. Start with the Beautiful Place and work your way back from there. Close your eyes. What could you smell.

I could smell...

...lavender. Heather. It was Scotland... Argyll! With Tamsin... Denning, after university. Got it.

No you dickhead that is not 'it' at all. Tamsin was about a foot taller than you with spiky blond hair. Met her at a party in Sheffield and you lasted about a month, until you went away for that week together and had both thought better of it by the time you got back. Start again. Smell...

...of lavender, it *is* lavender, the scent wafting up on the breeze, pushed up the mountain from past Scála down below. I'm sitting on a small outcrop of rock on a sweeping bend in the ancient cobbled road. I've been walking for ages up it from the town. It didn't look too far from down there, and I suppose it wouldn't be if it were a straight road. I had it in mind to get to the top and see the Monastery of Saint John but the heat is incredible even though it's still only mid-morning and so I've turned off to the Grotto of the Apocalypse. I didn't realise this was it until I got here, for some reason I thought it was part of the monastery at the top. But this is it, this tiny cave surrounded by several others, the spot where John the Theologian, banished to Patmos, received the vision of the apocalypse, that became the Book of Revelation. I read about it on the ferry. The most sacred of places, a hermitage for hundreds of years.

Looking down the hill the view is incredible. The small island is reduced to a busy knot in the middle, a ligature binding the arm of land tightly, the only town like a clot in a squeezed vein. Everything is so clearly visible down there, I'm sure if I stare hard enough I'll see Vanessa in amongst the white houses, bustling around the market, buying up knick-knacks amid the crowds swarming off ferries for the day. I lean against one of four tiny rough-bricked churches and bask in the heat tempered by a light lavender-scented breeze, a miraculous gap in the traffic of pilgrims that allows me to fully absorb the atmosphere of this holy place. I take in the panoramic view as if I might be one of the ancient monks, here to serve a term of religious exile in one of these hillside caves. The wide Aegean Sea all around me, dotted with islands under a curve of blue heaven.

Then?

Nothing. That's all, it was simply a Beautiful Place, time standing still, harmony of thought and setting, that's all.

Am I sure? Isn't there more to it than that? Hang on, what was the point of all this? It was to remember a name, to remember the name of the girl who looked a bit like Sophia and you got it, well done, you remembered her name, Vanessa. Mission accomplished.

Not true.

Vanessa bore only the most fleeting resemblance to Sophia, the tiny plateau of bone forming the bridge of her nose, possibly something about the straightness of the eyebrows. I don't want to think about this anymore, I want to have a beer and go to sleep, I want to rest on the sofa and look up and see Susan Sontag again, switch on the telly and watch some crap or other. Can't stop it though. Thoughts are piling up whether I like it or not, a chain linking together and tugging at me to reach the end. There is more to this moment than that,

something I haven't thought about for years. Sitting on those sun-bleached stones, attached to them like a native lizard, an organic connection to the world around me, and then
Then?
Fear.
Total irrational fear. A panic like you'd never known, something dark and awful pushing up through you, a Beautiful Place flipped over to reveal a terrible underbelly, a tortoise on its back with its vulnerable Jurassic limbs writhing helplessly. Your limbs, thrashing about, then tumbling off that hillside, legs spinning you down the winding road to the town below, where you crash screaming through the streets to the busy port and almost run Vanessa down, sweating and pale, a gibbering wreck spouting confused babble.
Sunstroke, the doctor said. Maybe, don't think so though. I'd experienced that before, this was very different. A knot inside my head slipping undone, unleashing demons.

I sat on a stone ledge and waited until a tour load of Americans from one of the cruise ships had boarded their bus to continue up the hill to the monastery. I wasn't interested in the impressive fortified building further along the road. I'd found what I was looking for. I went down the steps and re-entered the small cave. The resident monk was distracted at the entrance by a straggler from the party, a religious nut interrogating him loudly and enthusiastically about the authenticity of the site. I touched the three niches in the cave wall, ran a finger down the mouth rent in the rock by the power of God's warning. I knelt next to the small ledge, the stone pillow lined in beaten silver where the elderly John rested his head each night, a confusion of visions burning behind his clenched eyes, boiling in his skull, and I lay my own head there.

Nothing.

No revelation, no change, no conversion to religious belief or a message I must convey to mankind. I slipped out of the cool darkness into the light and
And?

And the light of the world consumed me.

*Hello dear, got to move you around a bit, sorry
love*

It's a bright summer's day, so bright that the light's hurting my young eyes

So odd, the way he lies there.

We're walking down a very narrow street typical of seaside towns along this part of the Welsh coast

*Can happen, though. You do sometimes find a
reluctance to come back to the world*

The side of a building runs the full length of the pavement. It's roughly pebble-dashed, sharp-looking and white

I don't think I can blame him really

A young man of about eighteen or nineteen is walking towards us, his head down, trying to keep as close to the wall as possible. Despite the summer heat he's wearing a leather jacket, zipped up and held tight around him

*Well you'd have to be pretty determined to put
up with this lot being in you. Not very nice, is it*

The street is very busy with holiday makers and he occasionally brushes against the wall. His face creases with pain whenever his shoulder touches it

No. He looks so peaceful though doesn't he?

His expression is so intense and tearful I can't take my eyes off him

Yes, I know what you mean. Like a baby

As he gets closer I can see his body is impossibly close to the wall

A big baby in a giant incubator

His left arm is missing and he's clutching an empty sleeve. He doesn't want anyone to see.

I never forgot that face. Never.

Events break down into their component parts, a never-ending series of vignettes displayed for my benefit, teasing me to find the connections. Each is a story so complex I barely have time to take in the next.

Two Asian boys walking casually along Bethnal Green Road, joined by a scarf tied around the left ankle of one and the right of the other
A film poster announcing that The Terror is Not Knowing
A scrap of newspaper that wraps momentarily around the foot, the headline How I Became Somebody
A playing card in the gutter, a naked woman smiling seductively through the grime
A teenage girl attacking another with a stiletto shoe outside a pub, hopping to avoid getting her bare foot dirty

I'm lost for words. There is so little left to say, I'm not saying it. My own voice is becoming a stranger to me. He got bored of the long awkward silences and doesn't answer when I call, anymore. But I will keep looking. Use my eyes properly to see things around me. The business of being gets simplified every day and as my own life gets simpler I see the complexity of everything else. It's in the smallest of things, even the most banal. Every crack in the pavement, every dog turd or piss stain is filled with nuances and barely concealed meaning. More significant than the lines on one's palm, or tea leaves at the bottom of a bone china cup.

Each night I walk around the city and look into the empty offices. I peer in through soundproofed windows at the brightly-lit unoccupied spaces. Rows and rows of desks and chairs, endless banks of sleeping computers. I wordlessly record them so I will be able to examine them properly at my leisure, if I need to. I don't think anyone else does. I wonder about the people who work there all day, who they are and whether they like being there. And if they ever come at night and look in at their own desks.

Now you see me, now you don't.

Crouched in the gloom of a pub's side passage with only the stale malt and piss air for company or strolling around Soho in sparkling light, I'm unseen, like the invisible man. I walk in circles all day and see the same faces, over and over. See them so many times, over so much time. But there's no recognition. No 'hello how are you'. Not even raised eyebrows 'fancy seeing you round here can't stop'. You stare at the floor or suddenly see something fascinating on the other side of the street that gets your full attention. I live in hope of you walking straight into a lamppost. But I understand, I do, I do. It's embarrassing, isn't it. Uncomfortable, even. It's fine. I don't want to talk to you either. If I step inside a restaurant or shop, cross the threshold of a bar, then I'm seen. Seen very clearly. They attend to me so quickly, approach so rapidly it is almost endearing. I do it out of sheer boredom, to break the spell of not existing at all. Walk in turn and walk out again. Experience the small explosion of activity I create, the impression I make, and leave again. It makes me laugh. But usually I just walk, walk all over town. When my head is clear, when the demons are away and I can think, I look at the buildings, I watch you. I watch money getting spent. It's amazing. You rush around on a Saturday afternoon, desperately shedding what you've been locked away earning all week. And when the shopping is done you feel decadent with all the spending. And so you go to a bar because the idea of drinking at a time of day when you would normally be working is too tempting to resist. And I come past with a blanket worn like a robe over one shoulder and I open the door and walk right up to the bar and smile at you and you look at your pal and you look at the barman and you smirk awkwardly and I turn and leave before I'm asked to.

Now you see me, now you don't.

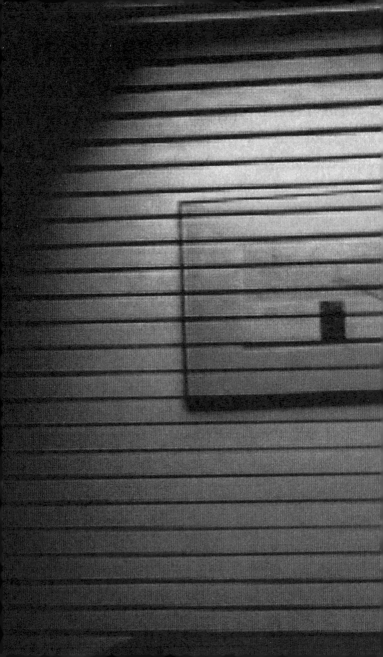

Small things that need attending to, that prevent me from leaving. The opening of the eyes, the in and the out of the lungs. The pulling back of sheets. And so on. Other things that beg for attention and are refused it. The washing of dishes and bagging of rubbish. The opening of curtains and windows. And so on.

It is all a matter of focus and careful consideration. The avoidance of any futile action is the goal. Petty anxieties must be dismissed, doing for the sake of doing cut out completely. Inner motion is brought to the forefront, every heartbeat experienced resonating around the body. The vibration of the universe is triggered right from in here. Every thought staying in the present. Total awareness of one's immediate surroundings to the exclusion of everywhere and anything else.

But being in the present is very difficult. The mind can be disciplined to allow only a minimum of thoughts but there is always a queue, notions waiting their turn, becoming impatient and pushing others aside, demanding to be considered. Thoughts, like the poor, are always with us. The mind finds meaning where there is none, wrings out the optic nerves for every drop of information and delights in processing even the most banal detail.

And the degree of smallness to be allowed is hard to judge. Eyes don't stop seeing because they are closed. The mouth is a boundary between universes when shut. Colonies thrive along eyelashes and brows, my body is the apathetic host to countless lifeforms, all equally unaware of their own existence. Their fate linked indubitably to mine, and mine to forces beyond comprehension.

The pulse pirouettes. A reminder to the brain that it is still here. Loyal until the end.

– And how are we today?

We are fine thank you.

– You've been out of danger for a while now and I think it's time you said a few words, don't you?

Personally? No, not really.

– You've been very lucky.

Oh yes, that's my middle name, Lucky.

– You were lying on that footpath for a long time. If you hadn't been spotted when you were you'd have been dead minutes later. And we nearly lost you again, once.

Lost me? Surely not. You're too careful. But then I went missing a long time ago.

– You've had an operation on your stomach and still need more treatment. You'll be here for a while yet, so why don't you just tell me your name so we can at least do some of the paperwork, Hmm?

Oh alright. Mark. Mark 'Lucky' Taylor.

– Your throat will be sore after not using it for so long, but the sooner you start, the sooner we can feed you properly and get rid of some of these tubes. And the sooner you'll be able to leave.

– Mark. Taylor.

– Sorry? Can you repeat that?

– I said Mark Taylor. My name.

– That's great, thank you Mark. That's a big help. I'm glad you're with us again. Now drink some water for me and I'll arrange to have you tidied up a bit.

– Thanks.

Mark Taylor. Curious. I haven't thought about him in years. Kid at school. Wonder what made me think of him now. Anyway, he'll do.

I'm visible again. I'm speaking again. I wonder if I'll be understood.

You stay indoors and keep the curtains closed all day. You simply find it easier with the room held in a reassuringly constant evening, that's the rationale. A lot of people do that, though you imagine most of them must work nights. It always used to signal a recent death, closed curtains during the day. A house blinding itself in grief. No one's died here, of course.

You have measured your living room. You know exactly how many people of exactly the same height as yourself could lie end to end lengthways and widthways. Whether this is useful information isn't known yet, but you have the calculations, should you need them. You never know.

You pour a glass of chemical-tasting tap water and gulp it down. Just passing through. You're a one night stopover, a conduit, like all the bodies it's passed through before yours, and the who knows how many after. You wonder who will be next to taste this water once it has completed its cleaning and filtering. Someone with their own life, their own problems. Unaffected by you and yours, untainted by the treated water.

This thought process tires you and your mind slumps again, languid and torpid like a dog against a wall on a hot day. How do you know you're alive? You look in the mirror but don't recognise the face staring back. A pale mask. You ask it for some confirmation.

Mirror: Do you reflect on what you see, or mirror the views I present?

What is your name? For a moment, a split second, you panic. Don't be so stupid, it's fine, of course you know your own name. You take a sheet of paper out of a drawer and find a pen. You sit at the kitchen table and write your name, over and over. Once the page is covered you put down the pen and stare at it. The first few lines are wobbly, as though you weren't entirely convinced. By halfway down it's a bit more confident. The last couple of lines are in capitals, the ink scored deeply into the paper. You turn it over, and pick up the pen again.

You draw. A spiral intersected at regular intervals with spikes. A staircase with enormously deep risers and nothing at either end. A headless mouse. Then numbers, numbers that at first you don't recognise. You search them for some meaning, try to break the code. Now you have it; flat number, bank account, date of birth, phone number. You feel satisfied. Aspects of your identity reasserted, your hand moves swiftly over the page at a dramatic angle. You stop, you're out of breath. A surge of electricity rushes through your mind. You laugh out loud, and quickly get more paper from the drawer. It's coming now, it's all there in your head. You must work quickly to get it all down, whatever it is, before it dulls, before the electricity fades and the ideas and images go with it, this is it, the first time in ages, real energy, real thoughts, a desire to do something, anything, all the things crowding your head, jostling each other, merging changing twisting and turning get it down get it down

You open your eyes and the window is a vertical rectangle of deep blue. You slowly lever your head off the table without moving your elbows which are spread wide on either side of you. Several sheets of paper fall limply away from your forehead, the glue of your sweat unable to hold them. Your left ear throbs, you must have been asleep for a long time. You rub your eyes. Your right hand is sore, sore from teenage twisting and tight pen holding. Look around. There's paper everywhere, dozens of sheets all covered with a tight network of scribble. You pick a couple at random and turn on the main light. Stand under the bulb; you need to scrutinise the words. There must be something in all this. Lists. Long lists of names, places, dates. A mixture of people you have known, family and friends, ex-girlfriends, all mixed with historical events, famous people, celebrities and politicians. All with thin straight lines connecting them, criss-crossing endlessly, drawing parallels, associations. Random meaning. You carefully gather all the pages together, collate them as if there is some order you are imposing. You find an old work file and score out the title on its spine. You write 'File' next to it and put the paper inside. You take the bulging file called File into the living room and file it between a couple of books on the shelf. Go back into the bedroom.

Dog lies down again.

– So, how do you feel?

– I tend to use my hands, generally.

– Alright, Mark. You don't mind if I call you Mark, do you?

Why not. Good a name as any. Ironic. Making my mark, finally. Marked my card.

– That's fine. What should I call you?

– I'm Doctor Stephenson, I'm the resident psychiatric doctor here. I'd like to ask you some questions.

I know who you are. So obvious. The caring words, the nice smile. So young and eager. Where do they find people like you?

– Nice to meet you.

– And you too. Mark, I need to ask you first of all, can you remember anything, anything at all about the night you were brought here?

– No I can't.

– I see. Well, the police will no doubt ask you the same thing shortly, so do try hard to remember if you can. Do you have any idea how long you've been here?

– No. Why, is that important?

– Well, you have been unconscious for quite some time, and we haven't been able to find any record of someone of your name being reported missing.

– Who would report me missing?

– Well, family, your friends, workmates.

– Don't have any.

– You don't have any family, no friends who might have been concerned?

– No.

– I see. So, where do you live?

– Anywhere I like.

– Are you saying that you're homeless?

– If you prefer, yes.

God, this is boring. Why did I wake up?

– I see, I see. Well, you have been extremely lucky.

Not that again.

– Your life was hanging in the balance there for a while. You were heavily sedated for some time but we've been concerned recently that although you were medically stable and displayed normal brain activity, you still weren't showing signs of full con-sciousness, remained entirely unresponsive. Do you have any comments about that?

– Didn't feel like coming round.

– Why not?

– Bored. Felt like a break.

– OK. And why, when you opened your eyes again, did you not respond to questions, or say anything at all?

– Got bored. Being in my head. But didn't want to talk to anyone, yet.

Don't say too much, don't make him too happy.

– That's interesting. Let me make some notes here. It's encouraging that your self-will reasserted itself, that can be vital in cases such as yours.

– Really.

I should have stayed where I was. I knew it. The moment I open my eyes and move, they're on me, bothering me with questions. God, he is so keen.

– Let's leave that for now. I'd like to ask you about your arms.

– What about them?

– Can you tell me anything about the scars and where you got them?

I made a pact a truce you idiot.

– Mark?

– I'm sorry. I'm very tired. Can't this wait?

– Yes, yes of course it can. We can continue with the evaluation later.

– Evaluation?

What am I, a house? Or more of a bungalow? Semi-detached? No, very detached indeed. Am I worth much? Is it a buyers' or a sellers' market, currently?

– Of your needs.

– My needs? I don't have any needs.

Apart from the one involving you pissing off permanently.

– I may be able to help you get proper treatment, possibly a place in a residential care unit or even somewhere of your own.

– Really. That's very kind. No, thanks.

– Hmm. Mark, I understand that you may feel compromised, confined to a bed at the moment, but there will come a time when you will be well enough to walk and you know as well as I do that shortly after that you'll be discharged. The weather is getting worse and it will be cold and damp by the time you leave. It may prove to be very hard to readjust to the harsh reality of living on the street after so long spent lying here.

– I didn't ask to be put in here. I didn't request to be knifed, left for dead then found. It's in the grand scheme of things for me to be out there, that's my place in the overall picture, the natural order, and you don't meddle with the order.

Shit, he's writing it all down, I'm saying too much. Stop talking stop talking.

313

– Interesting. I'm going to leave you now. You mustn't get too agitated if those wounds are going to heal properly. Would you at least think about what I've said today, and agree to discuss it again soon?

– I will ruminate at length.

Ah, bless him. Quite dejected. I'll bet he's a month out of training, tops. I may be his very first case. The honour is all his.

You haven't felt this good in ages. You can't quite remember the last time you felt so together. As if by magic you are, really, almost your old self. You feel ready to face the world. You clean the front room, behind the sofa, the TV, everywhere you'd be mad to even look normally. You do some laundry, dig out some clothes you haven't felt like wearing in a while. You've decided to get out of the flat, maybe go for a walk. Cheered even more by this sense of purpose you root out your good shoes. You're feeling hungry now, but you polish them with relish. With relish! Hah! There, a gag, a small pun. Evidence of your return to form. At this rate you think you might go back to work any day now. But first, go and see her. You haven't spoken since before everything went wrong and you gave up talking to anyone. She won't believe it. You have a picture, a film playing in your head of the reunion. A sweeping aside of it all, no need for apologies or explanation. Good for you.

You are feeling good. You are. Feeling so good, you decide to go out, take the air, visit a pal. Make the most of it. Make the most of it, it can't last. Carry on. Carry on like this and you'll be in tears. No. You are out and about, feeling good, taking the air, going to visit a pal. Looking around. Look, around these parts it doesn't do to stare. Stare at the ground. Two retards kissing in the street. The dull ache in your left testicle. The light through the blinds playing across her face. A slow even heat applied to the base of the surface. No longer under guarantee. Please return to place of purchase.

Purchase; your grip has loosened. Unravelled. Trouble ahead, a head full of trouble, the doors off its hinges the cat's out the bag, it's no good, you can't pretend. How do legs work? How do they *know*? You are slowing down, each step is a nightmare You've turned to jelly, kneecaps swimming in butter. Don't think like that.

You have a broken film playing in your mind, a jerky picture of her face combed by sickly early evening light, seen through a jagged blind on a balcony. The shitty street swims in front of your eyes. Black dots. Dogs mock you – don't laugh, it's not funny.

You sink to the ground.

The filthy asphalt rises to greet you and swallows you whole devouring your stinking carcass in one go.

I was right. She is pretty, she does have a nice smile. Not plump, though, not at all.

– Hiya Mark. I'm going to change the bandages on your stomach today. Is that OK?

– Marvellous. I didn't have any other plans. Help yourself.

– Oh dear.

– What?

– You're not going to turn out to be one of the difficult ones are you?

The Difficult Ones. That's good. A good way of describing all of us, out there.

– No intention whatsoever of being difficult, Nurse Richards.

– You can call me Julie.

– Why, is that your name?

Lovely eyes. Dark brown, so dark the pupils don't show. When did I last notice a girl's eyes? When did I last see them this close?

– Ah, you're a funny one, I see.

That lovely throaty laugh. I got them mixed up, then. Maybe

317

there was only one all along.

– Funny peculiar, you mean.

– I won't comment on that, Mark. I'm in charge of your physical state, not mental. I leave that to Doctor Stephenson.

– We've met. I presume I'll be seeing more of him.

– You will indeed. In fact, I think he will be coming along shortly after I've finished with this lot.

– Oh good.

– Knew you'd be pleased.

– Hello again.

– Hello again, Doctor Stephenson.

– I wondered if I might ask you some more questions.

– Fine, go ahead.

– Have you ever received treatment for any mental crisis or chronic disorder, and if so where and when?

Straight in there, this time. No messing around. Anything you say will absolutely definitely be used in evidence against you.

– Crisis?

– Yes, a psychotic episode, or seizure, anything of that sort?

– No, I haven't.

– Really? You're quite sure?

– Absolutely, definitely.

I haven't received any treatment I'd invited or accepted willingly. There's never been any crisis, any disorder. Others insisted on applying their own criteria and I suffered as a consequence. I was labelled and deemed in dire need of assistance, some correction. And I resisted, and attempted to suggest otherwise, and everything escalated and before I knew it, I was treated to something I would rather not have been.

– Look, Mark, I'll talk completely frankly with you. I think you could use our help, and it's a long shot but as I said before, I think we could assist you to get off the street permanently. But the two things go hand in hand. You won't be eligible for any long-term accommodation if you refuse point blank to accept

318

your problems and won't agree to proper medical treatment.

– Look, I understand. It's nice in here and I don't really want to be back out there, you know. And it's so much worse when you've got… problems, you know?

– It's OK, Mark, there's no need to upset yourself, I merely wanted you to understand that you do have some options at this point. This doesn't have to be a dead end, you can turn the situation round, if you want to.

– Thank you. Just let me rest, if that's alright, and I'll continue thinking it over. I appreciate what you're trying to do.

I remember them picking me up from school.

Their faces are pale and drawn. They exchange a few muttered words with the teacher who has brought me into the staff room, a place I have never been before. Uncle Graham lifts me up and carries me, unnecessarily, I feel, to the car. We sit in silence for a few moments, which I'm used to, when I'm with my uncle and aunt. Then Uncle Graham starts crying hard, his hands shaking as he grips the steering wheel, and Aunty Beth is holding my hand too tightly. They're scaring me and I start to cry. They take this as a sign that I have guessed already, that I know why they have come to get me and what has happened, which is impossible, of course. Uncle Graham keeps saying 'It's alright, son, don't worry, it will be alright' and Aunty Beth wraps my head in her arm and shouts 'What are you talking about Graham? How can it be alright? Don't tell him that, for God's sake.' And then he is pounding the wheel with his fists, the clenched tan leather of his driving gloves, his skin very white through the holes on each knuckle, against the spiral perforated beige leather binding on the wheel, and this detail which I can see through a fuzzy gap holds me, the blurring of the two things. His head drops forwards into view, and as it rests on the wheel all I can see is a nostril, a tuft of moustache and a gingery sideburn. It looks funny, like an animal I've never seen before. The animal disappears again and Uncle Graham takes some deep breaths and turns around, giving me an awkward smile, as though seeing me for the very first time. 'We have to go now,' he says. 'They're expecting us. We have to go and speak to someone about, about an accident, something terrible that has happened.' His eyes blur again. 'You will have to be a very brave boy.' 'Okay,' I say. He reaches back and I feel the smooth fingers of his glove against my cheek, and smell the strong animal scent of the leather. I wonder what they are made from, is it cow? Or horse? I would like to ask Uncle Graham but he turns back and starts the engine.

They called me a bright spark, so I burnt the place down.

They didn't have much sense of humour. Had I been them I would have just laughed, but they didn't. Punishing the younger ones was part of their job, and they did it with great dedication and seriousness. Baden-Powell had a lot to answer for.

I hated the hut, and all the bastards in it. I was early for our weekly session of bullying and ritualised humiliation and couldn't help myself. The vicarage next door had been freshly painted a nasty shade of pink and a bit of board leaned against the wall warning WET PAINT. I was standing there thinking how awful the colour looked when I noticed a tin of paint and a brush sticking out from behind the sign. It didn't take a moment to decide. I knew what to do to relieve my boredom.

Three Venture Scouts came around the corner just as I had finished and was standing back to admire my handiwork. I tried to run but they tripped me up. They dragged me to my feet and over to the side of the scout hut.

– What's this?

– What the fuck do you think you're doing?

I kept my mouth shut. It was fairly self-evident. A simple statement, my little joke. WET GRAFITTI said the building. The pink stood out well on the dark creosoted panelling.

They weren't impressed with my work or my silence.

– You'll have to clean this up. We'll give you a hand.

They picked me up and smashed my body against the wall. With much grunting and swearing they keelhauled me along the letters. My nose and knees bumped and bashed on the rough timber ridges but I wasn't going to give them the pleasure of knowing how much it hurt me. When they reached the end of the wall they loosened their grip and I fell back onto the stone chippings. I sat up and gave my nose a gentle tweak to see if it was broken, and plucked at a splinter in my cheek.

Two of them walked around slowly, getting their breath back. More exercise than they were used to, obviously. But the third stood over me, snorting. He must have felt more insulted than the others. A real bastard, seventeen and angry about it. Tall and thin with an awkward face; no longer the neat smoothness of a boy's features and not yet organised into the angles of a man's. He grabbed the scruff of my collar and lifted me up to the messy surface again. My face was squashed in the paint and I coughed and spluttered. I could feel his hot teenage breath on my neck, all nicotine and sweet fortified wine, his spittle on my cheek. His whole body pressed hard into my back, his stiff dick against my spine through the thin material of my uniform. There was nothing sexual about this performance. He was simply enjoying himself too much. This opportunity to demonstrate his power.

I wouldn't beg and he got bored. He pulled me away from the wall and threw me down. The three of them prodded and poked me with their boots, as if turning over a hard turd or a dead cat. I kept still until they were done.

– Let that be a lesson to you, you little shit.

– Think you're clever. A real fucking bright spark.

They walked away. I got up and examined my green jumper. It

was ruined, the oil paint rubbed deep into the fibres, obliterating the badges on my breast. I tugged off my neckerchief and chucked it away from me angrily. I never wanted to see it again. I swore at it, told it this was the end, the last time. I wasn't ever going back in there. It just lay all twisted on the ground and I think it had had enough, too.

My anger would not subside. A fury whirled inside me that could not be calmed. Not going back was not enough. That hut continuing to exist was too much to bear. I needed to erase this place.

The next day I stopped on my way to school and watched the plumes of smoke rising from the gutted remains, the tangle of blackened metal chairs, charred roof timbers and unidentifiable debris. I had seen the hut from my bedroom window in the night, a flicker of flames through the trees, across the cornfield. The last sign of life, soon extinguished by the great arcs of water falling over it. The corpse was dreadful, a mutilated mess. I picked up an anonymous blob of plastic with a buckled nail set in it and put in my pocket. A small souvenir of the exorcism I had performed.

I wonder what happened to my memento? Does it sit somewhere in that house by the fields, neglected and forgotten, pining? No. It has no feelings. As dead as Mom and Dad already were when I fashioned it from a whole scout hut, and just as forgotten now. They were killed in a car crash, and I went to live with Uncle Graham and Aunty Beth. Time passed and things changed. Uncle Graham died and Aunty Beth moved away. I don't know where, and it doesn't matter now.

The moon is casting so much light, it reminds me of night scenes in lots of films, where everything is as visible as in daylight but tinted blue. The torch I brought is still in my pocket, I definitely won't need it until I'm inside. I crawl through the gap in the wire fence and follow what I remember to be the path around to the rear of the silent building.

I walk into the dark remains of the ballroom, stepping around the black patches on the parquet floor that represent holes. Moonlight filtering through broken windows describes the space well enough for me to cross it without hesitating. I stop at the foot of the enormous staircase and peer up. The floors grow darker approaching halfway up the hotel and then lighter again towards the top; a square of sparkling deep blue sky, where the roof should be.

I start to climb the remains of the staircase, my feet occasionally clipping chunks of marble debris. The elaborate bronze handrail runs out by the first turn, reduced to a number of twisted spindles and then nothing. I push my body closer to the wall as I get higher, peering harder as the night regains its darkness. I reach for my torch but then decide I don't want to use it; there is only one more very dark floor and then the light from above starts penetrating, and if I switch it on now I might find it harder to see again when I turn it off.

There is a strong smell of damp that I hadn't noticed before. Plants sprout from gaps in the walls and floors, and I have some difficulty getting around a fully-grown bush sitting in the middle of a corridor. I check each room, but I can't find what I'm looking for. Each is as empty as the last one, all of them featureless apart from splintered floorboards and fallen plaster from the ceiling.

I reach the top floor and take deep lungfuls of the clear air. The derelict suite glistens under the stars, its grandeur regained. The walls are stunning under the giant moon. The light shivers across the silver paint, each repeated fleur de lys as perfect as the next, painted in deep red turned maroon by the night's blueness. An optical illusion makes the shapes appear closer than the surface of the wall. I extend a forefinger and touch one and my finger sinks into it. I try to yank it back sharply but it keeps going in. I slam the palm of my other hand against the wall for leverage and there is a cascade of dust as the plaster collapses, the whole wall seems to give way while holding on tightly to my right hand, I can feel the blood being drawn from my arm, a violent sucking that is draining me, I shout and set off an alarm of buzzing in the hills all around, the night is filled with the crazed frenzy of a million tiny legs scraping, wings vibrating, a demented bombardment of sound that drowns out my screams help me somebody please help

The buzzing stops when I open my eyes and blink in the semi-darkness. I try to lever myself off the sofa but my arm doesn't work and I flop back down. I rub the dead flesh hard until I feel the sharp tingling of pins and needles. The doorbell breaks the silence again and goes on longer this time. The sound is shocking, I'm not sure I've ever heard it before. I stay quite still in the darkness and listen. The letterbox squeaks open and a voice calls my name.

'Hello, It's me. John. From work. Are you in? Brian asked me to stop by, see if you were OK.'

I don't recognise the voice, or understand what it's saying. I don't know a John, from work. What work? I don't know anyone called Brian. There is a bead of light around the lounge door meaning I must have left the hall light on. I wait a while longer and then I hear the letterbox squeak again and something drop onto the hallway floor. Once I'm sure no one is still there I go out to see what it is. I pick up the scrap of paper from the mat. It has a transcript of the voice scribbled on it. I scrunch it up and toss it at the open binbag in the kitchen, missing it completely.

Sleeping on the street went from being pretty dangerous to positively lethal in the space of a vicious cold snap that came without warning. Bodies were found frozen solid, people lost fingers and toes. I was forced to rethink my nomadic lifestyle and after some searching I found a good place to sleep regularly. Probing through the confusion of buildings behind Waterloo one night I slipped between some giant metal bins and came face to face with a breezeblock wall. A black gap ran along its top edge through which hot air drifted invitingly. I stood on tiptoe and peered into the dark aperture. My eyes took a moment to adjust to the gloom and then I made out the shape of the underside of a stairwell. I levered my body up and fed it slowly through the slit. My heart was beating fast as I lowered myself into the unknown. My toes just reached the floor with my fingers still hooked on the rough lip. I turned and examined the space carefully. A poorly insulated heating duct poked out of the wall opposite, with enough room around it to lie down comfortably. It was completely enclosed on three sides, the gentle roar of the vent keeping it very warm. A thin shaft of orange penetrated the gap I had entered by, casting just enough light to feel secure and read by but not enough to allow anyone to see me down here without clambering noisily over the wall themselves.

How good it felt each night to lie there, relaxed in a prone position without the constant threat of being attacked in my sleep, free of the bulk of dirty blankets and cardboard. I could leave the grimy holdall containing my few things each day when I went out, knowing it would still be there when I got back. This subtle shift in my daily routine made a big difference. Walking around town without that black albatross swung over my shoulder, I blended in more easily. People didn't avoid me as much or look so often. I could cover more ground each day, I didn't tire as quickly and being able to strip out of my clothes every night meant I could keep cleaner too.

One night I got back desperate for warmth and realised I wasn't the only one using the space. My bag hadn't been touched but the cardboard sheets I used as floorcovering had been rearranged, covering the concrete better than the way I had laid them. When I sniffed the air I was shocked to find the lingering odour of deodorant. The tangy smell confused me. I was certain no one else was there whenever I was. Who could be coming and going without leaving more evidence or crossing my path?

The bitter cold forced me to return one afternoon. I climbed the wall, dropped down the other side and collapsed on a dark bundle that let out a yelp. I shouted and jumped to the other side of the vent. The shape scrambled to its feet and into the strip of light. A small olive-skinned man of about twenty with dark eyes, high cheekbones and a hooked nose was staring at me, his arms extended forwards.

– Please, no trouble.

He was sweating and his hands shook.

– You cunt, you nearly gave me a heart attack. What do you think you're doing? This is my place.

– I'm sorry, very sorry. Want no trouble, just sleeping.

I muttered and pushed his hands away.

– Well you can fuck off. I sleep here.

He bent down and hurriedly gathered his things together. I was angry but as I took him in properly, I felt curious. He was dressed in a hooded sports top, jeans and cheap but fairly new trainers. He folded a towel that looked clean and rolled it up with a toothbrush, toothpaste and shampoo inside. He stuffed it into a rucksack.

– Sorry, I go anyway. I only sleep here in day. Before work.

– Work?

Now I was totally confused.

– Yes. At hotel. I work in kitchen at night. Then I go to work in petrol station in the early morning. Then I sleep here.

He said all this with a smile that disarmed me.

– My name is Mirsad Feijzic.

I watched without saying anything as he took a pen from his pocket, and wrote his name on the cardboard we were standing on.

– Well this is where I sleep and I don't want you here when I am.

His friendliness had worn the edge off my determination to defend my territory.

–Thank you, thank you. I am grateful.

And then he strapped his rucksack onto his back and scaled the wall.

Like lodgers in a boarding house who never meet, we shared that small oasis of calm without seeing each other. Our routine continued through that winter. One night I returned and found a brown paper bag standing in the middle of the flattened cardboard. 'For You' was scribbled on it in biro. I looked inside and found chunks of sugary pastry that smelled of cinnamon. I bit a corner off and tasted it suspiciously. Walnut paste and vanilla. I lay down in the darkness and chewed on it contentedly.

A few days later I returned just as Mirsad was squirming his way out through the bins.

– Ah, my friend. Did you enjoy the baklava?

– The what? Oh, the pastry thing. Yes, it was nice. Thanks.
He beamed at me.
– Yes, very good. I make it in the hotel kitchen when my boss goes home.
I nodded, once again unsure of how to respond to what he was telling me. He said goodbye and jogged away towards the bridge.

This reminder of his surreal existence roused my curiosity again. That night I lay there wondering who this strange person was who slept rough but worked nearly all the time. It bothered me.

Mirsad was pleased to see me when I climbed through the hole the following afternoon. He was sitting on the floor going through his belongings, making sure everything was folded and packed as neatly as possible.

– Ah, it is you. I get worried when I hear someone. But you and I we share, so I'm glad.

I agreed with his simple logic and sat opposite him on the cardboard. Making conversation no longer came naturally to me but I hardly had to say anything before he started to tell me all about himself. About his childhood back in Srebrenica, about the massacre there when he was sixteen, the murder of his father and brother in the back garden by laughing teenage soldiers with machetes while he hid nearby in some bushes and watched, helplessly. And about the responsibility this passed on to him for his whole family, how they fled to the enclave of Zepa and how when that too was overrun they had been forced to make a terrible decision. A refugee camp had been set up in Zenica but he feared it was a Serb trap. They couldn't all take the risk of going there and they couldn't survive in the open. So the rest of the family made their way down the valley into the town and he went with other young men into the woods; they had heard of gangs offering to escort those who could pay out of the country to safety. Their only hope was that he would get away and find somewhere they could all move to one day. His family had given him everything they had left to pay for the long dangerous journey across Europe but it was an investment, in him and them.

I asked him why he had two jobs, and why if he had them did he sleep here? He explained that the hotel night shift paid him two pounds an hour. The job involved washing a mountain of dirty plates that never seemed to reduce in size and then hosing down all the kitchen equipment. There were two of them who did this every night. At six in the morning he would leave the hotel, walk the two or three miles to Acton, and work on a station forecourt until two in the afternoon, a job which was easier but paid a few pence less per hour. Then he would catch a bus back into town and walk across the river to where we now sat. This left him with six hours in which to rest before getting up and going back to the hotel. Once every few nights his boss left them to it and he would use a shower room. His pay was taxed at source and fines were often incurred at the hotel for things like being late or breaking crockery. He had tried renting a bedsit somewhere a long way out of town but found he couldn't send money home to his family via an uncle and stay there; no matter how little he spent he never had enough for both.

– Why don't you beg? You'd make a lot more than two quid an hour.

He frowned.

– Why would I beg? I'm not beggar. I am a worker.

I didn't have an answer.

– Why not just go back, find your family in Zenica? Things must have improved there by now?

He shook his head and looked sad and defeated for the first time. I could see now that his eyes were sunken and very lined. I tried not to think what images he must see when he closed them to sleep. He finished packing his bag.

– It is still much much worse there. Even few pounds I send each month is more than I can make in Bosnia. The war is long over but it is still very dangerous and poor. I want them to join me here once I have better job and house.

I didn't know what to say. If his home country was worse than the circle of hell it seemed to me he existed in here, then it was beyond my imagination.

– You'd better get to the hotel before they fine you.

He brightened now that home was far away again.

– Yes, I go now. Sleep well.

At some point that spring I became aware that Mirsad was no longer staying with me. The exotic smells had thinned and then gone completely. Everything was exactly as I had left it in the morning when I returned each night. I tried moving the cardboard sheets around, exposing gaps of grey concrete, but when I got back they hadn't been covered over again. It was as if he had never existed. I felt a loss that unsettled me. I didn't really know him at all. We had only met a handful of times. But a loneliness I hadn't experienced before was mine now. I was on my own again.

One day I found the address of the hotel where Mirsad had told me he worked and that night I walked to Queensway. It was late by the time I got there and it occurred to me that Mirsad must cover almost as much ground on foot each day as I did. It was a long time since I had been there and I was surprised by how busy the street was at night. The multi-ethnicity of the area meant it existed in a completely different timezone to most of London. Crowds of people streamed in and out of Chinese restaurants, juice bars and kebab shops. I double checked my A-Z and curved through the streets behind Bayswater until I found the place. I couldn't march in through the marble and smoked glass entrance so I hovered around in an alleyway behind it until I saw a door open and a small figure bob out, throwing bin bags onto a heap of others.

– Mirsad?

The girl jumped.

– Who's that?

– Sorry. I'm looking for Mirsad, Mirsad Feijzic. Is he here?

– Hang on.

She slammed the door shut and I listened in the darkness to the shouts on the other side. After a while the door re-opened. A burly man in a dirty white uniform leaned out, squinting.

— What d'you want?

— I'm looking for a friend of mine, Mirsad. He said he works here. He looked me up and down and grunted.

— Friend? I can believe that. He's doesn't work here anymore.

And then he slammed the door shut again.

I stood there blinking. Mirsad needed his jobs too badly to give either up. I didn't imagine he'd found something better. I was wondering what to do next when the door opened slowly. The girl's head appeared round it.

— You a friend of Mirsad's?

I nodded.

— He's gone, I don't know where. He got caught having a shower. There was a fight, I wasn't here that night so I don't know exactly what happened. I heard it was bad, though.

A voice barked behind her and the door closed for the last time.

I didn't sleep well after that. I spent days lingering in my cell, but his face never appeared over the wall. I couldn't remember exactly where he'd said the garage was, and I had a bad feeling that he wasn't there anyway. The weather was improving and eventually the space was too hot and airless to be comfortable. One morning I got up very early and packed my things in my bag. I took the top off a can of bright red spray paint I had stolen and wrote MIRSAD FEIJZIC 1998 in big letters across the grey wall. I scrambled out and walked away. I didn't ever go back there.

Why am I thinking about all this now? It happened years ago. I never think about it. What's the point? I moved on, I forgot all about him. I walked away from that place and within days I was at ease again, alone and happy that way.

I know why. My memory is filling in gaps, repairing holes that I punched out on purpose, to protect myself. The longer I'm away from the world outside, the more surely it returns to me. The streets are waiting for my return. They will have to wait. I don't know if I want them back.

She burnt better than I imagined she would. One moment she was there caught in her hell of frustrated luxury, imploring me, and then she bubbled and blistered and disappeared completely. Her relief was as tangible as the heat on my face. I felt so much better knowing I would be able to sleep, sleep without seeing her desperate expression. I had woken up that morning sure of what to do, the only course of action to take. Free her from that frozen moment, trapped forever as the face of that false building.

There was a pub at the end of the road and I deserved a drink. I went in and ordered a pint. I sipped the fizzing lager and then called the barman over again.

'I'm sorry, but this glass is really dirty,' I said.

He looked at me and then took the pint glass from my hand. He held it up to the orangy light behind the bar and examined the greasy handprint. He sighed and then silently poured the lager into another glass, plonking it back down in front of me. I nodded and smiled, taking a long sip. When I went to pick it up again there was another oily print around it. I looked at my hand up close. It shimmered like fish skin and a petrolly perfume made my eyes water. The barman was watching me and I went into the toilets. There was no soap or hot water so I soaked my hands under the cold tap for a minute and then rubbed them hard on the stiff roller towel.

When I went back to the bar a few people were standing at the windows looking out and blue light was strobing the patchy ochre ceiling. I could hear a conversation the barman was having with one of the regulars.

'Shame, they only finished them a month ago.'

'Yeah, half full already too, apparently.'

'Not much of a welcome.'

'No, but it's not surprising is it? Building places like that round here, I'm amazed it's not happened before.'

'Kids from the estate?'

'Yeah, so they think. Must have set fire to that sign and it spread from there.'

'Christ. How bad?'

'Don't know yet, Sheila reckoned it's mostly smoke damage, up one side.'

I knew the barman was looking at me and I carried on drinking slowly. I stared hard at my reflection behind the bar and tried not to listen. Something wasn't right. I looked as though I was wearing theatrical makeup, heavily smudged kohl making panda eyes and a dark smear around the sides of my nose. I rubbed the palm of one hand around my eyes but it was still greasy and felt unpleasant. I guzzled the dregs of my pint and left without looking at the barman.

And I have slept better, much better. I haven't seen her since, or thought about the building that tried to fool me, wrapped around that innocent corpse. When I close my eyes the pictures stop, just like for everybody else.

Before I open my eyes I'm aware of her scent, cutting through the sickly aroma of antiseptic and sweat. She isn't wearing perfume – it's the smell of moisturiser, deodorant, and the world outside this place. I doubt the lovely fragrance lingers on her all day. She must leave at the end of her shift with the unmistakable cloying odour of hospital life on her skin, in her hair. Would I be able to notice this difference normally, or are my senses heightened through isolation? Does any suggestion of the outside world set off signals in my head?

– What are you thinking about?

She smiles at me. Her lovely familiar smile.

– I was just thinking how much better I'm feeling.

She carefully brushes a tiny piece of lint from my arm. Don't ever, ever stop doing that.

– Well, you are a lot better, aren't you. You'll be able to walk around any day now, I think.

– Really? That's great. Every time I try to sit up I feel like something's going to pop inside.

How close is this to the real thing, to a normal conversation? It feels real. It's the closest I've come.

– Well DON'T sit up then, silly. You don't want to do anything to make your stay even longer, do you.

That smile again. Oh stop it Julie, stop before I go and spoil it all by saying something stupid.

– Have no fear, nurse. I will be off your hands in no time.

She looks sad. I must be imagining it. No, I saw it. A fractional, spontaneous curl of the lip. She's busying herself with the covers too much.

– I hear you might be able to get your own place.

– You heard correctly. Doctor Stephenson has been very helpful. It's not definite, but maybe I can start again. A new life.

– How nice for you. Just what we all want, isn't it?

Is she joking? Isn't there more than a hint of seriousness in her voice? Julie, is there anything I can do?

She pats my leg and walks out. How long, how long 'til we two meet again?

I'm unsure how much time has really passed in here. I've only got their word for it. But the tips of the trees I can see from the window have lost their leaves and the sky is a fairly constant pale grey. The people who occasionally go by the door tend to be wearing thick coats and Julie brings with her each morning an air of recent brisk walking in a chilly breeze.

Brisk walking in a chilly breeze.

I slip the covers down and pull myself up. There is a sensation as though something will tear inside me but I manage to sit upright. I gently turn and lower my legs to the floor. I've had some physio but I wobble about for a moment. Using the bed to support me I stand up and take a few deep breaths. I step away from the bed with my arms out. I'm on my feet, on my own two feet, and it feels fantastic. I take the robe from the hook on the wall. There's no need to check the drawers of my cabinet. I came in with nothing,

I'm leaving with nothing. My account is cleared. I wonder if I will be able to find my things, my keys and map? Did they land in the river, or on the bank? Can I remember where it happened? I can only try. I can only do my best, under the circumstances.

I wake up and look at my clock. I haven't woken this early for a long time. A thin shaft of white light enters through a slight crack in the curtains. It runs up the bed like a barcode scanner, reading me. I slip out of bed and stand close to the curtains. I can hear things outside. People walking past, birds singing. I peer through the crack. It's very bright and I pull the curtains apart. I can see people, people walking along the street below. They must be going to work. I wonder who they are, and where they work. I wonder what they are thinking about, and whether they will be late.

I get up and I want to go out. But the flat isn't looking too good and I need a wash, so I decide to have a shower and do a bit of housework first. I fill a couple of bin bags and put them by the bins downstairs. The place looks a lot better, but it's still full of *things*; every surface is cluttered with odds and ends, records and books lie all over the lounge and there are clothes everywhere in my bedroom. I find the roll of bin bags and load all of them full. I double check each room and notice the small table that my computer sits on. There are disks and shells all around it and I sweep them with my arm into one of the bags. The whole job takes ages and I'm sweating profusely by the time all twenty bin bags are standing in a line by the front door. A queue of fat black Labradors eager to be let out. I make several journeys ferrying them quickly to the bottom of the stairs and then climb slowly back up while my heartbeat steadies.

When I walk back into the flat I'm impressed by how different it looks. The results are quite startling. Almost everything that symbolised me has been eradicated. The atmosphere of decay has gone. Pleased by this improvement I find my good shoes and give them a polish. They too are quickly transformed and I laugh at how easily things can be made good again, how they can seem to be beyond all help and then with the application of one's will and some elbow grease they are changed beyond recognition.

I've had an idea. I will go and see her. She doesn't live far away. A few minutes out in the open will do me some good, I think. It is much cooler so I get my coat, and I realise it's the first time I've worn it in ages, since the spring at least. It doesn't fit as well as it did, it hangs a bit loosely across the chest and shoulders, but it will do. I am very hungry, but there isn't anything here to eat. I go through the cupboards above the sink but all I can find is a box of teabags. I pop one in my mouth and hold it on my tongue for a minute or so. It makes me feel slightly nauseous and the taste is horribly bitter but the pains in my stomach recede.

I want to see her because I have a lot to say. This period of time has been important to me. The clouds that I now realise hung over me for years have parted. My eyes feel bright and wet, like a new-born foal's. Many things are now quite clear to me. How could I have been so misguided? How could everyone be living under such delusions? So, she is the first one to tell. She is clever, I think, so it shouldn't take long for her to grasp the essence of what I mean. She will be pleased. I mustn't rush into it, though. I must speak slowly and carefully. It would be too easy to give the impression that I am not in control, not making sense. My excitement must be held in check if I'm to make myself understood. I can't find my keys anywhere. It's possible I put them out with the rubbish accidentally. I can't hang about all day so I leave the front door unlocked and set off.

My breath pumps out little patches of fog as I walk along, clicking my fingers in time with the smart click clack of the metal tips on my shoes. I intend to take more notice of everything and I am going to memorise street names, I decide. I'm struck by the wild variation in architectural styles and periods. Maybe there was a lot of bombing around here, during the war. A church converted into flats, probably some time ago. A newly converted warehouse. A row of small council houses, with very 1970s detailing; the tongue and groove timber cladding, the porches with pitched roof that almost reach the floor and have a distinctly Scandinavian feel. This area is schizophrenic. One moment it is a chalet resort, the next a northern mining town. Then a 1920s German housing scheme, then a colony of nineteenth century textiles factories. Many buildings show signs of change of usage and status several times over, from industrial to live/work to office to decrepitude to artist's studio and then accommodation or office, again. Looking so hard at it all is making me dizzy so I walk faster and warm my hands by clapping them in front and then behind me.

This invigorates me but then I start to feel too hot. I open my coat and let the cold air wrap around my chest for a moment. I button up again and walk on, resisting the urge to run. In a few minutes I have reached the right street. But when I walk along it I can't see the house I'm after. I start to get upset and then remember the next street is almost identical. I hurry along and soon I'm in front of the right house, I'm sure of it. I ring the bell.

A woman I don't recognise opens the door. A small boy is standing behind her, looking at me through her legs. She smiles at me quizzically.

'Hello,' I say. 'I wonder of you could help me, I'm looking for a friend of mine, she lives here.'

My voice doesn't sound quite right, as though I've borrowed it from someone else.

The woman frowns. 'I'm sorry, but I think you must have the wrong house. We live here.'

I'm very confused and my ears are getting hot.

'I haven't seen her for a while. This is definitely the right house. Perhaps I could wait?'

The woman steps forward and closes the door slightly.

'We've lived here for six months, she must have been the previous owner. What was her name?'

I stare at the floor. 'I'm not sure. We had an understanding, an agreement. She didn't know mine either.'

While I am talking the woman pushes the door to and opens it again very slightly. I can see a brass coloured chain bridging the narrow gap.

'Look I really can't help you, the house was empty when we bought it. I'm sorry.'

I want to say something else, something that is creeping into my head but isn't there yet, not entirely ready to be said. Then it arrives.

'Sophia,' I say, quite definitely.

But the door is shut.

My head is a jumbled intersection of railway lines. I breathe deeply and some patterns emerge, the lines untangle. Carriages shunt up and link together and a train slowly pulls away. Sophia, the girl, whose ex-husband died, she sold the house. Of course. How stupid of me. I stood waving to her, I shouted my name, a name she doesn't know, didn't hear. How could I forget a thing like that, that emotional scene outside that very house? I feel a little better and the train whistles and steams around a bend.

I carry on walking and my hunger becomes an issue again. The blood in my veins is thin and watery. My stomach is a flat paper bag. I pinch the palms of my hands hard as I'm walking, a little trick to fool my blood sugar momentarily. I don't have any money. Or a job. What about work? I stop suddenly and another train almost runs me down. Shit, I stopped working, didn't I. I never called that person, Brian, Brian my boss, glasses, older, that one. I never called as I said I would. As he said I should. It must be too late by now.

And does it matter? Haven't I discovered all sorts of things not shared by those who blindly and willingly tether themselves to the drudgery of work? Who spend their lives in the pursuit of things, things that have no real meaning or value, that exist only to ensure that people continue to get up and go to work? Have I already forgotten everything I've learnt? No, it's fine, this is simply a momentary lapse. They will have to go on without me; I have other things to do.

But I am hungry. I don't know when I last ate. I pass a line of people queuing for a bus and they all look at me. Did I say that out loud? And that? And that? I think so. I clamp my mouth tightly shut and carry on. It's getting colder. It must be getting late. I have to think, I need to make a plan. I fall into step behind a girl. She swings her bag over her shoulder and I hear a soft thud. When I look down there's a smart black leather purse in front of me. I pick it up quickly and tuck it into my coat. I jump into a doorway and look inside the purse. There are a few credit cards and different bits of paper. I open another compartment. Cash. Forty-five pounds and some change. I go hot all over and grin. I pocket the money and close the purse.

I don't feel totally victorious. I've made this happen but I feel bad about succeeding at someone else's expense. The girl is far along the road now and disappears around a corner. I quickly shove all the money apart from one twenty pound note back into the purse and run like mad along the street, pushing past people, I pelt along at full tilt, my shoes going clickclackclickclackclickclack. My chest is tight and my legs ache but I keep going. I turn the corner and see the girl about to get on a bus. I shout and wave, and run up to her.

'I. You dropped. This.'

She is shocked for a moment until she sees the purse I'm holding.

'Oh my god, thank you. That's very kind.'

I'm pleased and watch as she hurries aboard, opening her purse for the fare. I wave at the bus as it pulls away and walk back onto the main road. I notice that the cars have their lights on and the light is fading fast. I must have been walking around all day. It doesn't matter.

I'm delighted with this. Who would have thought it could be so easy? I can get something to eat anytime I like. I've spared that girl the nuisance and upset of losing a purse and cancelling all her cards and been compensated for my effort by the comparatively small profit I've made. We are both happy. I wonder what I should eat. There isn't anywhere just here but it's not far to the market, there are several nice places along there. I might go to that pub, the one that does good food. I haven't had a drink in a long time and my mouth is watering at the prospect of a pint of lager and a burger and salad.

I pass by a block of new flats. The building is beautifully floodlit and lights are on in most of the windows. The effect is very pleasing, set against the clear early evening sky. It is marred slightly by what appears to be a huge scorch mark up one side, as if a giant match has been struck against it. A large sign stands in front, with several lights angled onto it. 'STUNNING LOFTS' says the sign and it describes my mood perfectly, these thoughts that transport me, the stunning lofts of my mind, the elevation of my soul. I am walking and looking and thinking and feeling fine, better than ever, with a sense of really understanding it all for the first time. I take in everything around me, absorb everything I see. I can feel it under my skin, coursing through my blood, pulsing up my spine and into my brain. I come to a junction and a red road sign agrees that I have 'CHANGED PRIORITIES'. The bad times are indeed behind me. Another smaller sign says 'One Way', and I'm pleased with its prognosis. One way it is, isn't it. No diversion, no side routes, one life one go.

It's getting late but I'm not afraid, nothing can harm me. My coat protects me from the evening chill and my mind shields me from insecurity, safeguards my passage into the night and the future. The looming gas towers don't trouble me and the black mirror of the canal below doesn't reflect my thoughts. I walk through a pair of large metal gates into the unlit park and the dark trees greet me with open arms.

TOM GIDLEY

Tom Gidley was born in 1968 and lives in London. A co-founder of *frieze* magazine and former member of all-electric bass guitar band Big Bottom, he has exhibited widely over the past fifteen years. His work encompasses a broad range of media, including film installation, sculpture, painting, music and literature. *Stunning Lofts* is his first novel.

CURRENT TITLES FROM METRONOME PRESS

Metronome Press is dedicated to developing fiction
and new styles of writing in relation to contemporary
art practice. The following titles are the original creations
of artists of international renommée, published
for the first time by Metronome Press.

For price lists, mail order, and all enquiries, contact
www.metronome.org.uk

Manuscripts are welcome and should be sent to
Metronome Press, 6 rue Cavallotti, Paris 18, France.

PHYLLIS KIEHL

---

*FAT
MOUNTAIN*

SCENES

METRONOME PRESS

FAT MOUNTAIN SCENES
by Phyllis Kiehl

At the Weiko Sud Diet Clinic, a slimming farm completely isolated from the outside world, a group of extremely obese patients undergoes unconventional therapy, one that doesn't necessarily produce the desired effects... Until one day, Dr Ariel Tense, the new straight-laced and vicious senior consultant, arrives at Weiko Sud from Brasilia bringing with him his own arsenal of slimming tools. Soon the tension builds up between the sinister Dr Tense, ready to whip his new herd into submission, and Dr Sago, the mysterious guru-like manager of the farm. As the XXL fashion show comes to an ecstatic close, the situation in the clinic escalates uncontrollably... This page-turner written by German artist Phyllis Kiehl is available from Metronome Press. 168 pages, English. ISBN 2-916262-03-2

TOM McCARTHY

REMAINDER

METRONOME PRESS

REMAINDER
by Tom McCarthy

Traumatised by an accident that involves something falling
from the sky and leaves him eight and a half million pounds
richer, REMAINDER's hero spends his time and money
obsessively reconstructing and re-enacting memories and
situations from his past: a large building with piano music in
the distance, the familiar smells and sounds of liver frying and
spluttering, lethargic cats lounging on roofs until they tumble
off them... But when this fails to quench his thirst for authenticity, he starts reconstructing more and more violent events,
including hold-ups and shoot-outs. As his addiction grows,
the whole drama spirals out of control... Find out how this
breathtaking story develops by purchasing Tom McCarthy's
REMAINDER from Metronome Press. 288 pages, English.
ISBN 2-916262-00-8

CHARLES HENRI FORD
& PARKER TYLER

THE YOUNG AND EVIL

METRONOME PRESS

THE YOUNG AND EVIL
by Charles Henri Ford & Parker Tyler

At last it's available again! The book that Gertrude Stein was
mad about, and that was originally published by Obelisk Press
in Paris, in 1933. Written by American poets Charles Henri
Ford and Parker Tyler, THE YOUNG AND EVIL tells the story
of Julian and Karel, and their friends, somewhere between
the gay bars and poetry scenes of Greenwich Village, and the
drag balls of Harlem. This queer coterie spends much of the
time getting drunk at parties, swapping beds and apartments,
avoiding the hostile attention of police and sailors that cruise
the parks, meeting up at all-night 'coffeepots', generally
looking fabulous in make-up and gowns, and – occasionally
– creating art. A masterpiece proudly brought back to you by
Metronome Press. 176 pages, English. ISBN 2-916262-01-6

FORTHCOMING TITLES FROM METRONOME PRESS

ODESSA STEP
by Bella Woodfield

IDLE
by Craig Garrett

MY RECENT LIVES
by Nancy Strasbourg

LA CAZADORA AND HER BROOD
by Douglas Park

LA JOIE
by Paul Baruch

DÉSORDRE
by Boris Tiago

QUITTER LE JEU
by Claire Guézengar

LE VERDICT DES VAINQUEURS
by Marc Atlas

DA WATERMELON VENDING MACHINE
by Olivier Babin

and many more…

Financed with the generous support of

Mr Harald Falckenberg, Hamburg
Mr Antoine de Galbert, Paris
Anonymous Patron, Barcelona
Ministère de la Culture et de la Communication, France
Centre National des Arts Plastiques - (aide à l'édition)
American Center Foundation, New York
Hessische Kulturstiftung, Frankfurt

Achevé d'imprimer sur les presses
de l'imprimerie France Quercy
113, rue André Breton
46000 Cahors

Dépôt légal : octobre 2005
N° d'impression : 51839